THE FIRST MAN TO TIME TRAVEL

By Alex Leam

Find me on Twitter @alexleam

CHAPTER ONE

Welcome To the White Room

Doctor Gavin Dawes worked for an organisation like no other. It was an agency that policed time travel. He belonged to the Federal Bureau for Accounting and Monitoring Time travel and its Effects

After he completed his history doctorate, and two years of field training the agency sent him on his one and only field assignment. The result of which landed him a six-month spell in the White Room on admin duty.

The left-hand side of the desk he was working at had a stack of files in his in tray that he swear hasn't gotten any smaller no matter how hard he worked. He reached over and took another field report from the top of the pile that needed logging, he read the opening question.

'After the device was discharged on London Road, did/do any civilians need a memory wipe? (If already completed, please detail your methods)' he glanced at the question number, this was question 1 of 796. He then noticed the date on the form. It was forward dated to two years from now. Two years? He groaned. He was now getting admin from the future.

He hated being stuck behind a desk. Day in and day out there was a never-ending schedule of deeply dull paperwork to wade through. This wasn't him. Admin? No! He was a man of action. Probably.

The only action he saw was on his maiden mission, the agency sent him back to Canada in 1941 to monitor the reopening of the South Fork Bridge.

He was beyond excited to finally get out in the field and prove himself. So excited in fact he skipped two vital parts of his training. Both parts were covered in depth in 'field craft 101'. The jist of which was to 'blend in'. Meaning he had to take a trip to the vast wardrobe the agency had to outfit himself with time appropriate clothing and belongings.

The agency had clothing to fit all sizes, ages, genders, and to suit every time period. The clothing archive was so vast it crossed two time zones. It also boasted an accessory range that could have filled a Spanish island, anything you could want to make it look like you belonged to the time you were going to. From bowler hats to era specific mobile phones, silver dollars to Roman coins, time specific watches to anti-gravity running shoes. However, the process of getting anything out of the continent crossing wardrobe took forever.

The agency argued that the system they had in place to procure anything from the wardrobe could be streamlined and made more efficient thanks to time travel. You could for example file what you really needed for your mission after you get back from it, nip back to the past to drop off the paperwork and hey presto! What you need, and nothing more would be delivered to your desk within hours of you going out on your mission. The bonus of this being that the agency could save money, and the staff could be cut. Problem was, they cut the staff a bit too far, and the entire wardrobe was now run by just one woman, an overworked and perpetually stressed woman named Karen.

Karen did all the paperwork, did all the picking and packing and deliveries. She also catalogued all the items returned and took them back. It didn't take long for the agency to realise that one woman in charge of the wardrobe was a massive mistake, but they didn't admit it. They were far too proud, bordering on arrogant to show any form of weakness, or admit that they had made a mistake. So, they stuck with just one woman and told the agents any delays where due to bad planning on their part, and nothing to do with them, thus skilfully absolving themselves of any blame.

The inevitable delays were starting push Karen's stress level to the limit. Her complaints to management that there 'wasn't enough hours in the day' where addressed by her immediate superior, who took no time at all to match her up with some special medication from the agency's pharmaceutical department called 'Nonixdormi', which after a weeks' worth of taking completely eliminated the users need for sleep. Karen could now work a seven-day week flat out with no sleep.

She was already half way through a 168-hour shift (with no breaks) where nothing was going right when she got the irate message from Gavin.

Karen had so many angry messages from agents wanting the earth and wanting it yesterday that she honestly didn't care anymore. Which was why the entrance to the wardrobe had the cheerful sign on the inquiries desk that greeted everyone that said, 'Bad planning on your part, doesn't mean an emergency on my part'.

She was catching a flight back to distribution from the subcontinent of shoes (having picked up the sandals for the nativity), when he got a curt text message from Gavin wanting to know where his stuff was as he was going out that afternoon. Karen had the form on her desk that Gavin filed two months ago, but she was forever fetching stuff and never at her desk. So, as she was beyond breaking point, she turned her phone off as the automated pilotless plane taxied along the runway and gleefully thought that Gavin could 'go get shagged'.

This was tricky, he didn't have the right cloths. But it was a simple one-day mission. Plus, the cloths he was in wouldn't stick out that much right? He threw caution to the wind and went for it and took his phone just in case.

The mission went perfectly. The bridge reopened without a hitch, nobody battered an eyelid about his cloths, and no enemies of the agency attempted to disrupt anything. Everybody seemed happy, including the reporter from the local newspaper.

Thanks to his wrap around shades Gavin didn't see the flash of the camera bulb as he was nestled in the crowd. But the camera caught him, looking massively out of place around the suits and hats in his t-shirt, sunglasses and zip up hoodie holding his iPhone.

The photo went undiscovered for eighty years until a website in 2014 found it and ran with the story 'Is this man a time traveling hipster?' It was meant as a joke article, as far as they were aware there was no such thing as time travel. But Gavin was rumbled, he had broken the rules about blending in. The boss of the agency was waiting for him the instant he got back.

Which is why Gavin was given an admin job as punishment duty. A dull admin job would have been just bordering on unbearable if it were in the regular office. But he was in the White Room.

The White Room was the nickname given to the agency's panic room, as everything in its sparse interior was white. White walls, white ceiling, white floor. No windows, blinding strip lighting. Just a white desk, a white Bakelite phone that could call anywhere in time and space, a white computer on a secure server, and a kitchenette with a years' worth of non-perishable rations which was joined by a single berth living quarters. The only item in the room which possessed any colour was the red emergency light that flashed when there was an emergency. But the bulb was broken.

Not that the panic room ever got used for a panic in its 1190-year history, as thanks to the nature of the agency's work they were never caught off guard, so it found a new use. Punishment duty. Any agent who broke the rules of the bureau would be sentenced to live and work in the White Room for a period of time determined by the boss, who had final say on all matters of discipline and procedure.

Gavin had been sealed in, living, and working in here for the last five and a half months. And he hated every bit of it. But thankfully, today was his last day. Sort of. His main duties over the past five and a half months was providing admin support for the boss's final field mission before she hit retirement. It was the most prestigious mission in the agency's history. Protecting the first man to time travel and protecting the discovery of the secrets of time travel so they couldn't be misused.

Many volumes had been written about the first man and the discovery. The events that took place so long ago, (and also currently on the white rooms mission clock in front of Gavin's desk) had been theorised and debated many times, as had the exterior agencies who wanted to steal the secrets of sophisticated time travel. The agencies themselves had the ability to travel in time, but the methods where very crude and ineffective by comparison. The agency had a Lamborghini, everyone else had a pushbike with two flat tires and no breaks.

Most missions caused paperwork, but this one was the motherlode. Everything was happening on this mission, and everything required paperwork. If it wasn't attempted theft of the bureau's secrets, then it was the attempted murder of the first man.

Many believed that the accident that caused the first man to go back in time twenty years (which the bureau went to great lengths to ensure happened as planned) was a bad thing and would lead to the destruction of life as we know it. So, Gavin had to catalogue and file every botched assassination attempt that happened and would keep happening on a paradoxical loop for the rest of eternity. But they persevered, there were even some brand-new attempts that they didn't bank on. Like the one he was currently typing up. The one that took place outside the nightclub.

He had so far typed up over 72,000 field reports that contained a murder attempt. Many of which had been neutralised without the first man noticing. But Gavin couldn't help thinking you'd have to be a bit dense to not notice a war going on under your feet. Completely missing the point of the clandestine nature of his employers work. Still, the excitement of today being the last day of the mission was seeing him through. He could then take it easy, and when the Boss's second in command got back to base they would see what a good job he had done and release him.

Gavin glanced up at the mission clock. In the field it was 11:22pm on the 4th October 2002. Just thirty-eight minutes then it was all over. A sense of relief filtered through Gavin like a man who's had a bad year looks forward to midnight on New Year's Eve. The bureau have a one hundred per cent success rating in the field, so the last part of the mission was a formality.

An unfamiliar 'ding' sound on his computer made Gavin look up from his paperwork to check what had happened. Finally, the results of the deep background check he started were in. He almost didn't open it, as something at this late stage couldn't be that important. He saw the subject line 'URGENT, New information uncovered. Report to head IMMEDIATELY'. Still, he didn't expect much as he glanced over the message, he took a slug of coffee as he read. He wasn't even one paragraph in when he saw the worst of it.

He was mid sip of coffee when he froze. Liquid started pouring out the sides of his mouth and he was rooted to the spot in disbelief. He put the cup down and dabbed at the spilled coffee with a paper towel, the majority of which landed on the crotch of the suit trousers.

How could this have happened? Why now? Sure, he had heard rumours but... they were just rumours. He tried to get the boss on her phone at her office in the field. No answer. He checked the timetable. At this point she was on the roof, unable to read the info he had to send. Dammit! He sent a message to her wrist comms device.

He had pointed out before the mission began that it seemed unfair that he was on punishment duty for use of anachronistic clothing and tech when the boss essentially gets a smart watch in her mission sixteen years before they were invented. He was told that the circumstances were different as the mission was so important, she needed to be connected to HQ at all times, plus a watch can be concealed easily in the field, and also he was told many times that unlike Gavin, the boss isn't a twat.

He sent a message to her watch. 'URGENT, New intelligence gathered. LOG ON NEEDED!' He estimated by the time she got the message she would still have enough time to act on it. It can't be that bad, I mean, if it were then the red alert bulb would be flashing. If that was on, then it was pretty much goodnight Vienna.

What Gavin didn't realise was, it would be flashing right now. If somebody had changed the bulb.

PART ONE

Meet Simon Radcliffe.

The Same Man Made Different by Time.

CHAPTER TWO

Enrolment

Tuesday 17th September 2002.

9:45am, University of Derby, Kedleston Road, B Block.

Meet Simon Radcliffe. Nineteen years old. Still at the age when people just called him 'Si'

Today was the day. Enrolment day. The day Si had spent the last nine months preparing for. Although, his plans did have to alter a bit. Fate saw to that.

He flunked his first year at uni once already the previous year, when a combination of new friends, personal issues, and the student loan check clearing meant he spent most of his time in the Arms Bar (the on-campus students' union pub) rather than the lecture halls.

He'd done well at college and wanted to do a history degree, but he didn't want to go far from home. So, it made sense to go to his local university in Derby. Most of his friends would be going there, so it seemed like the logical next step.

Nobody told him however, until the day he enrolled that the university had dropped the particular degree we wanted to do. It had been rolled into something called the 'combined subject programme' to save money, and it was every bit as uninspiring as it sounded and thanks to some of the modules being outsourced to a local college required travel he didn't bank on, meaning seeing his old friends was next to impossible, and making new ones was exhausting as he was never in the same place, or with the same people from one day to the next.

Feeling as lost as he did would have been enough to drive him to drink rather than attend a lecture, but one of the biggest reasons why he spent most of student loan money on alcohol was one of his lecturers struck the fear of God into him. Dr Rhonda Jarvis.

Rhonda was cold, patronising, and brutal with essay feedback. Dr Jarvis was a historian without comparison; however, she was pretty cutting with everyone's work but for some reason more so with Si. Despite his complaints being dismissed as paranoia, Si was certain she had it in for him. On top of all that she would also regularly accuse him of plagiarism when he had done no such thing on almost every essay, this argument even went as far as going to an academic board review once, that found in Si's favour. This did little to deter Rhonda though, if anything it seemed to make her worse.

Si didn't give up easily. He persevered, but the harder he tried the more savage she seemed to be. Friends said he was imagining it, but he knew full well she didn't like him. Like the caustic feedback wasn't enough, she would also show up late for every tutorial and make him wait for her to finish an email to her publishers before finally giving him some moments of her 'precious' time, and generally signalling Si out for treatment that made him feel like she'd be a lot happier, if he just left.

Over time this started to get to Si, he had high hopes for uni, and he was now getting into a very dark place. Rhonda had knocked all the fight out of him, and his brain was going down some depressive routes that scared him, thoughts he never had before.

By January 2002 he had had enough. He was depressed. His grades were low, Rhonda was being particularly vindictive with him missing her lectures and he was becoming a bloated borderline alcoholic. Not that many people noticed his problems, as come the spring term most first year students looked like that anyway.

The only way now was out. So, he withdrew, got back most of his tuition fees and the timing was such that he hadn't officially left until his January loan check cleared, so he decided to take a half gap year to sort himself out, and go back to Uni in September somewhere else. Somewhere new, somewhere without Rhonda.

He thought long and hard and settled on Southampton Solent, it had the perfect course for him, and it would be a kick out of his comfort zone as this would force him to go the whole hog. Move away and into halls. To take the edge off how scary this plan was, and to broaden his horizons a bit in the meantime, he decided to travel.

The plan was simple. Work a summer season abroad somewhere, in the meantime join a gym and get a job somewhere local. Early in February he booked four months accommodation and his outward and return flights to Ibiza. He'd always wanted to go since seeing 'Ibiza Uncovered' in the late nineties. Now he can. To fortify his resolve to go he played his considerable collection of 'Chilled Ibiza' CD's on a loop to get him hyped up. But being chillout music this just made him relaxed.

His excitement did build when he heard from one of his old school friends, who had done what he planned to do, that bars and clubs are crying out for people to work the front door to get people in, and he'd have no trouble getting a job so he could just go out on spec.

He was now fully booked for five months on the white isle, he felt excited at the prospect for many reasons. Mainly adventure, but equally as mainly he might get some action. He wouldn't admit it out loud, but sex was his major motivation. Up until this point he'd always been a tad shy around women, so he pinned all his hopes on an alcohol fuelled summer and a party atmosphere to help his limited experience. He didn't care much that this trip had already wiped out all of his money, he was bang up for what was going to be a summer to remember! Roll on May!

At the peak of Si's excitement was when disaster struck. Exactly

48 hours to the minute after Si booked the trip, the company he booked with disappeared. It didn't simply cease trading or go into bankruptcy. It literally disappeared off the face of the earth. The shop had been gutted and locked up. He only found out when he called the branch to double check his flights, he was a tad concerned as he saw on the news the airline had gone into administration.

The phone number for the travel agent now got him through to an Indian takeaway that was next door. The owners of the takeaway were equally as puzzled as they were annoyed, that they were suddenly having to deal with a load of angry holiday makers who had absolutely no desire to order a curry.

No matter how hard they tried to talk them round.

His mum gave him a lift back to the shop where he made his grim discovery. They'd gone and so had his money. He, and many others had seemed to have been scammed. He picked up his Chicken Tikka Masala from next door and went home deflated.

None of it made sense, that travel agent had been there since the eighties. They'd won awards and had several branches all over the East Midlands. But overnight they had all disappeared without a trace. There wasn't even a trace of them on the Companies House website. Not that Simon could check, as the internet his mum had at home (56k dial up, evenings and weekend package) stopped working that night. And didn't work again for the next month, no matter how many engineers came out to check the line and no matter how many times they called Customer Service, who were equally baffled.

He had no chance of getting his money back, he was screwed. The day he admitted defeat and gave up trying, was also the day the internet started working again.

So, he decided to stay local and took a menial job while his finances recovered and worked to undo the damage to his waistline and his mood. He got a job working in a restaurant, meaning he was more active, so he had no need for the gym, plus mixing with new people did wonders for his social skills and for burying the memory of being fleeced for over a grand by the fake travel agents.

That summer Si became a late bloomer cliché. By the time he hit his nineteenth birthday in July he was down to the slimmest weight he'd ever been, muscle tone that had never been there before had developed. He got a new haircut; his once lifeless blonde centre parting was transformed into a trendy spiky cut. He was fighting fit and increased self-confidence was getting him noticed like never before.

Sadly, he had no idea how to handle the female attention he was now getting, as up to this point he only had one sort of girlfriend the previous summer, before he started his disaster of a first year at Derby. He was just 'getting the hang of it' when she dumped him. But for now, he continued to work on himself and enjoyed getting noticed. It was inflating his already growing ego.

Things were going well for a change, after an almost year long run of bad luck things were looking up. Right up until the mix up. When his plan for September came crashing down.

He got a phone call from UCAS late August. Unusually it was an American sounding woman on the clearing line, who apologetically told him that for some reason his application got lost, unprocessed and his space at Southampton had gone.

This was beyond a joke, the travel agency earlier in the year NOW THIS!? He felt two conflicting emotions almost split him in two, he was a once both on the floor with hopelessness and was ready for a fight as he was so livid.

"There is space however at a university close to you" She said with hope in her voice, Si could hear the clacking of the computer keyboard in front of her as she got the details up, she continued "they've just started up a new history undergrad programme starting next month that pretty much identical to the one you were going for, they've even set aside a discounted rate for residential. There's a space going on clearing. I think you'll get in if you can go down and talk to them now"

Discounted Halls of residence rate? Pretty local. Well, that sounded perfect!

"Where is it?" Asked Si, enthusiasm slowly being reborn in his voice

She tapped a few more keys and clicked the mouse

"University of Derby" she said. Three little words that aborted the rebirth of his enthusiasm.

He was told that a position was being held for him if he went in today to talk to admissions. On the bus in, his more optimistic outlook on life he acquired that summer had rationalised that if he was out to prove to the world he was capable of a degree, then where better than going back to where it all went wrong. He'd be on the same campus three days a week mixing with the same people and living in discounted halls to give himself the full experience.

He was coming around to the idea, his upgraded image and self-confidence would carry him through. The hurt of last year could stay in last year. This was a new start, not going anywhere near the old bad habits of before. He wouldn't let himself down this time around.

He felt it as he walked back in through the revolving doors of the main entrance of the Kedleston Road campus. The sun shone brightly through the vast glass atrium, everything felt brighter compared to when he was last here eight months ago. Granted that was January and this was August, but he didn't mean the weather. His senses were heightened. His head was clear and focused. For the first time ever, he actually felt like a grown up.

Admission was a no problem at all, he was sorted with a place confirmed in a little over thirty minutes. He was amazed. What happened the place that was so bureaucratic it took a month just to get a cup of tea agreed on? This wasn't the place he remembered with a shudder. It was the same building, but it was different, he couldn't put his finger on why. Everything seemed more straightforward, to be working out for him with extraordinarily little effort.

He had a coffee at Blends, the students' union owned coffee shop then went to the library to use the computers to fill in his student loan application. Something he forgot about till his mum called him while he was having his coffee and reminded him.

The loan progress was equally stress free, at a time of year where you would expect a backlog and a whole load of upset and aggro. It was sorted and paid into his account on the day he moved into his Halls of Residence.

Now here he was, enrolment day in a place he vowed never to come back to. But he's glad he did. It's different this time, better. Easier. Like coming back was meant to be. Si was never a big believer in fate, but if there was ever a time for fate to sign him up to their mailing list today was the day.

He'd already met one of his course mates, Paul Kimmel the previous weekend who by chance lived in the room next to Si's in the flat in Peak Court. Paul was a mature student who was giving uni another go at 26, and on the surface at least was a good laugh. He and Si hit it off instantly, although Si's boundless positivity and naivety blinded him to Paul's main character fault. He couldn't see the fact that Paul was a monumental bullshitter.

Paul insisted that his nic-name from his previous job he'd just left be carried through to his Uni life. Up until the previous week he had been the store manager in the main Derby branch of Blockbuster video, where the staff called him 'Small Paul', on account of him being five foot and one inch tall. This had been refined from 'Not-so-tall-Paul' initially a play on the name of the famous DJ 'Tall Paul' until 'Small Paul' finally stuck.

"This doesn't bother you?" asked Si in their kitchen, as Paul reached up for the kettle

"Nahh not at all" Paul replied, in an affected cockney accent he sometimes forgot to put on. "I like it. If you work somewhere and they DON'T take the piss out of you, then you're not one of the lads".

Paul's lack of self-awareness blinded him to the fact that he was disliked by almost everyone he worked with at Blockbuster, the name calling he experienced was more to do with venom that comes from not being liked and not from good natured banter amongst friends. Paul's very obvious small man syndrome meant that he tried too hard in almost everything he did. Secretly Paul found this constant over effort in everything he said and did exhausting, and deep down would have loved to be able to give it up. But he'd been like this for so long, forever 'on stage playing the big man' he's forgot how to be any different.

Si was slightly in awe of Paul to begin with. He took in every phrase and pearl of wisdom he came out with as gospel. All the stories of his life, all the 'facts' and all triumphant wins that tumbled out of his mouth Si soaked up like a sponge.

They were having a pint at The Standing Order in town the night before enrolment, Paul, Si and a few others from their flat where sat around an oblong table chatting when Paul interrupted to say the most memorable of the many pearls that Si took in, he jumped in and without being asked dominated the conversation when he heard someone on the table drop the F-word.

"Changing the subject. But did you know, the word 'Fuck' is actually an acronym?" Paul said to Si sagely, but also with enough volume that all the table could hear.

Si wrinkled his forehead. This was news to him.

"Really?" he said a tad higher pitched. An octave his vocal cords tended to go to when he wasn't too sure of something.

"What does it stand for?"

Paul put his drink down and leaned in, like he was about to

impart the meaning of life.

“Forbidden Use of Carnal Knowledge” as Paul finished saying ‘knowledge’ he rapidly raised and lowered both eyebrows in unison one time so they peaked and troughed around the top of his glasses to visually punctuate the end of his sentence. If eyebrows could talk, Paul’s eyebrows had just said “Bet you didn’t see that coming!”

By now half the table was listening to Paul’s nugget of wisdom which was completely untrue.

“It was a Police term” he started to give an explanation nobody asked for “used in the Victorian era for arrests related to sex”

There was a quiet that was only lifted by a shout from the far end of the table.

“I think it’s your round short arse”. Everybody laughed including Si until Paul looked at him, and he abruptly stopped. His face sagging like a punctured balloon. Paul winked at him as got up to go to the bar.

When he got back with a tray of drinks, he found his seat had been replaced with an infant’s high chair that was at the other end of the bar next to the cutlery, normally reserved for family diners, or in this case for a group of people winding up their short flat mate.

Despite Pauls good intentions to give uni ‘a proper go’ he would drop out at the end of the first year when he blew most of his loan money on booze and drugs. Si tried in vain to persuade him to stay using his own false start at uni as an example of how you can turn it around. But he’d made up his mind. Paul was always easily distracted by the next new shiny thing that life jingled in front of his face and was always quick to abandon the previous shiny thing that was the ‘be all and end all’ a short time ago.

He stayed local and he and Si remained friends, up until a couple of months before his death in 2006. He was thirty-one.

Si and Paul stood in an enrolment queue on the first floor of B Block that seemed to have no end in sight, but at least it was moving at a pace. By this stage they had met someone else from their course. Kirsty, who had moved to be here from Oxford. While they were in the queue they got chatting to a man who didn't speak much who went by the name 'Hose'.

This puzzled everyone else. Nobody could quite place Hose's ethnicity. Paul was convinced he was Indian. Kirsty thought he was Iranian (because he reminded her of her ex whose parents were Iranian) and Si thought he was of Mexican decent and that he misheard him saying his name was José. They were collectively puzzled, and Hose was not giving much away. He shifted his weight and smiled a lot.

They all starred at each other, being as awkwardly British as they possibly could be when trying to be politically correct around race. They all then looked at Paul to egg him on to say something first.

"Hose?" inquired Paul "Is that a nic-name or something?"

"No" said Hose simply

They all reviewed his last answer trying to pick up a hint from his flat accent.

"Hose?" Kirsty echoed. "As in Garden?"

Hose just nodded.

They both then looked at Si, waiting for his question. Si had lost interest before Kirsty started talking. But he felt compelled to say something. Before he could draw breath, Hose's phone started ringing, the familiar 'num-a-near ner, num-a-near ner, num-a-near ner, nerrrr' of the Nokia 3310 that caused 42 other students in the queue to check their pockets.

Hose answered. They couldn't hear what was being said to him, but they could make out the voice on the other end was angry for some reason, Hose's eyes widened with fear, then he ducked out of the queue and into the gents.

“That’s a relief” said Si when Hose was out of earshot.

“Why?” inquired Paul

“Thought nothing would shut him up

They were getting close to the front of the queue. Hose had not caught up with them, which caused Paul and Si to make ever more outlandish jokes about where he had got to.

“Bet he was called out for an emergency with the fire department”

“The fire department?”

“Yea.. he’s a fire Hose”

And that was the best joke they managed. This was then followed by disproportionate levels of laughter, which had more to do with the excitement of being somewhere new and making new friends than actually finding something funny, that was half heartily reined in by Kirsty who wanted to laugh along with the pair of them but felt the burning eyes of other people in the queue who were getting a bit sick of them pratting about.

They reached the enrolment room for their faculty; Si went in first, handed his documents over to the woman by the door who glanced over them, handed them back and pointed to the table in the right-hand corner with the A4 Laminate ‘BA (Hons) History’ sign blu-tac’d to the front. He handed his admissions documents over to the red cheeked man on the other side of the desk and sat down.

He was over the moon it wasn’t Rhonda. It was in the back of his mind how he would feel if he saw her again. He looked around the room, he couldn’t see her. Had she left? It’s possible.

Simon entertained a few fantasies of Rhonda facing the University’s board of governors, struggling to answer their probing questions, and being given her marching orders, in his mind’s eye he could see her employment contract having a red ink stamp being thumped over it that read ‘Sacked for being a bitch, do NOT reemploy’.

The man who was sat in front of him seemed nice. Must have been hired over the summer, Si had never seen him before. His staff ID lanyard he was wearing around his neck said ‘Dr James Wells, deputy head of history’ even though he was sat down Si could see he was tall. His genial nature somehow at odds with how thin and bony he looked, and how sharp and angular his features were. Si guessed with his slightly receding dark brown hair he was in his forties, and not from too far away with the faintest whisper of a Yorkshire accent. So far, he seemed to be the polar opposite of the frosty Dr Jarvis.

“This all seems fine” Said Dr Wells smiling “I see you were here last year” he said looking up

“Yes that’s right” confirmed Si

“You withdrew in January this year is that correct?” Si nodded “It doesn’t state your reason, mind if I ask why?”

Si paused. Part of him wanted to say the truth “I pissed all my loan money away because Rhonda drove me to drink” but he thought better of it.

“I wanted to take some time out” he said eventually. “Travel” he added putting a veneer on what actually ended up being his summer.

“Fair enough” said Dr Wells reaching into a leaver arch file and flicking through the document wallets

“Here’s your timetable” he said handling over a photocopied sheet of A4. “Starts Tuesday next week”

Si froze when he saw Tuesdays at 9am. ‘Approaching History’ with Dr. R. Jarvis. ‘Don’t panic’ an optimistic voice said inside him ‘maybe she still has gone, and they haven’t updated the timetable’

“My first session is with Dr Jarvis?” inquired Si, slightly

panicked.

Dr Wells took the timetable back off him to double check.

"Aye that's right" he confirmed

Si looked around the room.

"Why isn't she here?" asked Si trying to hide the tension in his voice.

"Book signing tour ran over by a day, her new one about the Tudors is more popular than they anticipated"

10:52am B-Block, ground floor

"She the one you were telling me about?" Asked Paul slightly out of breath, finding it hard to keep up with Si's pace

"Yes!" Replied Si. All the bitter memories he felt last year that he thought were buried came rushing back.

"Blimey" Thought Paul. "We got more detail out of Hose". He almost repeated this out loud but sending Si's mood he thought better of it.

"What did she do that was so bad?" Paul followed up as they left B block and into the open air, heading to the direction of the Students Union building. Si's feet now on autopilot.

"I'll ... I'll tell you over a pint" They stopped. "Where's ... what's-her-face" Si clicked his fingers a couple of times trying to jog his memory"

"Kirsty?" Paul offered.

"Yea"

"Still in enrolment"

"Can you text her and tell her to meet us in there?"

"Why can't you?" asked Paul

Si paused before opening the main door.

"I'm out of credit" he explained

"So am I" replied Paul

The two men stood awkwardly for a second.

"Tell you what" Said Paul, figuratively being the bigger man "You get 'em in and I'll nip to Keddie's and get a top up card"

The main corridor that led down to the students union office looked like any other corridor on the campus, except half way as you were walking down on the left was a completely incongruous looking set of double doors that looked like they didn't lead to an office, but to a pub. Like a worm hole to a different time and place.

That was because they did lead to a pub. The Arms bar. The on-campus student pub that Si was walking into almost nine months to the date since he walked out of vowing to never return.

Alan, the bar manager who served him remembered him from before.

"Long time no see Si!" he said with a smile, that wasn't returned.

"Usual?" he inquired.

CHAPTER THREE

What ever happened to Simon Radcliffe?

Tuesday 22nd September 2022

9:45am, Derwent Pharmacy

Meet Simon Radcliffe. Thirty-Nine years old. Now at the age when people call him Simon. Or 'Mr Radcliffe'.

Today was the day. The day Simon had been dreading for the last six weeks.

'Usual Mr Radcliff?' asked the unnecessarily breathy pharmacist.

Simon nodded. He didn't feel much like talking.

The pharmacist scurried off to the back storeroom to collect his prescription. Simon mused for a moment how he always wanted to have a 'usual', to be so well known in a place that they know what you want before you even ask. He would have preferred it to be a coffee shop or a pub, but still here we are.

He couldn't remember if he did have a usual once, there was a vague flicker in the back of his mind that he couldn't tell was truth or if he were misremembering. He sat down on the row of three plastic chairs that where next to the counter with a world-weary sigh.

The sigh gave way to a yawn. He didn't sleep that well last night. Sinus trouble again. One way or another he'd had a lot of trouble with his nose. He was pretty sure it all came from when he broke it during his second attempt at the first term at Uni. He can't remember how he broke it though, although he was told he did it when he fell over when drunk on a night out, he somehow has a vague low-definition memory of someone hitting him, but he can't remember who.

He glanced up at the flat screen TV that was above the counter. Nothing on it of any interest, it just showed a rolling presentation of general health advice that looked like it was put together on PowerPoint (with the smallest amount of enthusiasm), interspersed with the occasional advert that he'd seen on TV from various pharmaceutical firms. Although one of the slides Simon incorrectly guessed was half finished. It just said, 'It's a Trap', this made him think of Admiral Akbar when the slide changed and played an advert.

The adverts changed to suit the time of year. Cold and Flu stuff over the Autumn and Winter, Hay fever stuff over Spring and Early Summer. And all year round an advert about how you can get Viagra now without a prescription, that Simon felt had taunted him.

Every month he came in here for his prescription, he always ended up watching the TV while he waited. There was something about a TV on silent in the corner of a room that Simon couldn't take his eyes off. He was the same every time he was in a pub and the TV was on. It could be the dullest programme imaginable, but he couldn't help himself, he was always transfixed. Last time he was in a pub, which was a while ago now he couldn't keep his eyes off The One Show that was playing on mute with the subtitles on. Much to the annoyance of his Tinder date.

As he waited for his medication, he was mentally totalling up how long he spent waiting for his repeat prescription over the last five years, one or possibly two days in total over the past half-decade were spent in here. Time that could have been better spent doing...

His mind went blank. What could he have been doing? Pressure wash the drive? Dig the garden? Could turn them blackberry's he picked into Jam before they turned. He sighed. He didn't like how middle aged his thoughts had become. Still, better to mull over jam making than dwell on what he was doing this afternoon.

The Viagra advert started playing on the Pharmacy TV. He tutted to himself and took out his phone to double check his appointment and check his emails. He put his thumb on the home button and the built-in fingerprint scanner unlocked his phone. It was still on the weather app 'Derby, dry and sunny 18 degree, 5pm 10% chance of rain' He cleared the weather app and opened his calendar 'All day event, pick up meds' and '2:00pm RDH appt'

The pharmacist reappeared, holding nothing.

"Was it just the one item?" she asked.

With a monumental effort Simon drew breath to speak.
"No, two. Mirtazapine and Quetiapine" replied Simon, whilst suppressing an eye roll. She went back to look again.

Mirtazapine and Quetiapine where his mood stabilisers and anti-psychotic medication. And it had taken five years of trial and error to get him on the right combination.

He hated that term 'anti-psychotic'. As was pointed out to him, on more than one occasion by more than one mental health professional that the term refers to Psychosis and was a run of the mill term in psychiatry. But Simon felt the stigma of having a mental illness bad enough without taking meds that drew up images of Norman Bates.

Simon had always been aware of his depressive side, right from his teens. He was pretty sure looking back that he had a minor breakdown when he flunked his first attempt at uni, as he didn't feel that way again until his full breakdown in October 2017 when he was living in Southampton with his now ex-wife.

Attitudes towards mental health had come a long way in the last twenty years, in 2001 he was too scared to say anything to anyone about how he felt, so he hid it. Convinced himself he was fine, and for a while he was, or so he thought. One of his therapists, Shaun, a trainee councillor who saw people locally for free to help his studies, correctly theorised that the 'golden era' of his life that he keeps harping on about was in fact an elongated mild manic episode.

This rubbed Simon up the wrong way. Sometimes thinking back to when was nineteen was the only thing that cheered him up. Remembering how he felt he could do anything and could take the whole world on. It was a buzz that lasted a couple of years. It wasn't mania. He was just young and full of it. Oh, what did Shaun know anyway. He wasn't even qualified.

"Sounds like to me you were under illusions of grandeur" Shaun theorised.

What? Surely a manic episode is frantic, irrational, high risk taking, requires you being bunged in a padded cell with electrodes on each ear?

"Not really, seems to me like you're on the milder end of the spectrum. That's why you had a hard time getting diagnosed".

He explained that manic episodes are harder to spot in milder cases as the person going through it is actually having a great time. They're full of energy and ego, exactly how he felt when he was in that 'golden era' as Simon put it, but on the flip side can easily go on a downer with little trigger and start self-medicating with booze, sex, or drugs. Or all three.

Simon could think of several occasions where his mood would change wildly over the years, and the booze, sex, drugs, and even kebabs he'd binge on to make himself feel better. One barley memorable Saturday night in 2019 involved all four at once, it was something of a relapse and he certainly didn't want to tell his doctor about it. His mates, sure. But not this doctor.

The pressure cooker that was his sanity had been bubbling away for a decade or so. It all came pouring out one day in a spectacular explosion in 2017 when he was working at

Southampton University. He did his master's degree there in 2006 and got a job in the Students' Union after graduation, initially he felt very comfortable working there and he stayed for ten years. He worked his way up to be Chief Financial Officer. Over time, and thanks to various budget cuts, he ended up doing three roles that were merged into one, on just the one salary that was just about making ends meet.

He had long forgotten his high ambition and dreams he had when he was nineteen and had become an early-thirties cliché. He spent his weekend days mainly in Ikea (on Zoe, his ex-wife's insistence) and nights at dinner parties or housewarmings for a seemingly never-ending list of Zoe's workmates where having. All of which were in vastly superior houses to the crummy flat he was in, none of which seemed to be as stressed as Simon was. This didn't seem fair. Where was he messing up?

Stress and depression where taking its toll. He was now roughly three stone overweight, with a shaved head to mask the fact he was losing his hair and was also the proud owner of a check Shirt that seemed like the uniform for men in their early thirties who had given up on life.

He grew a beard to compensate for the hair loss and to hide the extra chins he was getting. He thought this helped him regain some of his individuality, when in reality he just looked like every other bloke his age.

One day he couldn't hide his poor mental health any longer. He sat in front of his desk at work, rendered catatonic by the pressure cooker lid firing off in his mind. The stress of the job, the underlying and untreated depression, the decade and a half long existential dread, and the problems in his marriage all came up to the surface and dragged him down to the lowest possible depths.

Simon doesn't remember much about what happened next. Apart from all colour disappearing from the world, it looked like he could only see in greyscale. Time slipped passed him in a matter of seconds, three hours he was sat alone at his desk staring at the screensaver, only interrupted by the cleaner who wanted to know if it was alright to lock the office up.

Unable to comprehend what was happening, he checked his phone. Hoping to see several missed calls from Zoe wanting to know where he was. No calls, just a text message from her at 6:30pm saying she was going to the gym then off out with her work mates to a pub in town for somebody at work's leaving do.

"She cares about that job more than she cares about me" he said to himself frequently. Now, in his darkest hour he was certain of it.

He'd been signed off with stress on a couple of occasions in the past year, which Simon didn't disclose to this workmates as he didn't want to appear weak. Zoe, who was becoming increasingly distant showed little empathy and gave zero comfort.

Sure, she was matter of fact and didn't sugar coat stuff, that was one of the qualities that Simon liked about her, at least he did when they first got together. But just a crumb of comfort, something. Anything would have given Simon a lifeline to grab hold of. But no. Nothing.

Zoe was concerned about him, worried sick in fact. She'd never been so close to someone who was clearly not well. She didn't know what to do. She was an only child and the only time her Uber strict parents gushed with emotion was when she achieved something they thought she should be great at. Like playing the piano, even though she hated it. But she persevered as it got her praise, but this made her grow up with a perverted view of empathy. She thought if she carried on as if nothing was happening, Simon would somehow 'snap out of it' and everything would be fine.

But this had the reverse effect. Simon was convinced that she, and indeed everybody would be better off is he was just not here anymore.

A voice took his head over. He didn't recognise the voice, it was snide, vile, and very abusive. Worryingly Simon was doing what it was telling him.

"You're in pain. Everyone who you thought loved you is sick of you. What a burden you've become. What a disappointment you are. There's a way out of this, there's an easy way out. All your pain will go away"

The voice didn't leave him alone from the short drive from the Uni to the West Quay Shopping Centre car park.

He threw away his parking ticket as he knew he wouldn't be needing it and walked to the dockside edge.

"Do it" the voice was on and on at him. "It'll be quick".

He looked down, it was a straight drop into the water, no boats anywhere. He closed his eyes, trembling he swallowed hard and lifted one foot over the side of the ledge. He was a millisecond away from feeling the jolt that would have pushed him over when his phone rang.

The vibration in his pocket shocked him out of his brain fog, his knees buckled, and he fell backwards onto concrete. One leg left dangling over the side. Still lay on the ground he reached into his pocket and got the phone. It took this call as a sign that he had been saved, that someone up there was looking over him. He answered without looking at the screen to see who was calling.

"He......" he was short of breath. He composed himself and tried again.

"Hello"

There was a pause.

"Hello, am I speaking to Simon Radcliffe?" said the friendly voice at the other end

"yes" said Simon, a little disappointed this wasn't Zoe

"Hello Mr Radcliffe, my name's Nia and I'm calling about your accident?" said Nia, her voice going up at the end of the sentence

Simon was somewhere between confused and irritated.

"What accident?" he asked, some power returning to his voice.

"The road traffic accident you were involved with" continued Nia, sounding scripted.

It dawned on Simon what had just happened. An intervention had happened of him committing suicide not made by a loved one or a well-meaning passer-by. But by a cold caller.

He got in that night half an hour before Zoe. He didn't tell her about what did, or rather, tried to do. He told his boss the following morning and broke down in her office, his Boss insisted he go home and see a doctor at soon as possible. He was signed off again, this time with depression.

His knew his life as he knew it was effectively over. He had to do something. He told Zoe why he was signed off, not that this made much difference. As close as she got to being supportive was saying that he should 'visit home' as she 'can't be at work worrying about you'. He was signed off for an extra two weeks and that's where he went. Home. Back to Derby. And he never came back.

Time in familiar surroundings and back near family assisted his recovery well. Seeing what was wrong in his life in black and white he took any and all therapies that where going, registered with his old GP (who he knew would be a million times more helpful than the ones he was seeing in Southampton) and got on a treadmill of medication that would eventually lead him to what he was on now, and as soon as he was able he ended the marriage once and for all.

But no matter how much strength he was able to muster, how much he persevered. That day at Southampton quay still haunted him.

Simon blinked a few times to try and refocus himself, and to shake off thoughts of the Quayside. He found it difficult to concentrate on a regular day, worse so when he was stressed.

He took the day off, he had some holiday days he needed using up so he thought today would be best as he had to pick up his prescription, then head into Hospital.

He had particularly good intentions of getting out of bed at his usual work time, so he could get a decent breakfast and tidy the flat up a bit before leaving. But as usual his good intentions when stressed died quickly.

His alarm on his phone went off at 6:30am as normal. He reached over to hit snooze, only half opening one eye to see what he was doing. Simon's half-awake logic was such that he usually didn't commit to more than half an eye open first thing. Two eyes open, he thought, meant you were fully committed to getting up. And if you fully commit before your memory wakes up then its best to keep your options open. If you keep one eye closed, you could drift back off back to sleep with relative ease.

His memory woke up.

"You have the day off" it informed him, with the speed of a dial up modem.

"Great" thought Simon. "Both eyes shut then" and he rested back into the warm groove of the pillow where his head was a few moments ago. His early morning 56 kb/s speed memory whirred and fizzed some more.

6:39am.

The nine minutes snooze time passed, and his phone's alarm buzzed into life once more and jolted him out of his doze. He opened half an eye again, tutted as he swore he turned the alarm off. He made doubly sure he switched the alarm off and in a half-asleep temper he switched his phone off for good measure. He settled back down. His memory finally processed another fact and reminded him just as he was falling back to sleep.

"You have to set off early to pick up your prescription, you're meds are clean out"

"I'll do it this afternoon" he muttered out loud to no-one and turned over.

"You can't you've got the hospital appointment this afternoon" he memory counteracted.

His phone alarm brayed once again into life. He jolted awake, reached for his phone, and turned it off.

Shocked awake he pondered for a second how that could have happened. He was one hundred percent certain he switched it off. He dismissed it wrongly as a feature that switches the phone back on to make sure you don't oversleep

He rolled onto his back and opened both eyes fully awake.

"Bugger" he thought to himself. Promise of a weekday lie in dashed. He lay there starring at the ceiling. At this point, when both eyes are open, and Simon was committed to being awake was when his depressive inner monologue decided to launch an attack on his self-esteem before he had even had a chance to lift so much as a leg out of the duvet.

He lay there, alone, and vulnerable as he watched the dawn light lift the colour in the room up a shade, while a voice inside his head reminded him what a waste of space his is. How he's got nobody in his life that cares for him, due to him being fundamentally unlovable and how much of a burden he was and how useless he was at his job.

This was followed by a loud and cruel attack on his personal appearance. How 'stupid' he looked since he started to lose his hair. How his head shape was all wrong for carrying off the blade one all over buzz cut look he adopted, as he had little left on top, so the lot had to come off.

"Who are you kidding" his inner depressive monologue would say with all the malice it could muster, "makes you look nothing like Jason Statham. More like a Bond Villain.'

And all this would be launched at him before he even got out of bed. It was a persistent voice that never gave him a minute's peace. He regularly had to contend with all this before it even reached 7am.

All this plus the dread about his hospital appointment just about capped off the worst start to a day possible for Simon. He hated doctors and hospitals (and right now as he sat waiting for is meds, pharmacists!) to such a degree that his therapist said he had all the hallmarks of Post-Traumatic Stress Disorder, as if an incident took place in his youth at a hospital that scarred him for life. But nothing happened that he could remember.

He was referred by his GP who was a tad concerned during his last check in, he had only gone in for a medication review and mentioned he noticed blood in his urine.

His GP referred him to be checked out by a prostate cancer specialist. He had a family history with the condition, his dad died because of it when he was fifteen. Plus, he was he was approaching forty and was coming to the age range where both factors where a red flag.

“It’s probably nothing” his doctor reassured him holding his palm out flat in front of him to indicate to his worry to stop “But better to be safe than sorry”. Simon was a little touchy about his age and any time he had to confront his mortality, both coming at once was a blow, as both reminded him about how much of the last twenty or so years he had wasted.

He thought back to all the things he thought he could be when he was nineteen. Novelist, TV Historian, teacher, lecturer, he even wanted to stand as an M.P in a general election one day.
Five general elections had passed since he was nineteen and he’d done nothing. (Apart from a quick google search of ‘how do I become an MP’ shortly after the 2010 election, but that was as far as he got.)
The closest he got to a job in government was his current sole sucking excuse for a job as procurement manager in the accounts department at Derby City Council. Thirty-Nine years of life had amounted to this. Middle management in a finance team of a regional council that had its budget repeatedly slashed

to the bone. By now he thought he'd be going to his dream job wearing Hugo Boss suits, not making do whilst head to toe in Primark.

His office on the second floor of the council house overlooked the main square of the city. He had a direct view of the QUAD, the arts centre opposite the council that looked like a first draft Guggenheim discarded for looking too over the top. He would look out and see the various arty types going in and out. Pensioners catching a matinee screening of a classic film, tech crews setting up for various events and the most popular thing the QUAD was used for. The toilet.

It was a prime location in town, where people seem to want to go to the toilet the most for some reason..Then when they left to exit, they were greeted with a four-foot-tall see-through donation box that was half full of 20p's the odd fiver (and the odd Euro) with a sign attempting to guilt users to contribute to the toilets maintenance costs.

No matter who they were going in and out the Quad, Simon looked on with envy. He was jealous of their apparent freedoms. He wanted to live. He wanted to do something spare of the moment like he used to do. He was fed up with feeling trapped. Trapped by his condition. Trapped by his past. Nothing he ever did seemed to quite live up to the standard he set of himself when he was nineteen. Trapped by his uninspiring life living for each payday and barely making ends meet in between.

"Mr Radcliffe!" the pharmacist returned holding a small white paper bag containing his medication. Simon stood up and walked towards the counter.

"What's the address?" She asked as a security question. This always puzzled Simon why they did this. If a thief or a pill head were chancing their arm and happened to guess at a million to one odds his hard to pronounce combination of tablets as well as pluck his name out of the air, Simon would have handed the pills straight over, impressed at the odds defying thief.

"24a Duffield Road" he said flatly. She handed him the bag then moved on to the next person in the queue.

Simon put his pills into his bag and walked through town to the bus station, while he had his bag open he double checked if he had his referral letter, and his phone charger as he was down to 46% already.

He decided to take the bus into the Royal instead of driving. He remembered when he last went the extortionate parking fees, and the buses where every ten minutes. As he reached the city centre he pondered over all the shops at length, putting off actually getting on the bus until the absolute last minute he could.
When faced with a task he found unpleasant Simon became a world class procrastinator. If it was an Olympic sport he could have got a gold medal in wasting time for his country.

The closer Simon got to a deadline, the more wild and vivid ways he would invent to waste time that could be spent getting on with the task in hand, a bad habit he had nurtured over these past ten years. His last quarterly review for work for example, he kept putting off until the day before it was due, and even then he found inventive and creative ways to put it off on the day, or to make a start on it in a not-really-starting it way. By 4:30pm he convinced himself he would be ok to do it that night at home after work. So, he emailed himself the word document he started, that was one page long and only had the words 'Finance department Q2' written on it.

He was utterly certain that he could write a detailed and comprehensive report that would normally take a month between the hours of 5pm and 10pm. Actually, would be less time than that, he didn't get in till 5:30, sometimes 5:50 if the traffic was bad. So, at best he'd have four hours between getting in and the usual time he got to bed. Not that he turned the lights out and went straight to sleep at 10pm. He'd usually be on twitter getting angry at people who he never met, because they didn't share his political point of view.

When he did get in, he lost another hour watching The Chase, then another hour getting dinner, he usually lived on ready meals and take aways but tonight, in full procrastination mode, he absolutely had to cook fresh and from scratch. After this he also managed to kill another fifteen minutes on Candy Crush just for good measure.

By the time he sat down at his desk, in front of his computer in his spare bedroom it was 8:20pm. By that point, his stress levels had beaten up his concentration levels, so he managed to waste a further ten minutes reading Wikipedia.

During his brief walk to the bus station, he couldn't help but roll his eyes slightly at the charity shops that still had funeral clothing on the dummies in the window. The thought occurred to him that as it had been over two weeks since the Queen died, and if you were one of the great and good who attended the funeral, why would you buy a dark suit or dress from a charity shop in Derby? As he was mulling this over he stopped suddenly and became transfixed by a travel agents window.

The last-minute deals board he found particularly appealing. His eyes fixated on a deal for 'Rhodes. Seven Nights, all inclusive.

Flights from East Midlands Airport Thursday 24th September, £199'

He was tempted. Would the bunch of ungrateful tossers in his team even have noticed he was gone? If he just booked the flight and buggered off? Under £200 all in? It wouldn't break the bank. He'd never been to Rhodes, in fact in the last 20 years the only times he went abroad was for a booze cruise to Calais in 2009, and that was only a day trip. And his honeymoon to Paris in 2012.

He was desperate to get away. The more he thought of it the more excited he got, an excitement he hadn't felt in far too long. He was just about to take a step to go in and book it when he felt a vibration on his watch. It was a calendar notification.

‘Last chance to get bus’. His faced sagged. His shoulders slumped with defeat, and he walked off towards the bus station.

As he walked a thought came to him that he instantly dismissed as ridiculous and pushed to the back of his mind. Which was a pity as the thought was true.

And the thought was

“Hang on, I don’t remember setting a reminder in my calendar to get the bus”

And he was right. He didn’t.

CHAPTER FOUR

This takes me back

Tuesday 22nd September 2022

4:38pm, Royal Derby Hospital

The anger that comes from feeling helpless and powerless is almost like a superpower. And right now, Simon was using that superpower to storm out of the hospital at great speed.

He breezed through the automatic doors of the front entrance of the Royal and into the car park with such a pace the lag of the CCTV could barely pick him up. One second he was there, next moment he disappeared into thin air.

Inconclusive! Incon-bloody-clusive! As he exited out the front entrance of the Royal, Simon kicked a discarded Costa coffee cup that was lay on the ground in temper. He hit it with such force it vaulted over a bus stop, with drips of coffee cartwheeling out as it spun.

All them weeks of worrying, going to the darkest possible outcome in his mind just to have his hind quarters probed with no clear results. Anger, mixed with a short-changed feeling, with a dollop of anxiety teamed through Simon's veins so much it made him twitch, and he was barely able to finish a sentence in his thoughts with temper. Let alone talk out loud.

He didn't feel like getting on a bus, he needed to vent so opted to walk from the hospital back to his flat. With his current mood, he could probably do the two-mile walk in about 30 minutes, hopefully by then he would have calmed down and got his head around his results. His irrational hatred of hospitals, now at an all-time peak.

In his mind he had prepared how to deal with positive and negative results of the day, he was ready for both outcomes and how to deal with them both, but not ‘inconclusive, come back in six weeks for further tests’.

An hour and a half he waited for his appointment, alone. He noticed while he was navigating his way to the outpatients area waiting room, that he was one floor below the palliative care ward, which did very little to sooth his overactive mind. Being passed by ghostly looking people who looked like they didn’t have long left sent a chill right through him, this didn’t get any better when he reached the waiting room where he was surrounded by concerned looking quiet men of a certain age.

All men that is, apart from Brian.

Simon didn’t actually talk to Brian during his wait. He only knew his name as his meek looking wife who was sat next to him, regularly gave him a playful tap on his arm when he was being ‘hilarious’ and said in a voice that had all the impact of a talking doll who’s batteries where wearing down

“Ooh Brian, stop iiitttt”. And then she’d giggle.

Brian looked like he was in his late sixties, overweight, bald, and had a red complexion on his face that showed the world proudly, that it had been many years since his last piece of fruit. His coping mechanism at times of great stress was humour. And he was sat in the waiting room next to his low battery wife using humour. Badly. Laughing too loudly and too much. Cracking inappropriate jokes at the top of his voice, talking at a volume that was one notch above what was acceptable, especially to the pale looking man sat next to him.

The poor bloke who couldn’t escape looked so beaten up by life that any attempt to stand up would kill him off in an instant and having Brian talking at him seemed to be the cherry on the cake of torture, he had no fight to escape. Brian mistook this as somebody who was genuinely interested in everything that came out of his foghorn of a mouth and didn't pick up on the subtlety tortured edges of this poor man's expressions, who couldn't escape the story about Brian's last cruise, and about how the Radiotherapy course 'isn't going to stop him from going back on the same trip this year'.

Simon could see right through Brian. Blokes like that always have a tell, a sign that they are denying their true emotions. When he wiped his face after cracking yet another joke, Simon spotted a tear he wiped away, a tear that he knew instinctively wasn't one of joy.

Simon was mentally reviewing the day, the last six weeks and then by extension the last thirty-nine years of his life. Walking on autopilot, he barely noticed the world around him.

It was an awful day, and Simon's brain liked to give him a depressive episode when he was having a bad day. It relished kicking him when he was down and dishing out punishment he didn't want or deserve. The door was wide open for him to be reminded of every mistake he ever made, every stupid thing he ever said, a large dose of paranoia and anxiety all delivered with a lovely side order of crippling depression. His mind was so scrambled, he hadn't noticed the rain starting. Or the wrong turning he just made. He was walking into the centre of town.

He tried desperately to fight the onset, but once again came that all too familiar sinking through quicksand feeling.

"Deep breaths" he thought. "In through the nose, out through the mouth"

He knew the drill well, he'd adapted a neurolinguistic programming technique he learned to calm himself down, it had various stages, firstly it involved deep breathing and 'anchoring his calmness' by trying to remember a happier time, list all of his achievements in order to negate the nagging voice that was inside him, telling him that he never amounted to anything, and to make it as vivid and real as possible.

He pinpointed, with extraordinarily little guidance from one of the many therapists he saw, when his happy time was. His second-first term at Uni when he was nineteen.

He got out his Bluetooth headphones and put them in his ears, they made their familiar 'dum-dum' noise to indicate they were connected. Then he got his phone, opened Spotify, and looked for his 'September 2002 playlist'. Music usually helped when he was feeling like this.

"Ok, keep calm. Remember your achievements. And breath"

He ran through a list of great things he'd accomplished. The first thing that always sprang to mind was that time he rugby tackled that confused looking old man out of the way of an oncoming car that was seconds away from smacking into him. The CCTV footage of that happening made the front page of the next day's Derby Evening Telegraph, which he still had framed. The frame was in his hallway on the floor, he kept meaning to put it up since he moved back.

He was in town with his mate Paul, he'd had a few and the Dutch courage had egged him on smack into this bloke and pull him out of the way. Funny thing was that was all he could remember. He remembered the man was wet for some reason, even though it was sunny. Couldn't remember that man's face, or what happened next. Next few weeks were a bit of a blur truth be told.

Then there was going back to uni and making a success of it. Making Captain of the Rugby first team in his first year, that electrifying relationship with Hannah that lasted till the Easter. Feeling real Love and being Loved back.

Fine, she buggered off down south and he never saw or heard from her again, and it left a scar that he still has now. But boy what a few months they were. His heart still skips a beat when he thinks of her, even now.

Let's see, what else. What else. Oh yes! Getting a first in his history degree and graduating.

And that was usually as far as Simon's list of life achievements got to. One year of living his life to the full when he was nineteen, bit of a gap, graduation, then sod all since.

At least that was how his mind liked to frame things. If Simon were to let himself off the hook a little and really look for big life achievements he could have found loads more. Like having the strength to end a toxic relationship. Being able to reject a life that wasn't working for him and make a bold move away from it all. To take his mental health issues head on and not give up (at least, not succeed in giving up. Yet) But Simon was way too hard on himself. He was his own worst critic and own worst enemy and had utterly convinced himself he peaked in absolutely everything by the time he hit twenty.

He was challenged on this recently, when he bumped into an old uni mate of his, Kirsty, by chance at a festival they both happened to be at.

She hadn't seen Simon since 2006 and noted with some surprise (although she didn't say it out loud) just how different he was. Kirsty, who was now a secondary school teacher was camping for the weekend at the festival with her family, husband Tom who she met when she started working at the school she was currently at, and five-year-old daughter Grace.

Tom, who with his easy-going charm, full head of hair and zero sign of a stomach was the first to suggest Kirsty and Simon have a bit of a catch up while he took Grace to the fun fair. In fact, Tom was so nice, confident, and easy going, Simon couldn't see a single thing he could possibly like about him.

He and Kirsty got chatting, sitting outside her tent on two-fold away chairs. Tom even telling Simon before he left to 'help himself' to the cooler box of expensive looking fruit cider. Simon smiled and thanked him while internally thinking 'prick, no one likes a show off'.

They reminisced about old times and what they got up to since they last met. Simon was stunned by how little Kirsty had changed, different haircut and the odd laughter line here and there but you'd think it was five year that had passed, not twenty. Kirsty was always fond of Simon. In fact, she did once have a bit of a thing for him in that first week of enrolment. She was working up the nerve to make a move on him when he met Hannah at her flat party, they were together for less than a year, but by the time Simon was free again Kirsty was with someone else, and by that point they'd become just good friends.

Simon didn't tell her everything that had happened in his life. When you have limited time with someone you've not seen for a while, you tend to present a highlights reel instead of the whole truth. But Kirsty picked up on the fact that he was mentally hung up on his youth, particularly that first year they met.

She played devil's advocate saying that 'the past tends to be rose tinted; things weren't as rosy as all that' which Simon shrugged at. His response being 'well, it's not like I can go back in time and check is it?'

They ended the chat an hour later when Tom got back with Grace from the fun fair and another crate of cider he'd got from the car, to replenish what Simon had drunk. Which was pretty much all of it.

After he said his goodbyes and Simon shook that smug show off Tom's hand, he went off in the direction of his own tent. He didn't look back as he walked away, or he would have seen Kirsty looking at him with a mixture of pity, and relief that he'd gone. She felt drained.

As Simon's mind was all over the place, he only mildly registered he now was on St Peter's Street in the centre of town and not anywhere near his flat. But he didn't care much at this point. Reviewing his crummy life, and the six weeks of extra worrying that he might have the big C, kicked him down so far and so fast he was spiralling such a rapid rate, he was low. Dangerously low.

So, he didn't care he was in the centre of Derby in the pouring rain with no umbrella. He didn't notice the thunder that was rumbling overhead. But that was probably more to do with 'By the Way' by the Red-Hot Chili Peppers playing at full blast down his ears than his lack of awareness.

He hadn't had this feeling since that day at Southampton Quay. This was a shocker; he didn't expect things to go this dark. Now he had the hopeless feeling like the last five years of trying to sort himself out meant nothing thrown into the mix, as right now he honestly didn't care if a bus hit him. (Not that it would as almost all of Derby was pedestrianised.) But what he didn't realise was, when he reaches his lowest ebb something would happen that would shock him out of all this.

Pretty soon, by a freak accident of physics and nature and with zillion to one odds. Simon Radcliffe was about to walk into the history books.

The thunder and rain intensified along with the thoughts of the past inside Simons head. Shoppers dashed into the Derbion centre to escape the rain, the street leading up to The Spot, the local slang name given to a triangular paved area outside the London Road entrance to the shopping centre was deserted apart from a dangerously depressed Simon.

He didn't notice the lightning. The first bolt of fork lightning that hit thirty miles away, the second in quick succession fifteen or so miles away or the third that hit the stainless-steel metal ring sculpture located at The Spot as he passed through the centre of it. The Sculpture was installed in 2016 and is a series of chrome metal rings that you could walk through, that symbolised the city's industrial past, that the locals affectionately nic-named 'Derby's Cock Ring'.

He didn't feel anything as he passed through it. Not that this feeling had been ever documented by anyone until that point, but you'd have thought walking back in time twenty years would have been a bit grander. There was no rush, no pain or pleasure. It was as mundane and routine as just walking from the kitchen to the front room, and just as instant.

He didn't twig that the rain had instantly stopped when he passed through, or that the same bit of pedestrianised road he was on before was now open to traffic. He didn't notice that the ring sculpture had gone and the old underground toilets that had been filled in years ago were back. What snapped him out of his brain fog, was that he noticed out of the corner of his eye to his left, that Poundland has somehow become Woolworths again.

An underfunded department of his brain that looks for a rational response to bizarre situations, wrongly assumed that Poundland had shut down and when they removed the signage, the Woolworths one was still underneath. This would have been a great explanation if it weren't for the Woolworths sale signs in the window, the pick and mix clearly visible from outside and the shoppers leaving the front entrance with Woolworths braded single use plastic bags.

The music stopped; Simon took his phone out of his pocket to check why. No 5G signal, he looked up again open mouthed at the somehow newly reopened branch of Woolworths Derby in the... wait what? The Eagle Centre? It hasn't been called The Eagle Centre in years! Where's the rest of it gone? The huge unsightly grey box that housed the extended shopping centre, that should have towered behind the inexplicably reopened Woolworths had disappeared. And so had the extension that took up all of London Road. The run down 1960's concrete open plan shopping precinct was back, and on the other side...

"Zanzibar!" he mouthed. The nightclub he spent almost every Monday night at when he was a student was back, and the 'all you can eat' buffet restaurant that took its place had vanished.

He stood rooted to the spot desperately trying to find an explanation as to what was happening. A middle-aged woman wearing a Woolworths uniform bumped into him

'Sorry duck' she said as she held a hand out apologetically and headed for the front entrance. Simon noticed the uniform, why would someone be wearing a Woolworths uniform? He shouted after the woman, hoping she could shed some light on the situation

“Excuse me.. oi woman that bumped into me!”

The woman, who Simon knew was called Cheryl thanks to her name badge turned around, she clutched her handbag a bit tighter. Simon tried to find the right phrase to not make him sound like a weirdo

“Where am I?” he said. “Oh, bravo weirdo” he thought as soon as the words left his mouth

Cheryl just looked confused

“Don’t ask me duck I just work here” she replied, running into work away from the weird man. What did he have in his ears? Who wears headphones with the cables cut off?

Simon found it hard recovering from the sudden, yet not unpleasant jolt to his senses, he was still taking in his surroundings, head tilted up with his mouth ever so slightly open when he heard tyres screech, without realising he was in the path of oncoming traffic, he turned around to see a car had taken a blind corner at speed and was accelerating towards him.

The driver could see him, but for some reason, when he did, he put his foot down, then as he accelerated let out a huge yawn. Like the thought of deliberately knocking someone over bored him to tears.

From Simon’s point of view, what happened next, happened in slow motion. He half heard a familiar sounding scream that was aimed in his direction, then he felt a sudden thud. Not from the car, but from a rugby tackle that hit his midriff and knocked him forcefully out the way with a nano second to spare and he and another man hit the floor with a graceless tumble.

Simon didn’t see what happened to the car after it almost hit him. He had enough to process without seeing a 1998 Astra speeding off down London Road and very slowly getting more transparent until it faded completely out of existence.

A crowd was beginning to gather and surround the two men, a few locals and an unusually high number of tourists. Simon was winded on the floor with his eyes closed, so he couldn't see the assembling crowd take pictures with disposable wind on cameras. He could just about make out the chatter of the assembled onlookers

'That was close!'

'That was amazing'

'Bloody hell that kid were quick'

'Aww, I'm out of film'

'Why's that bloke so wet, been sunny all day?'

Simon could hear the other man's voice, the man who rugby tackled him out the way. It was familiar, but he couldn't quite place it. It was someone he knew; someone he knew a while ago when they were young.

'You ok mate?' asked the other man.

That was when Simon Radcliffe aged thirty-nine gently opened his eyes to see standing over him was, Simon Radcliffe. Aged nineteen. He was face to face with his nineteen-year-old self. And the reason why Derby looked so different was he was no longer in 2022. He was in 2002.

Under the extraordinary circumstances the elder Simon did the only sensible thing he could do. He passed out.

CHAPTER FIVE

D.R.I

Tuesday 17th September 2002.

Time unknown, Location also unknown

As he came to, Simon's senses gingerly went one by one back into action. First was hearing. He could hear somebody talking, it was muffled, but it was somebody official sounding. Then smell. A mixture of disinfectant and lino registered in his nose. There's only two places in his memory that smells like disinfectant and lino and seeing as he had the day off, he wasn't in the kitchen at work. That means, oh god, he was in hospital. Again?

His memory woke up a tad quicker than usual. Maybe he was still there? Hang on, that makes more sense. Yes.... yes it's all fitting into place now. He blacked out when he was in hospital earlier and had a vivid dream where he came face to face with his younger self. A very vivid dream, in fact his stomach muscles still ached from it. That is weird! Weird but not without form, this wouldn't be the first time some medication he was on gave him vivid and trippy dreams.

A couple of years ago when his GP first tried to switch him from anti-depressants to anti-psychotics, he had a week when he could smell what was happening in his dreams. Simon felt quite cheered by this thought. Confidence filtered through his body as he stretched and opened his eyes. He could hear a doctor talking to somebody, he caught the tail end of the conversation.

"...not even a fractured rib, thanks to you he's going to be fine. Hang on, your dads waking up"

Dad? Simon didn't have kids. What?

Simon bolted upright wide awake; he was on a hospital bed in a curtained off room.

"Relax Mr Radcliffe, you're safe and sound. You were bought into A&E to check you were ok. Thanks to your son you're gonna be fine" said the on-duty Doctor with impeccable bedside manner.

Behind him Simon could see his younger self staring back at him plain as day, and with an equal amount of disbelief. This can't be real? This was impossible, right? His brain was still not able to grasp what was happening, he searched desperately for a clue, a crumb of anything to apply some logic and reason to this situation.

"Which hospital?" asked Simon dry mouthed

This concerned the doctor a tad. Maybe he was more confused than he first realised? Perhaps he had a mild concussion?

"The Royal" said the doctor. Simon let out a sigh of relief. It was a vivid dream after all. The Royal Derby hospital was opened in 2010. He was up from Southampton visiting his mum and he remembered watching the Queen officially open the Royal on the local news. So far so good, but it still didn't explain why he was hallucinating a vision of his nineteen-year-old self though. Also didn't explain why the doctor could also see him. Still, one thing at a time.

The doctor could see this news was a comfort, so he repeated it while he picked up his clipboard and turned to leave. "Safe and sound in the Derby Royal Infirmary". The Doctor told Simon's younger self he was off to get his dads discharge papers and would be right back. Not that Simon registered this. He was getting his head around the fact a doctor had told him he was in a hospital that had been demolished seven years ago from his point of view.

The Doctor left and pulled the curtains. Simon and this vision of his younger self were alone for the first time. There was the mother of all awkward silences. Both of them wanted to say something, but what? How the hell could you sting a sentence together to sum up what was going on? Then they both drew breath to speak and said "Who..." in unison. The elder Simon backed down and gestured to his younger self to go first.

"Mate, Who the hell are you?" his younger self asked

"Was just about to ask you the same question" said the elder Simon as he swung his legs over the side of the bed.

"Why does your driver's licence have my name and Birthday on it?" inquired the younger version

"Have you been rifling through my wallet?" asked his older self, slightly indignant.

After the elder Simon passed out, the younger Si had to think on his feet and had to find out who this man was, and why this man who he had just rugby tackled to the ground looks so much like him. The unfeasibly large number of tourists had dispersed shortly after the incident leaving a few locals, one of which called for an ambulance.

"I had to find out who you where before the ambulance got there" said Si, replying to his older self's question

"and also, why you look like me but like..." Si paused. He was going to say "like me, but like fifty years old" but he checked himself, he didn't want to cause any offence, no matter who this bloke was.

Simon eyed his younger self dubiously.

"You were gonna say fifty then weren't you?" he said as his eyes narrowed.

There was a long pause

"wasn't" said Si, unconvincingly.

"Yea right!" Simon replied with authority in his voice, which quickly turned to incredulity when he remembered what the doctor said "Also, why did you tell the doctor I was your dad?"

"That wasn't me, that was the paramedics" His younger self explained that they guessed he was his dad due to how similar they looked, but older. He went along with it so he could ride along with him in the ambulance.

This was weird, but he had to know more. Nothing about this added up to Si. After he finished enrolment that morning and spilled his guts to Paul about his run in's with Dr Jarvis the previous year, Kirsty had joined them in The Arms bar for a drink. Which turned to two drinks. Then three drinks, then before they knew it, it was 2pm and they were all in the mood for a session.

They got the bus into town, (Kirsty making a point of sitting next to Simon on the bus ride in) and they all decided food would be a good idea before they drank any more. After eating, Kirsty declared that the Pizza that they stopped for, on top the bottle and a half of wine she drank in the middle of the day had made her a tad sleepy, so she ducked out, much to the protests of Si and Paul who were also feeling as knackard as Kirsty was but didn't dare admit it.

Si and Paul were on route to a pub near the precinct on London Road because Paul was absolutely certain that had an offer on for £1 a pint. He went on ahead to 'get them in' while Si stopped at a cashpoint near The Spot, where he noticed a bewildered man who was drenched in water, with two white things that looked like earphones but with no cables stuck in his ears. He was standing still in the middle of the road looking at Woolworths like he hadn't seen it in years when a car came at him.

He felt compelled to help. Si was no daredevil or have a go hero, but Dutch courage helped, mixed with and indescribable feeling, like an outside force was driving him on to get this bloke out of the way of the car. Like… it was like… how could he put this?

"Like your future depended on it?" offered Simon as he put his shoes on and went to get his coat.

"Yea" said Si, amazed that this man so was in tune with how he was feeling, and completely missing the quote from Back to the Future part three, a film that Si didn't watch until he was 24.

When they were in the ambulance, going the short distance to the demolished hospital that now exists again and is working fully, the younger Si remembered he forgot all about Paul. He found he still had 14p worth of credit, so he text him a vague outline of what had happened, he thought it best to leave out the weird bit about a man who looked like him, and that he was on route to the hospital. Not that Paul noticed, as when he got the drinks in he was then glued to the fruit machine for the next two hours until he got Si's text. This, as Si would later find out would be standard behaviour from Paul whenever they went to a bar. He'd get up to go to the toilet, then disappear for forty-five minutes as he'd been snagged by a fruit machine and left Si sat alone with nothing but what was left of his drink for company.

Paul would then spend the rest of the week moaning that he was skint.

The Simon's were in an impossible situation. You don't know how you're going to deal with an impossible and extreme situation until you're presented with it. Your reactions tend to surprise you, as you don't have the capacity to think about the ramifications of what has just been presented to you, you just work on instinct. You don't overthink.

You just do.

This was what was currently happening to both versions of Simon. The two men, although not saying it outright, they were extraordinarily at ease with this situation, at least for now, and they knew deep down who the other one was, and what had happened without saying out loud.

The elder Simon stood up. As he did a shocking dizziness mixed with queasy feeling overcame him, akin to a comedown you'd feel from a rollercoaster that was just a notch above what you could cope with. Sweat started to pour out of his forehead. He sat down on the bed. He mouth started producing way too much saliva.

"You ok?" Si asked his older self; aware it was a stupid question. Clearly he wasn't.

Simon had now gone from 'roller coaster come down' up several levels. What made the experience more difficult to cope with, was the mental flashes he was getting. Vivid Images popped into Simon mind of the current situation he was in, but not from his point of view, he was viewing them from the point of view his younger self, a few moments before they happened in front of him.

This was preposterous. Can't be a memory, this didn't happen when he was nineteen. He would have remembered meeting himself in his late thirties. Yet here he was, seeing his older self from behind his younger self's eyes asking his older self if he was ok, shortly before he said it. Was this a premonition? A side effect? Whatever it was it was knocking him for six.

Si guided his older self-back gently back onto the bed. The older man's breathing was shallow, and his pupils dilated. The younger Si pressed the call button above the bed to summon a doctor.

Simon battered his younger selves' hand away, despite the shakes he managed to grab the lapels of the younger Si's beige jacket.

"You, have to get me out of here" said a breathy Simon

Si protested that he was in the best place, and that the doctor with the world beating bedside manner would be back in a minute to see to him. But the premonitions, future sight, or whatever Simon was currently having flashed to him where coming in a rush. He was now several minutes ahead of his younger self.

For some reason he knew the doctor who had tended to him a few moments ago was now lying dead in his office, as he had a flash of his younger self being told this by current self. His younger self in disbelief went straight to the doctor's office, to see he had his throat cut while he was on the cusp of finding out that Simon's dad was dead, and this man taking up a bed in A&E was an imposter.

As Simon was explaining the doctors death to his younger self he dashed out of his cubicle while his older self was mid-sentence. Which was exactly what the elder Simon was trying to avoid, as when he did this the assassin who killed the doctor, disguised as a nurse would enter the cubicle where he was currently sweating through the bedsheets and wait for his younger self while the elder Simon was too sick to move.

As if this wasn't enough, the part of the elder Simon's brain that relishes in giving him a hard time decided that now was a good moment to connect some dots and give him some stick.

"Wow, all these years you prided yourself on saving that 'fat old man' from oncoming traffic. Your words not mine! And it turns out that 'fat old man' was you!"

Even time travel wasn't enough to shut his depression up.

As young Si was racing back the ward to get this man out, who looks like an older version of himself, who can also somehow see into the future, he felt his phone vibrate on his inside pocket. He put it on silent when he got to the hospital.

He took out his phone. A Nokia 3310 with a custom Union Jack phone cover.

One new message. Unknown number.

He opened the message, it read

"Don't Panic. Grab a wheelchair and take it back to the cubicle. The man in the bed IS who you think he is. You must walk into the trap set for you; Stand below A.C we'll do the rest. When done, take him back to your halls. Explain more when we see you. -F."

The assassin, who was sat on an orange plastic chair next to the bed usually used for visitors was casually cleaning the scalpel she used on the doctors neck with a blood-soaked tissue. She was explaining to a semi-conscious Simon how bored she was with trying to kill him, knowing full well that she fails. Saying that she would love to tell him her reasons, but she'd been stuck over and over doing this so many times in a pointless never-ending paradox. She'd honestly forgot.

"Oh bugger, forgot the straps" the assassin tutted, rolled her eyes then sighed. She looked at Simon. He looked pretty out of it; in fact, she knew full well he passed out in a minute. Wouldn't be the end of the world if she just went through the motions without ratcheting him to the bed? Them rachet straps were just a pain to get right just for all her work to be undone in a matter of minutes. Maybe there could be a compromise?

The younger Si found a wheelchair quite easily on his way back to A&E, as a follow up text message from the mysterious 'F' told him where they put one for him. Brand spanking new one, complete with a tartan blanket to put over the elder Simons legs.

He got back to the cubicle, drew back the curtains and saw his older self-passed out on the bed, and for some reason he was tied to it around his waist with a pair of tights.

He leaned in to get a closer look at the flimsy knot when an arm went around his shoulder, looped around his chest and pulled him back.

"Don't move, I've got a scalpel in your neck." She said flatly. She paused.

"Now, what came next... hang on. It's on the tip of me tongue" she clicked her tongue a few times as if to jog her memory.

The younger Si went from petrified for his life to baffled in a second. Why would someone who's trying to kill me sound like they were reading lines from a play? How is it possible to try and kill someone and to find it boring?

"W, w, who the hell are you?" he asked stuttering slightly.

Despite her disinterested demeanour, the blade in his neck felt all too real.

"Got it. Thanks. You say 'who the hell are you ..blah blah blah blah bla' she mentally went through some dialogue in her brain, then continued

"I am from an organisation that wants to stop the discovery of time travel, because a trap that is set for you that has terrible consequences. You Simon Radcliffe are the first man to travel in time. I have come back to the day you meet your older self to kill you so you can never become him in the bed, who is you from twenty years in the future. Now stay still I'm going to slit your throat".

She recited the whole speech in a monotone voice, and seemingly in one breath not pausing.

As she finished saying throat, the air conditioning unit directly above them started to judder and lurch about with such force it made the ceiling tiles shake. With a sudden and violent choke, a plume of black smoke and oil ejected from the unit, hitting the assassin square in the face, and only barely hitting the younger Simon, who used the confusion to break free from her grip and volt over the bed to untie his older self.

The assassin blinded by the smoke and choking on the flumes looked in the general direction of them both and said, for the first time like she properly meant it.

"oh I don't want to do this any..."

Before she could say ...more the air con unit came free of its housing and hit her on the head. Crushing her skull and killing her instantly.

Stunned and sickened by what he just witnessed and fired up with adrenaline, the younger Simon attempted a fireman's lift to the man the bored assassin and the text message from 'F' confirmed was his older self, to get him to the wheelchair. He stumbled on his first attempt. A mixture of skidding on the oil ejected by the air conditioner unit and skidding on the blood ejected by the assassin.

As he attempted his second lift, the blood started to fade. As did all the debris ejected by the air conditioner. And so did the assassin, or rather what was left of her. Everything in the cubicle was resetting before his eyes and was swiftly back to normal.

The only thing that remained was the queasy feeling left in his stomach from witnessing her violent death, which now didn't seem to have even happened.

Taking comfort from the text message he received from 'F' whoever they were, he went into action with the next part of its instructions. He managed to get his older self into the wheelchair, tutting greatly at his increased weight as he got older. He tucked the tartan blanket over his older selves legs and headed for the exit.

As he wheeled his older self-past the murdered doctor's office, the murdered doctor came out the door and walked past him. Alive and as genial as he was just half an hour previously. He waved and smiled at Si.

"Take care Mr Radcliffe" the doctor smiled as he waived, but he couldn't help the niggling feeling that he didn't sign off his discharge papers.

"Yea bye" replied Si increasing his speed as he pushed his unconscious older self closer to the entrance, not looking back.

Next stop, Peak Court.

CHAPTER SIX

If in doubt...

Tuesday 17th September 2002

8:31pm, Flat 34, Peak Court Halls of Residence

Si stared blankly at his reflection in the window. The strip lights in the kitchen were on as it was now dark, so he couldn't see much outside. Not that he was concentrating on his reflection. Even looking directly at his own face he couldn't see it, all he could see was the face of the man who almost got run over.

Everything that had happened today still hadn't sunk in, even now, three hours later. Since he got back to his halls Si had spent the majority of the time pacing the floor, making coffee, or starring out of the window. Enough starring he thought, back to pacing the grey lino of his kitchen and try once again to make sense of it all.

It times of great crisis, or even mild crisis. Any level of crisis in fact, Si would heed some advice his mum gave him, which was 'if it doubt put the kettle on'.

It was a flippant remark his mum said once when he was little, but for some reason it stuck in his head as gospel, to him it was the eleventh commandment so that's what he was doing, filling the kettle full of water for the fourth time this hour.

He turned the tap off, closed the lid, and slammed the kettle back down purposefully on its base and flicked the switch down on the bottom of the handle. He could have killed for a beer right now, or something stronger but he didn't want to leave the flat. When he got back from the hospital, somehow not managing to bump into anyone he knew while wheeling an unconscious heap of a man, who looked a lot like him halfway across town in a wheelchair, he put the unconscious so called older version of himself into his bed, then locked him in his room while he took the chair to the downstairs car park, as per the instructions of the mysterious 'F' in a follow up text message.

Even though he had his doubts and was assured by 'F' that he and this heap would be safe for tonight at least, he didn't want to leave and walk the short distance to the off licence around the corner. He felt compelled to stick around. Stand guard, the same compulsion he felt when he knocked this man out of the way of an oncoming car.

Nobody else in the flat had any alcohol (at least none that they left in the kitchen) and what with it being freshers week they were all out in town. So, Si was alone in the kitchen, with only a jar of instant coffee and half a packet of rich tea biscuits to help him mentally work through the events of today.

His phone beeped a 'derh derhh, derrh derhh' on the kitchen table as he was looking for a teaspoon. To Si's relief it wasn't another text message from 'F' but it was Paul who informed him he was on the second level in Zanzibar, it's two for one shots, and he wanted to know if he was coming out.

Si gazed blankly at the green and black screen, pressing the arrow button up and down to read and re-read Paul's message. He wanted to reply, and he was glad of a chunk of normality in a bizarre day, but he couldn't find the words. Today left him mentally drained.

All the thoughts of the day were swirling around his head, and he didn't like where they were taking him. He put his coffee down on the counter and rubbed his face with the palms of his hands, took two deep breaths and grabbed his drink. He'd have to deal with Paul later. One thing at a time.

He tried mentally listing the facts in smaller chunks to make them easier to digest.

That man in his bed was him. Him.

He is from twenty years in the future. 2022. 2022.

It wasn't sticking, this was like he was trying to learn foreign language.

That man in his bed is him aged 39. But what had happened? Si was just about getting his head around the fact that this man was an older version of himself, but that really wasn't how he pictured his future would be.

He'd just got himself into a good place. He genuinely believed he was destined for great things but no. Obviously not.

Si knew very little about the man in his bed, other than it was him aged 39, but he didn't strike Si as someone who had lived up to the high hopes he had for himself. What happened to his hair? AND his waistline? Although Si was not judgemental by nature, he couldn't help himself going on first appearances around what he witnessed. This felt personal. Well, this WAS personal.

He'd seen a bit of life working in the restaurant that summer, Si encountered a lot of people. And there was one specific type of person who bothered him more than most. The late thirtysomething man who had given up on life.

Although there were exceptions to the rule, Si witnessed so many different men who looked identical come to the restaurant so often he could swear they'd been cloned. They mostly followed the same pattern, overweight, bald or balding with a beard to compensate for the hair loss, and in a vain attempt to cover their double chins.

They would usually wear black, either T-shirt or shirt. They would usually be with their partner who they are only staying with for the benefit of the kids and the mortgage, as all the love and physical attraction died years ago.

You could see how trapped they were in the back of the eyes, you could almost hear their thoughts lamenting their lost youth and how they are hardly making ends meet, and their only escape is getting either their parents or there partners parents to look after the kids on a Friday or Saturday night so they could go out for a meal at a place their partner picked (as they lost any fight for their opinion a long time ago)

Five or six beers in they would then usually take their frustrations in life out on the waiter, (which Si had his fair share of) By the time the bill arrived at the end of the meal they would be ten pints in, and they would be brewing up a blazing row with their other half who was equally drunk and tired of life. They would pay up, and as soon as the front door of the restaurant closed, they would erupt and go at each other thinking that the door they had just closed was sound proofed.

Which it wasn't, and Si and the remaining diners would enjoy the entertainment value of the row with an underlying feeling of 'glad it's them not me'

Si was very glad that wasn't him. He said out loud on several occasions 'That will NEVER be me'.

But he was wrong.

It will be him.

Never mind the ghost of Christmas future, the spirit of disappointing days yet to come is now, and he is here, passed out on his bed.

The older version of himself fitted the cliché of the men he met in the restaurant perfectly. He looked exhausted. He looked like he'd given up a long time ago.

He wanted to know more. Maybe he was wrong, first impressions can be! A boundlessly optimistic part of his brain was trying to put a good spin on this. Maybe his older self is really successful, and the light that's gone out on his face was due to stress and the weight gain is due to him working long hours and getting takeout food. I mean, it can happen right?

Si had gone to the freezer to see if he had anything in as he was starting to get hungry when his phone beeped again, another text. He exhaled a weary sigh as he expected another text from the persistent Paul. Obviously it was him badgering him again.

But it wasn't Paul.

The message read

Unknown Number

01000100 01101111 01101110 00100111 01110100 00100000 01100110 01100001 01101100 01101100 00100000 01100110 01101111 01110010 00100000 01001000 01100001 01101110 01101110 01100001 01101000 00100111 01110011 00100000 01110100 01110010 01100001 01110000

Si looked up from his phone. Puzzled. He needed this after-today's events. He looked back down again as if the binary code was going to magically make sense in the two seconds since he first read it.

Wasn't that was a suspiciously long message for a Nokia 3310? All he knew was his brain was fried and this dumb message was clogging up his Sim card.

He deleted the message, mistaking it for one of those messages that are made of punctuation that make up a picture in a text message that had gone wrong. And downed the dregs of his coffee.

Glancing at the kitchen door when he put his mug in the sink, he noticed a faint light coming through the oblong window. His room was directly opposite the kitchen, peering through the oblong window he saw light around the door frame of his room.

He looked at his watch. 8:41pm. The 39-year-old version of himself was awake.

Si stood frozen to the spot. Minutes ticked past in what felt like seconds.

He had to face him at some point.

CHAPTER SEVEN

A coffee with myself

Tuesday 17th September 2002

8:41pm, Peak Court Flat 34, Room 416

For the second time today, the elder Simon came to in blissful ignorance as to what had happened, while his senses bickered about who was to go first. Before he opened his eyes he felt instinctively safe in his surroundings, they seemed familiar. He was in a single bed back in his old halls of residence.

It was dark. He reached for the light switch. A muscle memory of knowing where to reach was still with him, even though from his point of view he moved out of Peak Court nineteen years ago. He sat up, blinked a few times to focus his vision and to shake off the groggy feeling.

The feeling that came over him in the hospital, that was somewhere in the middle of seasickness, jet lag and a drug comedown had thankfully gone. As had the visions of the immediate future that were playing in his mind.

He took a minute to look around his old room, he couldn't help but smile. He had some of the happiest times of his life living here, he felt the warm glow of nostalgia that comes over you when you flick though old pictures of happier times, but the sensation was magnified, brighter and more vivid as he wasn't just looking at still images of the past. He was actually here. Looking at it, touching it, feeling it as it happened.

As it was early September, his younger self had only just moved in. So, a few things were still in boxes and the walls were quite sparse. It was a small room, basic but fairly luxurious by 2002's standards. En-suite with a shower and toilet. White painted breezeblocks walls. only broken up by the faded pinboard next to his bed and a light wood coloured fitted desk, with two shelves above it that joined to a fitted wardrobe. On the wall of the desk there was another pin board with his letter from admissions pinned to it, just above the phone line port which gave dial up internet access.

On his desk was his 'portable' TV, that was a giant box that's weight made it anything but portable. His combi DVD/VHS player he got for his birthday a couple of months ago. His CD collection stacked on the shelves above the desk. His small DVD collection was dwarfed by his Video collection and his rack of tapes filled the shelves with films and TV series he taped from home.

On the desk was his old laptop he got for Christmas 2001. Or currently I guess that would that be his new laptop? Newish I suppose. He opened it up with all the care shown during an appraisal of an ancient artifact on the Antiques Roadshow. He forgot there was a time when laptops didn't have widescreen and was as thick as the Yellow Pages.

Simon smiled as he remembered visiting a newly refurbished halls in Southampton shortly before he left. Which boasted a 24-hour gym on site, double beds in all rooms, a 4k smart TV in every kitchen with Freeview HD, and High speed WIFI throughout.

Simon went to use the toilet. When he finished washing his hands he turned off just the hot tap and cupped his hands underneath the water. He couldn't see a glass and he was desperate for a drink; the day's events had left him so dehydrated you could sand wood with the inside of his throat.

When he finished he went to the front door of the room to go and see where his younger self had got to. He was just reaching out to the door handle when he paused.

"Paul!" he thought, his heart rate increasing slightly "oh my god, Paul's alive!" his hand retracted from the handle and clasped over his mouth. With everything else he'd been through today, Simon wasn't sure if he could cope with seeing Paul as well and seeing as his room was next to Si's there was a huge chance he would be next door claiming he was studying, when he was actually wasting time on his GameCube.

After bonding during freshers week, Si and Paul became the best of friends very quickly. Some people even guessing incorrectly that they knew each other before the term started. For a while they were inseparable.

Even though Paul left uni after the first year they remained very close, right up to the argument. Simon had been haunted by how things ended, feelings of regret he still carried with him, and because Paul died seventeen years ago, these were feelings he could never put right. Seventeen years! Simon tried to remember his face, and his voice. But it was so long ago. And now, or at some point, he was bound to see him again.

When Simon finished at Uni, he took some time out to weigh up his options before taking the next step. He settled on doing a master's degree at Southampton and in the spring of 2006, he and Paul decided to go have that epic summer in Ibiza that Simon was robbed of five years earlier.

Everything was booked. This time with a national chain of travel agents, which although bumped up the price a bit gave Simon the peace of mind they weren't going to be fleeced. Paul told Simon he had been to Ibiza before many times the late nineties, which filled Simon with confidence that his good friend could be a guide to him, and that this was going to be a great trip.

In reality, Paul had never been to Ibiza as his mum wouldn't let him. It was one of his wildly embellished stories he spun the gullible young Si. Stories of epic nights out in all the world's best clubs (that he's never been to) where a speciality of Paul's. In fact, the closest he ever got to the White Isle was a school trip to the

Isle of Wight.

Fact checking the statements of a bullshitter was a little more difficult before smart phones. Even when Wi-Fi broadband became a thing, you still have to turn on a cumbersome laptop or your desktop computer at home. By the time you got online, you'd forgotten what you were looking to double check in the first place.

Simon, when he was younger at least, was a naturally a very trusting person who always thought the best of people. Plus, he only had laptop with dial up internet, so he was never going to see if Paul's statements added up. If he were more cynical, (which eventually he was) and had his iPhone to hand, his friendship with Paul would have crumbled a lot earlier.

What did crumble their friendship, was an argument that erupted a month before they were due to fly out. The cause, a woman named Chloe.

Long enough time had passed after Simons first serious girlfriend had disappeared for him to consider getting dating again. Chloe worked at the same branch of Blockbuster video as Paul, who had gone back to work there after he flunked uni and was hanging on to see if he could get his managers position back. After three years of hanging, he was still waiting.

He got to know Chole well, and they seemed to hit it off, and she seemed to like him. Paul had a tendency to get ahead of himself when any woman showed him any interest. Even if somebody was to flirt with him once he'd massively jump the gun and tell the world he had a new girlfriend.

In a rare moment of personal growth Paul decided not to tell the world he and Chloe were an item, until she actually agreed to go out with him. This unusual quietness coincided with Si getting to know Chole as well, whenever he popped in to see Paul on his way home.

Deep down Paul had always been a bit jealous of Si. He was better looking than he was and taller. If he were just one of these things Paul could have coped, but both? Well, that was too much.

Every time Si dated or went out with someone, anyone, Paul tried his best to steal whoever Si was with. It was like an involuntary tick. He couldn't help himself. 20% of the time he would just be laughed at, to his face and 80% of the time this would just be ignored by whoever Si was with, Si knew what was happening, but he overlooked it as well. A part of him found it funny. But another part was a tad wounded that his so-called best mate would even attempt such a thing. But he just swallowed his anger and got on with it.

After three weeks of flirting Chloe agreed to go out with Si for a drink one Saturday night, and when Paul got wind of this he went into overdrive to try and steal her from under Si's nose. As usual he tried everything in excess, laughing too loudly at her jokes, sitting to closely to her in the staff room, spinning too many half-truths and downlight lies to impress her, and slapping on way too much aftershave. His colleagues secretly found this hilarious, and one of them for a prank stuck a fake note in the customer suggestion box saying, 'can you tell that little dude to tone down the aftershave, I get a rash each time he serves me!" Which the manager took seriously and pulled Paul in 'for a chat'.

Chloe however was loving the attention and relished leading Paul on. She made sure she was looking at him whenever she left work with Si and told him about how Si and started 'staying over' on the weekends.

Paul, who was at this point thirty-years-old stopped calling and returning Simon's calls out of spite, when a well-meaning colleague who liked Si (the same one who put the fake note in the suggestion box) tipped him off as to what Chloe was like with Paul at work, her obvious baiting flirtations and spilling many personal secrets, Si hit the roof.

He dumped Chloe and exploded at Paul. Four years' worth

of pent-up aggravation and swallowed anger came out in a particularly heated MSN messenger chat. It got very personal, it ended with Paul saying 'I hope you're going to apologise for all this before we go to Ibiza' to which Si replied

'Fuck Ibiza and Fuck you'.

That was the last thing he said to him.

Paul spoke to Chloe to try and get her to come to Ibiza with him in Si's place. She declined, now she only had his attention he didn't seem all that appealing to her. So, he went on his own.

He died three weeks later when he fell off the balcony of the apartment he was staying in and broke his neck on impact with the floor. The day before he fell off the balcony he sent Simon a text which said.

'I'm really sorry mate. Wish you came with me, not the same without you'

Which Simon, who was still wounded and not being able to judge tone of voice in a text mistook for gloating. He didn't reply.

He didn't cry when he found out he died. He was so shocked he didn't show any emotion at all for a while, let alone grief. He read and re-read the saved transcript of the MSN chat over and over again to the point where me memorised every line. They fell out over something so trivial, that unearthed four years of tensions that were building up with them both. Simon was so consumed with regret he didn't attend the funeral, he wanted to, but it didn't feel right. In a stupid grief-stricken way, he felt like he caused Paul's death. Knowing how much he overcompensates when something doesn't go his way, he played out on a never-ending loop several scenarios in his mind's eye that caused him to fall. Knowing him, he was probably taking a bet he could jump between balconies or standing on the railing so pilled off his head he was convinced he could fly.

Simon was now sat on the bed, while every feeling about Paul was dredged up by this mind, having only just calmed down from today's events of now living in 2002, he was now reliving the grief of 2006.

He stood up; a sudden jolt upwards caused by his resolve to 'not think about Paul'. He could hear his therapists voice in the back of his mind telling him, how unhealthy it was to put things at the back of his mind. But he didn't take any notice. Needs must. He decided to wait for his younger self to reappear, he'd be safe in this room for a while.

Simon mooched around the room to find something to entertain himself with. He found the TV remote; he turned it on and flicked through the channels. "Four and a half channels? Was that it?" He switched the TV off in disgust and flung the remote on the bed. "How did I cope with four and a half channels?" he thought. Then he remembered, on his first year If he wasn't studying he was usually in the pub or with Hannah. He rarely had time to watch any TV apart from to have it on in the background as he was getting ready to go out.

As his eyes scanned the room, he saw it. Or rather he saw the black headphones first that trailed behind the TV. It was his Cassette Walkman.

He loved this Walkman; it was the first time he had mobile music that he stuck with. Sure, Discman's and Mini Disk players were around at the time, and MP3 players were in their infancy, but this simple mobile cassette tape player was reliable. And for a new model it was cheap. The younger version of Simon didn't realise it at the time, but as the years went on this humble oblong silver object became like a museum piece in Simons life.

Of all the things he threw out over the years, he always held onto this. And by 2022 it had stopped working altogether, was scratched, and dented and was pretty much useless. But he kept it as a reminder of happier times.

He picked it up. It was undented, gleaming and new, he opened the back and took out the clear plastic cassette and there it was. On a label on side A was Simon's handwriting, (neater than what his handwriting looked like currently he noticed) 'Mixtape Sept 02'. He couldn't resist it. He put the headphones in and pressed play. He felt the whirr of the reel to reel spinning around the few seconds gap before the song started.

The familiar opening cords of 'By the way' by the Red-Hot Chili Peppers started.

His younger self came into the room and saw what he was doing. He pressed stop and took the headphones out.

"Sorry" he said smiling. "Couldn't resist"

"Have it if you like" the younger Si replied. "Costs a fortune in batteries. Thinking of binning it anyway"

Simon was slightly taken aback. He put the Walkman back on the desk.

"You ok?" the younger Si continued "I was just getting dinner, saw the light was on" he said as casually as he could to disguise the fact that he had spent the last few hours pacing.

They both sat on the bed. The younger Si filled his older self in with the events in the DRI after he passed out. The assassin who looked like she was just going through the motions, the text from somebody called 'F' and air conditioner, and how they made an escape in the wheelchair that was left for them. He didn't mention the binary code text message, it was so random his overwrought brain had already pushed out that memory.

"Wonder how you knew what was going to happen?" the younger Si mused. His older self-shrugged his solders.

"Coffee?"

The elder Simon enthusiastically agreed, but he forgot two things. One, his tastes in food and drink got more refined over the years and when someone says 'coffee' he thinks instantly of the Columbian blended beans he has for his espresso maker at home. And two, his younger self was a student and drank any budget branded instant coffee he could find.

Simon saw his bag at the end of the bed

"Better charge me phone up" said the elder Simon, knowing full well that his iPhone didn't work in the past, it was more the comfort of habit of having it fully charged and by his side. His younger self offered his phone charger as Simon went for his bag.

"Nah it's ok, different make of phone. Got me charger in here" he said digging though his bag.

"Why do you carry a phone charger with you?" the younger Si asked his older self, genuinely bemused.

Simon located his charger from his bag and stood up.

"When you get an iPhone, you'll understand" he said to his younger self.

The younger Si was keen to see what mobiles in the future looked like. Simon hesitantly handed it over for his younger self to look at.

Si looked at the colour screen open mouthed, like he'd just been passed something from Star Trek. He looked up towards his older self

"Where are the buttons?" He asked, mystified.

The elder Simon explained it's not so much a phone as a touch screen computer that can makes calls and send text messages. And the only button was the one at the base of the screen that doubles as a fingerprint scanner.

"Screen's gone dead; how do I get it back?"

The elder Simon mentioned that you need the passcode to unlock it or use the fingerprint scanner. Just as he was walking over to unlock it, the scanner button read his younger self's fingerprint and unlocked. Simon tutted.

"Of Course," he thought "Same fingerprint!"

The Younger Si looked at the apps on his phone open mouthed.

On instruction of his older self, he swiped left and then right to see what he had. He paused on the final screen, so many questions. What are all these squares? He picked a title of one of the squares at random to ask his older self what it was.

"What's Face... book?"

Firstly, the elder Simon was mildly shocked, it felt like Facebook had been around forever. Must have started later in the decade. He thought back to the websites he used to use when he was 19 to find something he could compare it to.

"Erm, like a cross between Faceparty and Friends Reunited"

His younger self nodded in comprehension, he scrolled and picked another app

"What's Only Fans?" He asked innocently.

Looking mortified his older self-took the phone off him and insisted on that coffee.

9:01pm

The elder Simon tried not to wince too much as they sat in the kitchen, sipping his lukewarm mug of Happy Shopper instant coffee, as he remembered how proud it used to make him feel to be able to do his own shopping. He hated the taste of it but wouldn't openly slag it off to his younger self.

Everyone else in the flat was on a night out, much to both Simon's relief, so they could move about and talk freely, at least for now.

The day's events still hadn't quite processed with both of them. They chatted idly at first, but when they thought the other one wasn't looking, they'd stare at each other in utter disbelief. But the proof was there. There was no two ways about it. Simon Radcliffe had gone back in time twenty years and was faced with his younger self. And having only lived literally in the past for the last six hours, an attempt had been made on his life. Actually, thinking about it, it might have been two. That bloke who almost drove into him who yawned. Simon was certain he sped up when he saw the older Simon's face

"He yawned as he accelerated?" clarified the younger Si, putting two and two together.

"How can two people, try to kill both of us in one day, and look so bored by it all?"

Simon agreed he had a point. Neither men until this point had any real world run in's with hitmen or assassins, it's not a common occurrence when you work in accounts, but you would think the adrenaline and focus of an attempted murder would make you look a bit more interested at least.

They chatted about how outlandish the day had been, what the younger Si had been up to prior to the rugby tackle, what did the elder Simon remember about traveling back (which was very little) They got talking about the terms about what they should do while the older Simon was here, and while they tried to figure out who was this 'F' person was, and if they could help get the older Simon home.

In the meantime, they both eventually agreed that for now, the elder Simon had to stay here in Peak Court and pose as a relative of Si's who was helping him move in and get settled. After some considerable bickering they agreed that the elder Simon would pose as the younger Si's dad.

Simon wasn't keen on this at first. Granted at thirty-nine he was old enough to have a nineteen-year-old son, but there was something about that plan that rubbed him up the wrong way. In fact, it hit such a raw nerve, that he threatened to tell everyone that the younger Si had only lost his virginity the previous year, but he conceded after a while it that it did make sense.

Now they agreed on a back story and a plan of what to do in the meantime, the younger Si sensed a change of topic was needed. This was a golden opportunity, imagine you were sat opposite yourself, but they were twenty years older. Somebody was in front of you who had lived your life and knows your future. Si dug deep for something to ask his older self about the future. For some reason the first thing that came out of his mouth was.

"Why do you have a fake bank note in your wallet?"

"Sorry?" Simon was puzzled, fake bank note? What was he talking about? The younger Si continued.

"That fake twenty quid in your wallet, looks like something that came with a Fisher Price Post Office play set"

It then dawned on Simon what his younger self was talking about. He must have seen it when he was looking for some I.D. when he was rifling through his wallet. He explained to his younger self that it was real, and that's what bank notes would look like in the future.

"But it's tiny, and its plastic!" Si protested

"Yea, plastic bank notes are designed to be to be fraud proof" His older self-explained

Si shook his head.

"Right, well, I know bank notes look like toy money in the future, what else can you tell me? He asked his older self enthusiastically.

Simon took one final shuddering gulp of his bitter and gritty coffee

"Another?" the young Si gestured to the mug; His older self was quick to shake his head

"No to the coffee of no to telling me about the future?"

"Well, both" replied Simon "I'm not sure I can tell you about the future" he said apologetically.

Simon was no physicist, but as he explained to his younger self that he'd watched enough Doctor Who and Back to the Future to know some sort of etiquette when it came to talking about the future when you go back to the past.

His younger self screwed his face up and said only weird little geeky men watched Doctor Who, the older Simon then had to then explain it was back on TV and massively popular in his time. Even then he was worried he said too much.

"Surely you can tell me a little bit" his younger self said lowering his voice conspiratorially.

"Well, I'm a little scared to, to be honest. One little thing could mess with time, what if I tell you a tiny detail about the future and we wake up tomorrow and..." the older Simon struggled for an example

"And what?"

"And Hitler won World War Two?"

"It's 2002" his younger self eventually said. A dryly as he could.

"And you're from twenty years into my future!" he added

And so, the debate raged on. The older Simon was clutching at straws to hide the real reason why he didn't want his younger self to find out what happened and what he became. If your younger self were sat before you what could you tell? That your glittering career in the many avenues you wanted to try going down, never happened? That you fall out with his best friend over a petty argument, who then dies before you can make it up? That the passionate love affair with a woman who right now lives three floor below him would end in heartache, and not the happily ever after he imagined? That they wouldn't get married, live in a big house and have loads of kids. That she would go from saying she wanted to spend the rest of her life with him to rejecting him in such a way, that it would leave a scar on his heart he would still have to this day.

Well, not this day but twenty years in the future.

Well, you know what I mean.

Whatever, it still hurts!

Would you want to know from your older self that on the morning you travelled back to the past you had been to the hospital to check if he had suspected prostate cancer? And you were having a depressive downer off the back of it thanks to your Bi-Polar disorder which almost made you take your own life on a couple of occasions?

He knew that if he told any of this to his younger self it would hurt. He didn't want to crush his younger self, have him live with the knowledge that the older man sat in front of you had let you down so badly. That a once fearless young man had descended so far into mediocrity. Life would get to him and beat him down eventually; he didn't want to be the one to break his younger self's spirit.

There was a silence. Simon broke it by trying to say something that would get a conversation going with his younger self without giving too much away about the future.

"So, guessing you're not seeing Hannah tonight?"

The Younger Si wrinkled his forehead, trying to figure out who his older self was talking about

"Hannah...who's Hannah?" Si said eventually.

It then dawned on Simon that his younger self hadn't met her yet. All he remembered was he met her in the September. The twenty years that had passed had blurred the dates in his mind. September 2002 looking back in the grand scheme of his life seemed to last just a day, so he couldn't remember what date he was to meet the woman who would have such an effect on his adult life. That date was going to happen this coming Friday night.

CHAPTER EIGHT

Living in the past

Tuesday 24th September 2002

8:30am, University of Derby, Kedleston Road Campus

The younger Si had set off early to campus on foot, as it was a nice morning. The elder Simon had opted to take the Unibus that picks up from outside Peak Court and drops them off at the door of Kedleston Road. It had been an eventful week living in the past, but nothing was to top what they were heading for today.

Since the elder Simon's arrival in 2002, a total of five more attempts had been made to kill both the men, ranging from a straightforward drive by shooting by a bored looking man who said 'oh here we go again' before half-heartedly pulling the trigger, missing because the older Simon got a queasy feeling and a flash of the future in his head, and dived to protect his younger self, which then caused the assailant to drive off at speed into the distance, and then fade completely out of existence.

Then it went to the more outlandish and daring, (although high marks for its originality) a 2012 model drone carrying several pounds of Centex was flown and exploded outside Si's bedroom window, completely missing him on explosion as he and his older self were in the kitchen on the other side of the building at the time, with the debris and death the explosion caused being undone and put right in a matter of seconds. They also had a near miss incident with a poisoned latte, which was picked up by the elder Simon the morning after his first night in the past.

The memory of the previous evenings budget coffee was still stuck in the back of his throat, so the following morning, after a ropy night sleep on a makeshift bed, made up of sofa cushions on the floor of Si's room, the elder Simon borrowed £20 from his younger self, (who hammered home a point that this was what a 'proper bank note' should look like) and set off in search of Starbucks. Forgetting the first Starbucks in Derby wasn't going to open for another two years.

He was delighted however, when he found his former favourite hangout 'The Big Blue coffee shop' on Sadlergate, which by his time had gone out of business when he was living in Southampton, but now here it was, back open. After paying for the drinks, he went to the gents while the barista got to work. He got back, picked up his order, which were already wedged in a cardboard take out carrier and left.

He barely got back to the street when he was met by his younger self who was running at speed towards him, just before the elder Simon could draw breath to say, 'oh hello, here's your drink' the younger Si punched both coffee's out of his older self's hands, sending them flying into the air.

"What the hell did you do that for?" Simon asked with a mixture of bemusement and anger, his younger self pointing to the floor where both take out cups now lay. The two men watched as the several angry looking people who just got showered with hot poisoned coffee instantly dried off and then promptly forgot what just happened, and both cups that lay on the floor just faded away, and at the same time, so did the person who sneaked the cyanide into the Latte's, as they made a run for it out of the coffee shops front door.

He showed his older self the tip off text message from the mysterious 'F' who informed him just fifteen minutes previous what was happening, when he read it he raced off into town and got to his elder self before he could take his first swig.

Whoever this 'F' is, they were on the ball in terms of knowing what was happening. As they walked back to Peak Court the two men theorised who this 'F' could be. They both mentally ran through people from their time who had names beginning with 'F'. The younger Si thought of two blokes from his rugby team. Ferdy, who was a great player but hardly capable of masterminding impossible physics. Also, there was the fly half who the lads nic-named 'Fuckface', but he was out on account of his name actually being Leroy.

Only person the elder Simon could think of was his landlord Frank. But knowing his track record with maintenance around his flat, Frank clearly didn't care if Simon lived or died.

Almost as if 'F' knew they were thinking about them, the younger Si got a follow up message as they walked telling him to 'check his tray' when he was next in uni on Friday. Referring to the many racks of assignments trays that stretched the corridors of North and East towers faculty's with students names and ID numbers printed on the front, they were used mainly for lecturers to drop off marked essays, and for the students union to shove flyers in for upcoming events.

The two men were debating what this could mean as they walked into their kitchen, and that was when the elder Simon was presented with the sight of a very hungover Paul, who still hadn't figured out how to work the grill but didn't let this put him off trying to make a bacon sandwich.

Simon froze. Paul was in front of him, alive and well. And blaming the grill for not being user friendly. Unaware of what was going to happen to Paul in the future, the younger Si made introductions sticking to the agreed cover story

"Paul this is me dad, he'll be staying with me for a bit while I settle in"

Paul turned around; eyes bloodshot thanks to finishing the night on Vanilla sidekicks. He held out his hand to shake hands with Si's 'dad'. He Paused, looking at Simon a little deeper. He smiled

"Nice to meet you Mr Radcliffe, I'm Paul"

The elder Simon extended his hand out

"I'm….." Simon paused; his voice was cracking up.

The younger and elder Simons looked at each other, they both realised that they didn't agree on what elder Simon's name would be.

"…S..Simon" finished the elder Simon, somehow making his own real name sound fake.

"Simon Snr!" Paul beamed with the false charm he usually piled on when he met someone new and shook his hand with his trademark iron grip to show what a 'big man' he was.

Simon forgot he used to do that. It drove him mad at the time, as usually it made his hand hurt, but now he was in raptures seeing it again. The emotion got to him during the handshake, and he dragged Paul in for a BIG hug. Paul didn't put up a fight as the hangover and the surprise of his new friends 'Dad' wanting to hug him left him a little defenceless.

"It's so good to see you" the elder Simon whispered into Pauls ear, closing his eyes to hold back some tears.

Paul's bloodshot eyes were wide open at this point, not that you could see them as thanks to the height difference they barely made it past the elder Simons shoulder. He looked for an excuse to end this hug from Si's overly physically affectionate Dad.

"Best go, I.. I think the grill's just fired up" said Paul meekly, his face pressed up into the fabric of Simons jacket. Simon was dragged off by his younger self and quizzed in their room about why he felt the need to be so 'hands on' with Paul, which Simon declined to disclose.

Apart from having the attempts made on his life. The elder Simon was actually beginning to enjoy being in the past. He wanted a holiday, where better than a week living in a time he spent over half his life reminiscing about. This felt like the longest of long-haul trips.

Sure, he didn't know when or how he would be able to get back to his own time, he tried not to think about that too much, but for now he was enjoying many things about being back in the year when he was most alive. It was starting to rub off on him, dare he say it? He was actually feeling happy.

It was the small things that made him smile, like the price of a bus fare being so much lower, the shop windows advertising 'brand new products' just in, that the elder Simon saw just two weeks ago back in his own time in a charity shop, and the billboards around town advertising films and music that were out at the time. It felt like he was walking around a zone of a theme park that he been made at great expense just for him.

Friday 20th September 2002

5:20pm, Peak Court

The elder Simon had been given an 'allowance' of money from his younger self from his student loan to keep him occupied while the younger Si got to grips with student life. Friday afternoon he'd gone into town to get an airbed and a proper quilt so he could get some decent sleep after two ropy nights sleeping on sofa cushions. When he got back to Peak Court he buzzed his flats intercom to be let in. He was greeted by his younger self on the other end who said he had found what 'F' was talking about in this essay tray.

In their room, Si presented his elder self with the handwritten note on a white sheet of A4, that said

'Mr Radcliffe, can you please see me after the lecture on Tuesday 24th. 12pm my office. -Dr Jarvis.'

The elder Simons first thought was 'This can't be it' but it was Friday as instructed by the text from 'F' and after asking his younger self if this was all that was in his tray, Si nodded

"Well, apart from that there was a flyer for the Freshers Ball" he added.

Simon couldn't remember anything about Rhonda summoning him, ever. She wasn't the type. You went to her. It had been a few days since he got a queasy feeling that was usually followed by a flash of the future, so his foresight was no help. The Younger Si even tried texting this 'F' back to see if he could get any more information, but his message just bounced back as 'undelivered'. So, they both decided to go in on Tuesday and see if this did have anything to do with why he was here.

Si folded the note and put it on the desk.

"Anything planned for tonight?" Simon asked his younger self.

"Erm, Kirsty's invited me to a party in her flat downstairs"

The elder Simon paused. He remembered. This was it. This was the night. Tonight! He remembered now. Tonight, was when he was going to meet HER. Her, being Hannah Maberhill.

Although the younger Simon was a tad inexperienced with women, blonds weren't usually his type, but Hannah was different. Not just the hair, but everything about her captivated him from the instant he set eyes on her, he never forgot when he first saw her. She was downing a plastic pint glass full of white wine.

When somebody is so beguiling, has an indescribable aura that hooks you in, you don't care if the first time you meet them they're losing a game of wine pong against their flatmate.

The elder Simon was desperate to go to the party with his younger self, he knew what was going to happen and naturally he wanted to witness it again. The younger Si refused this point blank, as most of the building now knew him as his dad, and his dad rocking up with him to a flat party wouldn't do much for his street cred. So, the elder Simon was left upstairs, with just four and a half channels to entertain him.

9:56pm, Kirsty's Flat

The younger Si had been at the party for a couple of hours before he saw her. She was in the kitchen all the time, but until you really notice somebody, they may as well not be there. Paul had taken up a lot of his attention quizzing him about why his dad gave him such a lingering hug, it was the main thing he spoke about ever since it happened, and Si was getting a tad sick of it. At 19 Simon wasn't great at thinking on his feet, and after a couple of drinks his words got a tad scrambled. In his head he wanted to say the very plausible 'don't read too much into it, my dad's just a very affectionate person' but it came out his mouth as 'Don't worry, he just found you attractive'

Paul was not in the least bit homophobic, but he did look a tad puzzled at this response. Si knew he said the wrong thing, he tried to make it better but only made it worse.

'He just, really wanted to touch you' Si registered how static this made Paul, and how wide his eyes were. After a silence that went on a tad too long he gestured at the cans they were drinking from and said he'd sort out some more drinks.

When he was walking to the fridge was when it happened. He heard her voice before he saw her. It was different from all the other voices, she sounded posh. Royalty level posh.

"Oh, darling don't ditch me now, I need you"

Hannah's teammate in wine pong declared she'd had enough and couldn't drink another pint of Chardonnay as they racked up another game from the boxes of wine that were resting on the kitchen counter.

She'd only said a few words, but Simon was hooked, her voice did something to him. It reeled him in made his head swirl, when he saw her for the first time, all he could see was her. She looked more like a model on one of them pretentious perfume adverts that get forced down your neck every five minutes on TV in the run up to Christmas, pale porcelain skin, blonde shoulder length hair, huge doleful eyes. She didn't look or talk like your average student at Derby University. There was something about her. He hadn't got a clue what it was, but it was something.

When Hannah protested that she couldn't play on solo as this was 'mixed doubles wine pong' Si saw his chance.

"I'll play!" he declared with all the bravado of a knight in shining armour. Her friend that wanted to leave took this diversion as a chance to duck out.

Hannah looked Si up and down, she smiled.

"Hannah Maberhill, pleasure to meet you" she held out a hand and made introductions.

Neither could take their eyes off each other as they chatted, Si started to feel awkward by the two second silence.

"Say something man! Don't just stand there!" he screamed to himself internally, adding unnecessary pressure.

"Any... Any relation to Lord Maberhill?" He said out loud. Instantly regretting it.

Hannah looked puzzled

"No, why'd you ask?"

"Well, that's your surname and you talk pretty... well... posh" said Si, hoping that came out as a compliment.

"I'm guessing you're a first-year history student?" she asked Si adding a wry smile

"Why'd you say that?" he replied

"Not many 'lads' of your age know about English lords without having studied them that week"

Si was starting to feel a tad out of his depth, his inexperience was starting to unnerve him. Despite his confident demeanour and the chemistry between them carrying him through, his mouth was dry, and he was feeling a bit self-conscious about his increased heart rate might be noticeable through his shirt.

This woman was something else! Smart, beautiful, sophisticated (if you don't count the wine pong), and although as she pointed out her dad isn't the 7th Lord Maberhill, she was clearly from a well-off family, and for some reason, despite that woeful start she seems to like HIM! He'd never had a run of luck with the opposite sex quite like the one he was currently having, let alone feeling the major sparks with somebody who might just be his perfect match.

After losing their second game of wine pong, Si needed no convincing when Hannah suggested they ditch the party and go into town. They'd known each other a total of an hour and a half, but Si felt like he'd known her forever. He'd never felt this comfortable in someone else's company before. He felt happy, safe, wanted. This felt very real very fast.

After a heavy night on the town, they left Zanzibar night club at 3am, opting to walk back to Peak Court hand in hand. They laughed a bit too much when queuing to get in, when the doormen stopped them both saying to Si 'Hold it, you and your girlfriend gotta wait there a minute' When they finished laughing they couldn't help but look into each other's eyes. They couldn't hold off the attraction any longer, the top step leading into Zanzibar is where they first kissed. A passionate embrace that seemed to make the rest of the world melt away.

Nothing else was happening right now apart from him and her.

This was a memory that Simon replayed to himself many, many times over the next twenty years. He even remembered the exact time they left the flat, so the elder Simon knew what time to watch from the fourth-floor window as they both exited the courtyard.

As Hannah and the younger Si walked home, Si was enjoying something 'magical' was happening that didn't involve time travel. (Maybe magical was a bit sickly sweet, but right now he didn't care) A warm feeling passed through him that first he mistook for being a side effect for mixing his drinks all night. But no, this was contentment. Something brilliant was happening at once so quickly that also must not be rushed.

Not for the first time he was stuck in the dilemma of having an older head on younger shoulders and also being a horny nineteen-year-old. But between the two organs that were battling it out, his brain was currently winning. He was playing it cool.

He wanted more than anything to be with Hannah, he wanted it all. He'd never been so sure of something so quickly before.

Impressed by his own levels of chivalry, they stopped and faced each other before they reached Sadlergate. She put a hand tenderly on his face and leaned in to whisper to him.

"Have you ever had sex outdoors?"

And so it began, Si and Hannah. Cupids arrow had struck him hard, and from what it seemed her as well. There was no hang ups over the crazy ex, no seeing him just to keep their dating skills sharp till somebody better came along, there was none of that, or any of the other deeply unpleasant reason he'd encountered since his debut on the dating scene not that long ago. It just worked; it was. Well. Perfect!

His older self didn't protest that he didn't see his younger self much that weekend, as the younger Simon spent more or less every waking minute with Hannah, from the time they got caught having sex in the car park of Ram FM at 3:30am Saturday morning, to the Tuesday morning when both the younger Si and the elder Simon went into campus to see if the mysterious 'F' had anything to do with the tutorial Rhonda booked with him. He didn't protest one bit, as mainly he relished having the bed to himself.

The weekend was fairly quiet for the elder Simon. Left to his own devices he first thought he would try and get reacquainted with Paul, but for some reason after Kirsty's flat party, he was giving the older Radcliffe the widest of wide berths.

He spent the main part thinking back to his time with Hannah. The weekend he was currently having was bringing back memory's he's long since thought he forgot, especially when he saw her again. When she and his younger self briefly came back to his room, so Si could get a change of clothes.

By the elder Simons perspective, it had been nineteen years since he last saw her. And now here she was, exactly the same age as when they last met.

He could see how instantly in love his younger self was with her. He played the part of his dad very convincingly even though his gut reaction to seeing her again was anger. He wanted to rip the flat to shreds and shriek about how she left him. After everything, the passionate and intense whirlwind romance, the many MANY times she said she was deeply in love with him and she wanted to spend the rest of her life with him, just for her to transfer to Oxford-Sodding University the following Easter and bugger off without telling him to his face. All he got was a letter left on the kitchen table they were currently sat around. Her phone number was now a dead line. Even years later when an ex might pop up on social media. Nothing. And Simon looked for her, he looked for her A LOT.

All he had was that letter.

A letter he still had, that he kept in his bedside cabinet top draw. He could see his younger self going down the same primrose path he did, that would rip his heart and ego to shreds in just seven months' time.

Although Si and Simon were the exact same person, just twenty years apart. The elder Simon felt a paternal need to protect his younger self. Keep him from harm. But he couldn't, he knew what was coming and he couldn't say or do a thing.

Other than having the bed to himself, this was the other reason he was glad not to see much of his nineteen-year-old self that weekend.

As they both had early lectures, Si and Hannah agreed to get an early night and for Si to go back to his room. This lasted all of 40 minutes as when Si was getting something to eat with his older self she text him saying how much she missed him, and the plans changed to him going back downstairs and coming up in the morning to grab his things.

Tuesday 24th September 2002

11:45am, Kedleston Road Campus, Blends Coffee Shop

Si and Simon met for a quick coffee before heading up to Rhonda's office. Si needed something to liven him up following his first Rhonda Lecture he'd had in ten months.

Si told his older self that the weird bloke Hose who was in the queue for enrolment was on the bus in this morning. Seems to have changed his hair since last week. Si said 'morning!' as they crossed paths on the way out of the bus, to which Hose just looked at him petrified and scurried off.

The topic then moved onto the lecture.

"Swear she was looking directly at me for the whole thing" said Si between sips of coffee

"What, Rhonda?" the elder Simon Clarified.

His younger self nodded, adding there was something odd about her today. Maybe he was paranoid? Maybe 'F' would lead them someplace else.

They discussed how best to play things today. Simon feeling like he actually missed having a conversation with his younger self.

Both men set off to the lifts, Simon noticed how much his younger self was smiling more, and the certain 'glow' he had about him. He'd gone from missing him to being jealous of him in a matter of minutes. As he knew right now his younger self was at an absolute peak. A peak he thought at the time would never end. A peak he would spend the next twenty years trying to reach again.

Almost like it was contagious, paranoia was now starting to get to his older self. This was starting to feel like a trap

If Simon were a betting man, he would have staked his entire estate (which granted wasn't much) that Rhonda would attempt to kill either him or his younger self. It still wouldn't be the weirdest thing that's happened recently. And his lecturer trying to kill him would have been a phrase that would have seemed laughably unrealistic just seven days ago, when he was still twenty years into the future.

The younger Si pointed out that the mysterious 'F' hadn't steered them wrong so far, and if Rhonda did turn out to be one of the many assailants who lacked motivation, why would they put them both directly into their path?

They agreed that as Rhonda usually keeps her office door open during tutorials, the elder Simon would wait in the corridor outside her door, listening in while Si went in to find out why she had summoned him.

They agreed in the lift to the fourth floor to not speak as they walked to her office to avoid suspicion. They paused just slightly to the left of outside her open door, Simon mouthed 'you ok?' to his younger self who nodded, who took a deep breath and ventured forward. He knocked at her door; Rhonda was just finishing a phone call. She saw who it was and gestured for him to take a seat.

He sat opposite her desk for the first time in almost ten months. Memories of how useless she made him feel came pouring back now he was back in the same place.

"..anyway, I have to go I've got a student with me" Rhonda hung up the phone without saying goodbye.

"Mr Radcliffe" Rhonda said, squeezing an extra syllable's length into 'Mr'

"Dr Jarvis" he said back, trying to hide his nerves.

With as much grandiosity as she could muster, she started a long-winded speech about it being all well and good to return, but this time you really must 'make the grade' as she'd seen retuning students time and time again fall at the first hurdle when they realised how much hard work was needed.

The elder Simon, who was stood outside with his back to the wall listening in, felt more than a bit smug that his younger self had to listen to this and not him.

"Do you know why History is such an important topic Mr Radcliffe?" she said peering over her reading glasses.

Simon thought for a second, she could see he was stumped for an answer

"Because by truly knowing the past, we can plan for a better future"

Was that a coincidence? By saying this she now had Si and Simon's full attention.

Was that just a fluke? What does she know?

An alarm beeped on her watch. She slid her left-hand sleeve back with her right hand and glanced at it. Si never noticed before, but her watch looked a heck of a lot like the one his older self-had. Like a minicomputer screen was strapped to her wrist. He only saw it upside down, but he read 'Code Blue'

A look of relief washed over Rhonda. Her shoulder slumped and her face lost its stiffness.

"Oh, thank god, I can stop being an uptight bitch" she exhaled in relief. Rhonda's voice had totally changed, she stopped talking in an accent less upper class received pronunciation English voice and instantly turned into an American with a slight southern drawl.

Si was unaware of how wide his mouth had now swung open. The elder Simon was still stood outside but routed to the spot, unable to see what was going on. Although the cold sweats he was starting to get indicated to him it wouldn't be long until he saw what his younger self was seeing.

Rhonda, who was now a lot more animated when she spoke lent

forward to Si.

“Field craft honey, I was deep cover. Is your older self still stood outside?” Si shut his mouth and wanted to say ‘I think so’ but he was too shocked, so he just nodded. Rhonda shouted out the door.

“Hey, thirty-nine-year-old Simon, get your ass in here. We got a lot to talk about”

The elder Simon gingerly appeared in the door frame. He looked in to see his younger self was in as much disbelief as he was. In front of him was a woman who looked like Rhonda, late sixties, white dreadlocks, glasses, but her eyes were different. Kindly, welcoming.

“It’ll all make sense if you come in sweetie” she gestured for him to come and to take the seat next to his younger self.

Rhonda stood up, closed and locked the door. As she did she said

“Lots to get through, confidential stuff, can’t be disturbed”

CHAPTER NINE

The Tutorial

Both versions of Simon had to get used to some pretty mind-bending events this past week, time travel, living with a version of themselves who was twenty years older/younger, and for some reason several attempts had been made on their lives by assassins who looked like they couldn't be arsed. But this, right now, was just about edging both their brains to the brink.

Dr Rhonda Jarvis, the austere and to be frank, cold bitch who made their lives hell in the first year, was seemingly faking that British accent all along and somehow seems to know who the older Simon really was.

Si and Simon sat in total silence opposite Rhonda, then something clicked in both their brains, but the younger Si spoke first as he was closer to the memory.

"Why does your voice sound familiar? Your new voice I mean!" he said whist raising an eyebrow. Without looking, the elder Simon instinctively also did the same thing.

Rhonda sat back behind her desk. She paused for a second to consider her answer, then clasped her hands together and leaned forward and said

"Let's just say you weren't......

"...speaking to UCAS, that call was from me" the elder Simon cut her off and hurriedly finished her sentence, the words skydived out of his mouth. The younger Si looked over; his older self was looking seasick again.

"Sorry" said Simon, wiping the sweat off his brow. He swallowed the saliva that was building up in his mouth.

“I’ve been like this since I got here” he was starting to shake

“Relax, it’s perfectly normal” said Rhonda, as reassuring as he could. She continued

“It’s time lag. The time travel equivalent of jet lag. It’s not a premonition. It’s your memory is coming back is all, and that’s why you’ve been feeling queasy. Hang tight a second honey, what you’re feeling is normal. One thing at a time, I’ll explain what you’re going through in a minute”

When she finished talking she handed him a bottle of water.

What struck both Simons as odd was It wasn’t just Rhonda’s accent that changed. Everything about her was different. Her body language and overall demeanour was a lot… Well… Nicer. There was no other word for it. She turned to speak to the younger Si, as the elder Simon had his head between his legs taking deep breaths.

“You’ll no doubt have many questions” she said amiably

“Yes!” Said Si, going somewhat high pitched with disbelief. “Like why the hell are you suddenly American?”

Rhonda smiled. She explained that her name was Dr Rhonda Jarvis, and her doctorate was in History. Them parts were at least true. Knowing history like the back of your hand is an essential requirement for her job at the agency she runs that monitors and regulates all time travel.
Rhonda was a time traveller, whose job it was to police time travel technology, to make sure it isn’t used for selfish purposes, to regulate the time travel tourism industry and ensure that various ‘Anchor’ points (as she called them) in history took place without interference.

This was why her books on history were so good. As she was usually there when it happened. But this case she was on now, her final one before retirement was a biggie. It required her to be a deep cover agent who had been working as a lecturer at the university for the past five years, whist manipulating events in both the younger and elder Simons lives to make sure they were in the right places at the right times.

"Why?" asked Simon, with his head still between his legs

"To look after you both when the time was right" she beamed.

It was the highest honour of her career to be assigned the case to ensure the accidental circumstance that led to the discovery of time travel went ahead without interference, and that the first man to travel in time hit his mark as he was destined to do.

"Destined to do?" the younger Si screwed his face up. "What, this was fate?"

Rhonda, for the first time Si and Simon knew her looked impressed with something he said.

"Ah, you've heard of us then, most people have but they don't know what FATE stands for"

"What, Fate's an acronym?" Asked the elder Simon lifting his head up a bit too soon, big mistake. It gave him a mild case of the bends.

Rhonda worked for the Federal bureau for the Accounting and monitoring of Time travel and its Effects. Or FATE for short. The agents of FATE quietly go about their business up and down various time streams, gently nudging the great figures of history into going about their lives as they should do. Protecting them from various organisations that want to change the course of history for their own gain. Not that they ever prevail. FATE was a force to be reckoned with. The F.B.I's slogan was 'Fidelity, Bravery, Integrity' FATE's slogan was simply 'Don't argue'.

Previous highlights of Rhonda's career included the introduction of the protection of the T-Rex out of hunting season, from big game poachers who were on a time travel safari to the Cretaceous period.

She left a string of subliminal suggestions around Highclere

Castle, to persuade (without him knowing) the 5th Earl of Carnarvon into continue funding the expedition in Egypt, that would lead to the rediscovery of the tomb of King Tutankhamun.

Both of these missions would have been straight forward enough, if it wasn't for the vast quantities of time meddlers looking to profit on the dinosaur big game industry. Or kill the 5th Earl of Carnarvon so the money runs dry, and King Tut remained undiscovered.

FATE had a way of dealing with these sorts. On the first attempt to disrupt history they would succeed. But FATE would go back a little further in time with the knowledge of how they won and stop them.

This would annoy the would-be meddlers, as they are now part of events. So, they would be stuck, forever more in perpetual time loop, increasingly and half-heartedly trying to bring down a historical event knowing they fail. When they did fail, FATE rectified the damaged caused by their attempt, and any dead bodies, burned down castles or stolen wealth would evaporate within seconds and be reset to how it was before they tried.

Only on very rare occasions FATE would make themselves known. On the special cases where a direct intervention was needed. And assisting the world's documented first-time traveller in his safe passage home and protecting the secrets of time travel that came about as a result was one of them occasions.

The younger Si correctly guessed that the text messages he'd been receiving were from FATE, who have form for using localised and time specific communications devices to convey a message during the higher stakes missions. Text messaging, phone calls, telegrams, smoke signals, and on one occasion a very graphic and detailed totem pole.

Both Si and Simon were keen to know how, and why Simon

walked back so casually into 2002 that he barely noticed. As Rhonda explained how, they managed to understand bits of it, Physics was never a strong point for Simon. But they both knew there where scientific terms being bandied about that where hundreds of years in advance of their own time.

The bits they did manage to pick up and understand included the 'rapidly condensed and localised timeslip' that happened when the Ring was struck by lightning, this opened up a unique, almost tailor-made worm hole that was tuned into Simon's brainwaves because of his close proximity. It would only work if Simon were the one to pass through it though, nobody else.

Apparently this phenomenon happened a lot, but the only way someone could pass though and successfully travel would be if a time slip worm hole made a connection on the other end.

Rhonda could see she both Simon's where starting to glaze over, so she started to use so more relatable examples.

If the worm hole doesn't connect you can't pass through it. Like if you called somebody and they didn't answer the phone, you can't have a conversation. The worm hole needed to find somebody, or something at the other end with matching and opposite brain wave patterns. As time travel became more sophisticated, these patterns were able to be synthesised, duplicated, and expertly refined. But in 2002 and 2022, the odds of the worm hole finding your younger self on the other side with matching and contrasting brain waves are almost Zero. But buy a zillion to one chance, that happened.

The elder Simon asked what she meant about 'opposing brainwaves' between swigs of water

"Both of your brain patterns at the time of the slip have been well documented" She paused to see if they both followed. So far so good. She continued, pointing at the younger Si.

"Your brain was thinking of the future, and this was amplified to eleven by your day of enrolment" she rested her arm back down on the table and addressed them both

“Where else would you find a building rammed with people all thinking of the future?”

The elder Simon was catching on to the explanation

“A university during freshers week?” he offered

Rhonda nodded

“Exactly. Your nineteen-year-old self over here had spent a day exposed to an intense blast future thinking brain waves in..” she gestured outwards to indicate she was talking about the whole campus. She continued..

“What is basically an intensive battery farm of thought, when you left to go into town hit the bars you were riddled with the stuff”

The younger Si narrowed his eyes as a thought occurred to him.

“You said opposing?” Si looked at Simon “What made his brain waves opposite to mine?”

Rhonda looked at Simon, this was tricky. She wanted to be honest but not let slip to his younger self about the elder Simon’s hospital visit.

“Your older self-spent most of the day in a building, (she paused, choosing her words carefully) where the majority of the people in it were thinking of the past”

“What building?” asked Si, genuinely curious

Rhonda drew breath to speak again, Simon intervened

“Hospital” he said flatly, looking directly as his younger self. “I was…

Rhonda cut him off

“…..having a check-up that was near the palliative care ward.”

‘Brilliant’ thought Simon sarcastically. ‘I’d just forgotten about that’. Talking of sickness, that reminded him

“Can you explain why I keep feeling sick and getting these weird premonitions?” he asked

‘Like I say, they’re not premonitions’ said Rhonda shaking her head. ‘Your memory of when you were last experiencing all this is bleeding back though’

Si and Simon exchanged glances. Rhonda’s watch beeped three times. She consulted an already open spreadsheet on her computer.

She continued as she glanced over the data.

“The human brain at its current state of evolution isn’t built to cope with time travel, let alone meeting yourself when you were younger. When you go back your own time…” she put her hand on her chest then continued

“..with our help, your brain will seal all you experienced off for both of you and you’ll forget everything that happened”

Sweat started to appear on Simons forehead again, he groaned.

Rhonda pointed to the elder Simon

“You experienced all this once already when you were him (she wheeled her arm round to point at the younger Si, like a gun on the top of a tank, she wheeled her gun arm back around to the elder Simon) when you go back to your own time you both forget what happened and carry on as normal.”

She wheeled her arm back to the younger Si, becoming more like a metronome

“When you get to be him” she tocked back to Simon

” Your close proximity to these events for a second time will unearth these memory’s shortly before they happen, giving you the feeling of seeing into the future. Sadly, for you an initial side effect of this are symptoms kinda like seasickness. You’ll continue to get these flashes, but the sickness will subside”

Rhonda rested her arm on her hip and noticed the sweat on Simon’s forehead.

"It's happening again isn't it?" she stood up. Simon nodded

"Then you know what happens next don't you?"

Simons eyes widened as a memory of his older self-jumping on him on and hurling him to the ground came rushing back. Rhonda started counting down.

"Three....two.....one"

As she said one she noticed the red dot that was trained onto the younger Si's temple, and in a split second she screamed at them both

"NOW"

Simon launched his full weight at his younger self and hurled them both to the floor, a nano second before the snipers bullet cracked and passed through the window, missing them both by a millimetre and coming to rest in the wall off the office, passing through and smashing the framed copy of the book cover of Rhonda's best seller about the great assassination attempts of history.

The younger Si just about took in what had happened before he said, "what the hell did you do that for" the aborted the phrase as his mouth formed the W of "what?" as he lay on his back he could see the shattered window.

The shatter proof glass was cracking, but the creaking stopped abruptly and sounded like it was rewinding. Before his eyes, the window unshattered and began to heal itself. Before he could stand up and get his chair straight the window had repaired itself without being touched. And so had the framed book cover.

Imagine you owned a corrupt Wall Street brokerage, only concerned with profits at all cost, or you were a well-funded war lord who wanted to provide your clients with guaranteed victory? Owning a sophisticated means of time travel, like the agents of FATE use would give you the edge in business.

Think of the billions you could make trading having the

knowledge of how the markets are going to go. You could go back even further and make your family's money increase ten-fold before you were even born. Think of the investments you could make then!

Or, in a different line of work, imagine you could offer your clients the chance to not only own the biggest and best weapons from history, but the chance to also delete and reverse any defeat they experienced in the past. Alter the timelines so their best and brightest fallen soldiers could be reborn? Saved from being killed in the field and back in action with the odds stacked in their favour.

If this were you, and the possibility exited, you'd stop at nothing to achieve this.

Equally, there were groups of people who believed that time travel should remain undiscovered. They can foresee a time when FATE were unable to police their discovery effectively, and the timelines become so badly corrupted the whole sphere of existence was at stake.

Imagine you're so board of going on holiday to the same destination each year, then the option of a time travel vacation is presented to you. Wouldn't you want to spend your two weeks in the unspoiled beaches of Pangaea 335 million years ago? Better still take a city break to Jerusalem and stop off for dinner at a next table to Jesus at the Last Supper or go back to the year 2002 and witness the birth of Time Travel and see the first man to Travel, Simon Radcliffe as he comes face to face with his younger self.

All of this is exactly what had happened. And exactly why Derby was more crowded than normal. At the time Simon wrongly believed this was down to the city center being generally busier with a new intake of students. But no, it was because there were many organizations that had developed crude and inaccurate means of time travel who wanted to steal the secrets behind it and are not above fighting a dirty war to get it.

Equally, a faction who wanted to prevent time travel called 'Radcliffe Snr Must die', where littering Simon's timeline around the time of his traveling backwards, with the intention of killing him so none of this happened. They claimed responsibility for Simon's suicide attempt that was thwarted by an agent of FATE who was posing as a cold caller, and another agent who manipulated the weather to ensure a gust of wind came along at just the right time to help him fall backwards when his phone rang.

A splinter group of the RMSD, called the RJMD (Radcliffe Junior Must Die) believed pretty much the same thing as the group who they broke away from, but they thought it would be more effective to kill the nineteen-year-old version of Simon. The first attempt being a trap set for him in Ibiza in the summer of 2002, involving him being lured out onto a tenth-floor balcony that gave way, but FATE intervened again and made the travel agency he booked with disappear overnight so he couldn't go, and re-routed all calls to a 'A Taste of Bengal' takeaway.

Every time they were foiled by FATE they knew their punishment meant they were forced to repeat the botched attempt to kill either junior or senior for the rest of eternity. Two versions of the same man at different points in his life caused a loop, but each assassin retained their memories of last time.

For example, an assassin from the RJMD who had just taken a pot shot at Radcliffe Jnr with a sniper's rifle, was now on his 798th unsuccessful attempt. As he watched the elder Simon from his vantage point at the top of north tower save his younger self AGAIN he watched on with a familiar sinking feeling as the damage he did to the window righted itself, the picture frame got back to normal. After a quick conversational exchange with Rhonda, he watched as Radcliffe Jnr stood up, flicked the V's at him through the window and then pulled the blind down. This signalled the end of the loop he was stuck in, his shoulders slumped, and he looked down with a heavy heart as he and his rifle faded out of existence, to be respawned on the next loop, four hours earlier on the timeline on the ground floor on North Tower, all set to take his 799th attempt that was due to fail.

He was one of many lacklustre assassins that now infested the Uni and the City of Derby, like the man in the car who tried to run Simon over. The incident at the hospital. And thousands of other attempts that neither man even registered where taking place by potential killers with varied degrees of sophistication, who have to keep up the charade of trying to kill Rhonda, Si and Simon (as they were part of established events, and the universe would collapse if they didn't) a deadly army had been raised that couldn't be arsed, and it was growing by the hour.

Rhonda mentioned the thousands of time tourists who were here to observe history unfold, would probably get in the way a bit taking pictures, but they won't be any trouble. All time travel tour operators have a strict code of non-interference FATE enforce on customers.

Rhonda had handed both men a folder the size of phone book cheerily entitled 'glossary of attempts to kill you'. All data was uploaded to Simons phone calendar, so he'd get a notification on his watch at least when somebody, or something was about to pop up. This plus Simons flashbacks to when he was in the younger Si's shoes gave them the advantage.

"These are just the documented cases, that happen between now and the night you go back to your own time, the events we've already taken care of. More could pop up unexpected, so be on your guard at all times. And nobody, NOBODY is to know of this. It's just to be kept between us three, and any other FATE agents you come across. Understand?"

Si nodded; Simon was flicking through the files.

"Erm..." he said abruptly. He looked up.

"Why is Hannah's name listed under 'known agents/assassins'

Hannah? The younger Si repeated sitting bolt upright in his

chair, his voice going up an octave in disbelief. A state his vocal cords where getting a bit too used to recently.

Rhonda nodded. She went into detail about how Hannah worked for an agency who were hired to manipulate various events in history, by any means necessary. Try as they might, they couldn't identify who had hired them. FATE knew more or less everything, but this, and her background remained a mystery. A mystery they were still trying to crack even now.

Based on the other attempts at murder and manipulation FATE assumed that the younger Si's girlfriend, who he spent a large portion of his life hung up on, was nothing more than a mercenary and a honey trap. Tasked with making Si fall in love with her, then vanishing with no explanation to mess with his mental health and drive him over the edge.

"Didn't everything seem a little too perfect?" Rhonda said to them both

"I guess" signed the elder Simon who had years to adjust to the hurt.

"No" proclaimed the younger Si defensively, who'd only just started with the hurt.

The younger Si folded his arms, his lips got very narrow, and his eyes widened. He was mentally shutting himself down as his mind was overloaded. Not her as well. Please not her. Rhonda held up a thick looking folder.

"So, it's OK for him to know about stuff like this, stuff that I know from his future?" asked Simon pointing at Si who was trying to keep his head together.

"Oh yea, neither of you will remember any of this when you go home" she reassured him. As Rhonda finished saying 'Him' she reached into her top drawer

"One thing our guys in the field did manage to intercept was a mission brief, plus field report. Or rather what's left of it. They tried to burn it. Everything is in their including Hannah's field report she submitted when she completed her mission" Rhonda held the folder out to the younger Si who's arms where still folded, his eyes glazed over. Seeing his younger self's thoughts spiral close up, Simon took the paper and added it to the folder.

"Probably best if I took this" he said to Rhonda. Who nodded in agreement. She continued.

"Their unit's objective is to change history, and obscure situations to benefit the effort.. then it stops as the next sentence is burned up"

Simon, now used to spotting Rhonda's acronym talk, used his fingers to spell out the acronym of Change History and Obscure Situations.

"CHAOS!" He said triumphantly, like he just found a nine-letter word on Countdown.

"I'm sorry" Rhonda didn't follow "What?"

"The acronym of their mission brief spells 'Chaos'. She's an agent of Chaos!" Simon sat back in his chair pleased he spotted one.

"No" Rhonda said flatly. "They're not called Chaos. We don't know what they call themselves. Although I'll grant you they missed a tick not calling themselves Chaos" She turned back to Si who was now calming down.

"So, coincidence?" said Simon, still slightly hopeful he might be right

"No" said Rhonda. "COINCIDENCE were busy" She let that hang in the air for a second to see if either Simon would get the joke. Neither did. She decided against jokes and went back to explaining.

To clear the frazzled feeling in his brain the elder Simon got up to open a window.

He reflected for a moment, all the times FATE mentioned where they intervened and manipulated his life to ensure he would not deviate from getting here. All the times thought he was being followed and his doctors said this was 'classic paranoia' and it wasn't. He was right. And FATE and or some random assassin was trying to kill him or save him while adding to his poor mental health

"I never wanted any of this" Simon said flatly.

Rhonda looked at the melancholic elder Simon at the window, and the rage filled betrayed younger Si still sat opposite her. Sensing she was losing the room a little she tried a different tactic to lighten the mood.

Having studied this case at length she knew of the collateral damage caused to Simon's health and knew where his thoughts were leading him.

"You know because of all this; your name will live on forever more."

Both men looked at her, she explained that from here on in the name Simon Radcliffe would be up there with Neil Armstrong and The Wright Brothers for famous historical firsts.

"But I won't remember anything" whined the younger Si

"True, but you're heading for the history books, there'll be towns, airports, cities and off planet colony's named after you" she turned to Simon

"Just what is it that you want?" she offered

"Well, erm." Simon couldn't think straight, for some reason top of his list of wants was the holiday he was looking at the morning he travelled back

"I wouldn't mind a trip to Rhodes" he said tailing off at the end, aware of how pathetic it sounded out loud

"Rhodes?" Rhonda repeated in disbelief.

"Simon, your name will live on forever more. You are heading for the history books. Rhodes? Where you're heading you won't need Rhode......" she stopped. Aware of what she was now saying.

Despite his mood, Simon was unable to stop the smile spreading on his face.

“So” he proclaimed, starring back out the window.

“How do I get home?”

CHAPTER TEN

The Plan

Tuesday 24th September 2002

1:40pm, Students' Union, Kedleston Road

The elder Simon sat at a square table on the ground floor of The Arms bar, studying the vast arrays of folders, gadgets, and mission data Rhonda had given them. After a good hour and a half of mind-bending facts thrown at them both about their lives, and the people who were going to try and kill them, and the detailed plan about how Simon was going to go back to the year 2022, both men were more than ready for drink.

The younger Si got back from the bar carrying a tray with two pints of lager and two whisky chasers. The younger Si didn't like whisky, but apparently his older self-did and his older self had suggested it as it was medicinal and would be good for the shock. Si wasn't so much sold on its medicinal qualities as it alcohol content, as he was still reeling about the news about Hannah and therefore was massively in the mood to get stinking drunk.

You could see every inch of every thought that was going through the younger Si's head as he rested the drinks down on the table. He'd always worn his heart on his sleeve, you could tell exactly what he was thinking just by looking at him. This was why he was no good at poker.

By the time he hit 39, Simon had got a little bit better at hiding his true feelings, but not by much. Right now, his older self was engrossed on the page that gave them a full breakdown of all the people they were going to and had already encountered and if they were going to kill them or not. This felt like cheating a little bit, like skipping to the last page of the book to see the ending. But it made for fascinating reading.

"Well stone me" said the elder Simon without looking up

"Says here, that, that geezer Hose who we got talking to on enrolment day. Apparently, he was a time tourist. That phone call he got was from his tour operator telling him he was getting too close to events and should go back to his hotel" as the elder Simon finished speaking he jabbed the document in the area about Hose and handed it over for his younger self to see.

In his time, Hose was the most common name for a man in the UK. The trend at the time of his birth was to name children after things related to a garden, seeing as nobody had a garden anymore. It was a sort of nostalgia protest movement, that was in memory of all the greenspace in the UK that was developed to house the ever-growing population. By the time Hose was born, nobody had a garden as they were all used to build more houses. There were no parks, no fields, and no farms. Just houses. Many of which stood empty, as the industries that died in order for the houses to be built meant nobody could afford them.

Hose was number one in the list of popular baby names. Second was 'Sprinkler' followed by 'Shed' third was 'Spade' fourth place went to 'Hoe' (a boy's name) and fifth was 'Pressure Washer'. Mr Hose Templar, to give him his full name lived for his holidays in the past and loved coming to Derby in 2002 to witness Time Travel's discovery.

This was his fifth time coming here in as many years, there were five other versions of Hose wandering around town at this point. His first year visiting, he was one of the tourists taking pictures at The Spot when the younger Si rugby tackled the elder Simon out the way of the car, it was a magical moment. Just as the history books said! Made the trip worth every penny, he was determined he was going back next year.

And go back he did. At the exact same time he was taking

pictures of the two Simons near Woolworths, there was another version of Hose, but one year older sitting in the accident and emergency department at the old Derby Royal Infirmary, waiting for them both to come in from the ambulance. He was kicked out by a porter however when he tried to get a picture of the elder Simon on the stretcher.

Hose, year three was on the Bus with the elder Simon this very morning, he panicked when he said hello to him, and legged it as his tour operator had forbidden any interaction with historical figures.

This got Hose thinking, how did the first man to time travel know who he was? He must have bumped into him on a future holiday.

The fourth year he played it safe and just had a long weekend during Freshers Week. But year five was when the younger Si met him the first time around. Hose came with a friend of his, Rake Smith, who was an expert in the history of time travel but hadn't had the money to come before now.

Rake worked for FATE in their archive and found footage from the University's CCTV that showed Hose in the queue for enrolment. Hose was mortified and didn't want to join the queue, but Rake said he was part of established events, and not interacting with Paul, Kirsty and the younger Si would cause a shatter in time.

Rake, drilled into him to not give too much away, and coached him in the fine art of meeting historic figures without destroying the universe. Hose was tempted, he always loved this story. But getting too close? This made him nervous. All the nerves that would come with the possibility meeting your favourite band or movie star but mixed with the outside chance that with doing so, you might destroy time.

Rake kitted him out in period costume and outfitted him with a time specific phone, and student accessories (which took forever to get from Karen in wardrobe) and gave him an assumed name to go by. Soon as the younger Si and the others got talking to him though, his nerves got the better of him and gave his real name away. This caused some eyebrow raising from the others who quizzed him further. Thankfully, he was saved by his phone, his tour operator found out what he was doing and called him back to the hotel. He was issued with a fine and given a three-year time travel ban.

Simon looked up from the folder and saw his younger self's face, clearly on the verge of tears as he starred into his pint. He put his hand on his younger self's arm in an attempt to comfort him.

"You ok?" he asked, concerned. His younger self just shook his head. This felt weird, Simon remembered how much Hannah's eventual disappearance hurt him, but that was after they'd been together seven months and part of him was left wondering why for the next twenty years. Least now he knew why, but surely his younger self couldn't be this cut up after only being together with her for a weekend. No matter how intense it was.

Simon tried to console the lovesick younger version of himself, having literally been there. But he still wasn't completely hitting the mark. When talking about her, the younger Si was still saying tired clichéd phrases like 'It felt so real' 'I thought we had something special' and 'you don't know how you'll feel till it happens to you'.

"It DID happen to me" replied the elder Simon, slightly starting to lose his patience.

"Sorry, yea course" the younger Si snapped out of it, Simon reached for the scotch which prompted his younger self to do the same, the two men raised their whisky glasses, clinked and downed the shot, Si shuddering more than his older self. Simon's watch beeped. He read the notification that popped up

"Ah, that's handy. Looks like Rhonda's uploaded everything to me calendar" he read the notification in full, mistakenly thinking it was going to be harmless. His pupils dilated fully when realised it wasn't. He calmly looked up to his younger self, who was halfway down his pint and said

"We'd better move"

The younger Si thumped his glass back on the table with a satisfied 'Ahhhhhh'

"No, I don't wanna move, I'm comfy" he replied, not really hearing the full context of what his older self-had just said, but the booze at least did give him back some power to his voice.

"What I mean is if we don't move that speaker that's above us attached to the wall is going to come loose and brain you in about ten seconds" Simon pointed upwards, and he spelled it out to this younger self.

Si looked up. Speaker looked ok to him, but after the incident with the sniper in Rhonda's office he figured they'd better move, just as he reached for his bag the bracket came away from the wall and a twenty-five-pound weight lump of plastic was plummeting straight for him. The younger Si dived out the way sending his drink flying in the opposite direction. The elder Simon grabbed the files off the desk all with a split second to spare.

There was a sickening crunch as the speaker hit the ground. After the odd scream from the odd onlooker and the chattering had stopped, shock started to set in, Si and Simon, both unharmed regrouped and stood looking at the crater left in the wooden floor by the speaker. After Simon unnecessarily pointed out 'what could've been your head' Alan the bar manager double checked they were both ok and offered another round on the house. Which both men accepted with incredible speed of being asked.

They moved upstairs onto the mezzanine level, making doubly sure the only thing that was above them was polystyrene ceiling tiles. Simon handed over the files on 'who was who' over to his younger self, who now after two pints and two shots of Whisky was mellowing.

Simon attached one of the gadgets Rhonda gave him to his set of keys.

"What's that?" asked his younger self

Simon looked through the laminated A4 sheet titles 'gadget inventory, illustrated' and held aloft the two-inch-long cylinder with what looked like an LED light at the end that came on a key chain.

"Emergency alarm" Simon read from the sheet.

Although FATE had been successfully thwarting attempted murders on the two Simons. According to the laminate Simon was reading, that doesn't mean that new people who they haven't accounted for wouldn't give it a try. There may well be an attempt on both their lives that wasn't on the list.

The alarm (which looked like a novelty miniature torch you'd buy for your keyring) would automatically alert FATE HQ when activated, who would scramble a response team to the location to rectify any damage and heal the timeline. It also said that it was fully automatic, it would size up when they were in a situation that looked dire and 'instantly put a stop to the assailant, ONE USE ONLY"

"What does that mean? 'Put a stop to the assailant' Asked the younger Si

There was no other information. The elder Simon re-read the same sparse paragraph, as if the printed words would suddenly throw up extra information.

"No idea, still best to keep on me. Just in case" he shuffled the folders around on the table and picked up the thickest of them all. The one marked 'Friday 4th October, The Freshers Ball'.

When the elder Simon asked about how he was going to get home, Rhonda spelled the whole plan out in detail. A minute-by-minute belt and braces account of the night he's due to go back. So meticulous was she that both men glazed over after just five minutes. An expert if field craft, misdirection, and subterfuge Rhonda may be, but it seems her ability to not quite hold your attention she displayed in her lectures was very real.

Rhonda had already explained that positive and future thinking brain patterns of a vast quantity of people, can help secure a connection for a time slip to a time in the future. The next incident where they'll be sufficient quantities of that energy again will be at the Freshers Ball on the Friday night of the following week.

The Freshers Ball was one of three flagship gala events the students' union puts on during the year, the others being the Grad Ball in January, and the May ball in... well, May.

They take over the entire atrium of the university and most of the ground floor, rig up several stages and bars and put on a mini black-tie event festival that usually goes on till breakfast the following morning. This would be the last chance until enrolment in September 2003 that they would have to harness all that abstract future energy.

Rhonda had a more scientific term than 'future energy' for it, a term that wasn't even in use in the English language in Simon's lifetime. She said it a few times, and neither of them remembered. It was such a complicated and difficult to pronounce term that both Si and Simon forgot what it was, even when they were looking at it on the page.

The night of the Freshers Ball the agents of FATE would treat the Kedleston Road campus of The University of Derby as a battery farm and harness the future energy power via terminals they were currently in the process of installing, located on the flat roof of the building. They would transfer this to a turbine that would amplify it and relay it via electricity pylons to the weakest spot in space and time, to form a new worm hole for Simon to travel back to 2022 at exactly the stroke of midnight, at exactly the same spot he came in through the previous week. Like hitting the redial button on an old landline phone.

Simon asked when Rhonda was explaining all this, why FATE, an agency with all the relevant time travel technology at their disposal, are going about all this in such a Heath Robinson sort of a way.

Rhonda explained that delivering such sophisticated time travel tech to a time where it wasn't in common use carried such a high risk of theft and misuse, especially at this point in time, that they decreed that only locally sourced tech would be used to get him back. After the event, the equipment it could be easily disbanded, and nobody would be the wiser.

"How do you get back?" the younger Si asked Rhonda.

She explained that, although she could get back easily with the help of the other FATE agents who were currently at work in the city, she decided not to. This was her last mission, she was retiring. She was very happy in the early 2000's, her books were selling well, and she was a highly respected historian. She was going to live out her days here. The early 2000's were a very popular retirement spot thanks to the lower cost of living and the average temperatures being higher than other times.

The New Yorker even went as far as to dub the turn of the 21st century as 'the new Florida for retirees'. Aware that an increase in people of retirement age living on earth at the same time would arouse suspicion, FATE explained this away by labelling them all in the media as 'baby boomers' and were a product of post war prosperity and not commercial time travel.

On the night he goes back, Simon would be given a specially modified tuxedo to wear. The fibres of the jacket, trousers, shirt and even socks would have nano-receivers woven in them so he would soak up the maximum about of future energy possible, he would then be escorted from Kedleston Road to The Spot, where the Agents of FATE had prepped the city centre so that he could pass through the time slip without drawing too much attention from the locals.

For added security, this event was blanket banned from all time tourism as they couldn't risk a stray tourist messing the plan up, and the night he goes back both version of Simon will experience a beyond ridiculous surge in assassination attempts. Holidaying in this time zone would be like having two weeks self-catering in Baghdad during the second Gulf War. (Another time zone that wasn't open to tourists)

On the other side of the redialled time slip, they estimated that thanks to the residual energy left by the entrance point in 2022 he'll arrive back within a twelve-hour window from when he left. To all intents and purposes, it would be like he'd only been gone for a day.

Everything both the older and younger Simon had experienced and will experience during his older self's stay will disappear from both their minds. Which is why Simon had no memory of meeting his older self until he was back here going through it all again. Simon tried to use this to encourage his younger self on seeing the bright side, he may be hurting about Hannah now with everything he's learned, but all that will disappear and the end of next week.

"How the hell am I supposed to go on seeing her though, knowing what she really is?"

His younger self had a point. His heart let alone any other appendage just wouldn't be in it. He tried to argue that they didn't know that much about Hannah or her unit's true intentions, most of it was FATE guessing based on every other assassin's attempts. All these events are anchor points, and the laws of causality, that FATE patrolled wouldn't allow any deviation from it. Surely he could just fake it for a week, right?

The younger Si pondered this for a second. He knew all too well he couldn't muster a poker face, but what would he say to her?

"I'm busy tonight, mind if we don't see each other till after the 4th when I lose my memory?"

That wouldn't sound suspect at all. He asked his older self what he did when he was him, which he couldn't remember. Simon protested that he couldn't just switch the future sight on and off like a light switch.

The younger Si felt a dark mood clawing at him, he batted it away by asserting himself on the conversation and changing the subject to something his older self would struggle with.

"Seeing as we won't remember anything, guess you can tell me a bit more about the future now?"

Oh dear. This was tricky. Technically, yes Simon could. But he figured that the poor sod had suffered enough without learning that he doesn't really amount to anything.

"I could, but you've had a rough day" Simon said as reassuringly as he could.

"Nahh come on, it'll cheer me up" the younger Si insisted. Still possessing titanium levels of optimism about what lay ahead.

This was now beyond tricky and now just pulling in at awkward. Simon mentally rewound the last twenty years, pausing when he thought he saw a good bit. Something the lofty ambitions of his nineteen-year-old self would relish.

"Well, you do a master's degree" he said eventually. His younger self nodded; he accepted the news but wasn't bowled over.

"You get married in 2012. This month actually, pretty much bang on ten years from now" this seemed to make his younger self smile

"Hannah?" Said, ever hopeful.

"Nope, somebody you meet when you do your Masters" the younger Si looked a little crestfallen at this news, but with a side of hope attached.

"What's her name then?" he asked

"Zoe" his older self-replied, mentally trying to go a couple of steps ahead to try and not catch himself out with some painful truth. Thankfully this seemed to pacify his younger self.

“Well, if you can get over Hannah guess I can too.”

Simon smiled, a little better at concealing his true thoughts and feelings compared to his younger self.

“What’s Zoe like?” asked the younger Si in all innocence

Simon just about managed to control the reflex inside himself that wants to instantly reply to such questions about his ex-wife with the response ‘she was a controlling cow that gaslighted me so much my mental health took a nosedive’, and managed to say with some convincing levels of authenticity

“She lovely, really, really nice”.

The younger Si was just about to process his next question, which would have been ‘You got any kids?’ But just before he could ask anything else, his older self cut him off

“When were you planning on seeing Hannah again?”

The younger Si thought for a second and said ‘ooh’ with everything but his vocal cords when he remembered he still had his phone on silent. The older Simon could see the green and black screen of the Nokia light up as Si checked to see if Hannah had been in touch about tonight, he read the message and put his phone back to normal mode. The button sounds as he typed a message back delighted the elder Simon in a way he thought a Nokia 3310 would never do.

“So, I guess you can do more than just send a text message on that phone of the future you’ve got” Si said to his older self, glancing up at him between button presses

For some reason, the first thing Simon thought of was ‘Dick Pics’. Even though he’s never sent one and could never understand why men do, this still popped up in his mind as a future phenomenon, that on second thoughts he’d decided he’d put further down the list of things to tell his younger self.

As his younger self finished the text message he flicked through some more pages in the ring binger Rhonda had gave them. The page headings and accompanying data were mind bending, there was not a chance they'd get through it all in one sitting. 'Identified assassins' 'Tourists who get a bit close' 'Assassination attempts A to Z' 'Assassination attempts in Date and Time order' (seven pages of A4 dedicated to just the Freshers Ball, which made every available hair that was left on the elder Simon stand on end) and finally 'Assassination attempts, illustrated'

Simon rolled his eyes. Illustrated? Please! He hated the section even more when he saw how fat his avatar looked in the diagrams, then he got to the last page. A single sheet of plain white A4 that had seven words printed in a large font in the middle. Seven words that made Simon go cold. They just said...

She will cause the end of everything.

What on earth did this mean? Rhonda? No. Why would that be in a document she put together. The bit of paper looked so out of place compared to everything else, that was so meticulously planned even the font used and font size was the same throughout. Something in the back of Simon's mind flagged up that there were other messages like this that had been dotted around but he paid it no attention.

He slammed the folder shut.

CHAPTER ELEVEN

Back in The White Room

Date and Time unknown.

FATE HQ

Something had gone wrong. Horribly wrong. You did not need to be a genius to figure that out, and as luck would have it Dr Gavin Dawes wasn't.

He messaged the boss in the field and altered her, but nothing. And now Gavin was sealed off from the rest of FATE HQ and was on his own, desperately trying to figure out how to work the antiquated emergency evacuation device.

The arrogance of FATE's unbeaten field record meant that maintenance and upkeep of The White Room was always pushed to the back of the list of priorities, and had its budget repeatedly slashed.

FATE was notorious for slashing budgets and merging jobs together to save money, in an effort to become more efficient. Usually having the opposite effect. The wardrobe department, and permanently depriving Karen of sleep being the biggest mistake they didn't own up to.

Other mistakes they were too proud to admit included a clerical error in accounts that gave their annual staff wage budget accidently to the Kray twins, a discarded cigarette giving the 1990's a puncture, and closer to home putting the rifle range in the same room as the staff canteen during refurbishment. Telling staff in a round robin email that they had to learn to duck quicker during lunch.

The other mistake was making the librarian redundant and merging the role with the night security guard. Logically it was a pretty sound idea. They ran a study to see who did the least amount of work of everybody on the payroll, and the loveable night-time security guard Norman was tasked with ensuring the books in all areas of the building were kept in order.

FATE had a huge collection of printed books dating back to the start of the printed press, a copy of every book ever written was at FATE's vast main library, as well as the many corners of all other areas of all the headquarters. From first editions of the greatest works of fiction ever published to a Haynes manual for a Golf GTI, everything that was ever committed to print was here. FATE believed that the printed word was absolute in terms of preserving human knowledge, it could never be corrupted.

The mainframe computer at FATE HQ backed up the idea to place Norman in charge of the library, as it had picked up the fact that he loved books and listened to countless audiobooks when on duty. What the computer didn't pick up on was why he listened to audiobooks.

This was because Norman was short sighted, and even with his extra thick corrective lenses reading strained his eyes so much, he just found listening to the audiobook version easier. Norman was never one to complain, and passively took on his new duties in the library to the best of his abilities. FATE didn't pick up on the problem until he'd been in charge of the books for six months (with no training or assistance) and he regularly mixed up the catalogues and never put the dust jackets back on the right books after cleaning.

Gavin was praying that the messed-up book catalogue didn't spread to the white room, as he searched frantically through the book shelves and the storage areas, the alarm in the main building was still piercing the frantic noise of his co-workers trying to do anything to escape. The vault door to the white room sealed him off from the collapsing reality that surrounded him.

All he could hear was the sickening crunch of the building, and all of FATE HQ collapsing in on itself and frantic screams of his colleagues as they faded out of existence, desperately trying to prize open the sealed door, trying to get into The White Room.

The room was time proof. If all of reality collapsed, then The White Room and all persons in it would still be standing. It was built well, but not maintained well. All that was left of FATE's mainframe computer was attempting to sound the backup alarm, but over half of its terminals were in Southern hemisphere that Gavin correctly guessed no longer existed. So instead of sounding the backup alarm it got a tad muddled up with its remaining audio files and started playing 'the Shoop Shoop Song' by Cher on a loop.

Gavin wasn't sure which was more destressing. The frustration in his inability to work the emergency evac system, the sound of mass destruction and death, or Cher. Either way any of the three he didn't need it right now. The least experienced and least talented agent in the organisation was the only one that was left, and it was up to him to get the remaining agents out of the field before their reality collapsed.

Frantically tearing at the three bookcases as Cher started to sing for the fifteenth time he found it. 'Emergency evacuation teleport device, a friendly user guide' He had an uneasy and futile feeling as he felt the weight of the book in his hands, it was a thick as a telephone directory.

He got back to his desk. While looking for the book he also found a fully loaded colt 44 magnum hidden behind a copy of 'farewell to arms' that he used to shoot the three speakers out so at least Cher would shut up.

He sat down, he blew the dust off the front cover and opened the book. It read…

'This book is dedicated to my husband and three kids, Patio,

Barbeque, Trowel, and Grass. All characters are fictious and any similarities to persons living, or dead are purely coincidental'.

He took the dust jacket off the book. The dust jacket was for the manual, but the book was the erotic fiction classic 'My Kinky Billionaire Boss' by Fence McAllister. He slumped into his chair. Cursed Norman in a variety of ways and shoved the book off the side of his desk with such force it cleared three feet in mid-air before ending its journey by hitting the interface console of the evacuation unit. He searched the catalogue for where he could find 'My Kinky Billionaire Boss'.

Maybe, just maybe. It was a straight swap, and he could find the manual. The computer returned the results.

My Kinky Billionaire Boss, main library, level 669, sector X. Gavin slumped back in his chair. The book was in the library, and the library no longer existed. Now what?

The phone on his desk started to ring, it was the bosses right hand man in the field urgently looking for an update. Gavin stooped over his desk unable to respond. What could he say?

'Emergen...' He tailed off. He'd have to tell the truth. He looked over to the evac device.

'Hang on' he thought brightening up. 'Swear that light wasn't on a minute ago'

He asked for them to standby for a second while he checked something, which they bellowed back down the phone 'WE DON'T HAVE A SECOND' which he heard from three feet across the room.

The machine was working. It was working! The screen on the interface was on and displaying the message 'emergency evac go, waiting to receive'.

The crack in the interface screen confirmed to Gavin that it was a pure fluke that the force from 'My Kinky Billionaire Boss' landing on the unit jolted it into existence, and the settings that were programmed in from last time were linked to the field comms units.

He got back to the phone, and with an much confidence as he could muster said

'Ready to receive sir. Emergency Evac Go.'

As the unit sparked and fizzled into life, he could just about hear the conversation on the other end of the line. The boss didn't sound happy. As she finished wistfully saying something along the lines of 'Oh what have you done' the line went dead.

A blinding white flash emitted from the evac device in the white room that nocked Gavin off his feet with its brilliance.

As his eyes adjusted, Gavin could make out the silhouettes of three figures. The evacuation had worked. But who was the third guy? He'd never seen him before.

All he could make out was, he was quite short.

PART TWO

Nineteen.

&

Thirty-Nine.

CHAPTER TWELVE

Mr Monday Night

Monday 30th September 2002

6:15pm, Peak Court

Simon had been living in the past for almost two weeks now. Like a holiday maker who had gone a long distance to see a different culture, he'd adapted quite well to his new (and I guess, at the same time old) surroundings.

He'd officially gone native. He didn't miss much about his life 20 years in the future. And he'd been feeling the upsides. He'd never admit it aloud, but he knew that less time spent in pointless arguments on social media or mindless scrolling on various apps was actually improving his mental health. Not being bombarded with a consistent stream of your peers telling the world that they are doing so much better at life than you, was refreshing.

It was like one of them holidays he saw advertised on remote Scottish Highlands that were billed as 'digital detox' as they were so remote that they had no phone signal, let alone 5G.

Another thing he dare not admit was that he was feeling Happier, not a big shift in his overall mood but a noticeable one. He didn't want to admit it as his condition petrified him. He didn't want to acknowledge positive emotions anymore in case depression got wind of it and came after him and gave him a sound thrashing. Simon lived a lot of his time in fear. It was exhausting.

When he first landed, being back in time was at first a little jarring for Simon, seeing himself at 19 in tip top shape upset him. A high-definition reminder about how far he had sunk into mediocrity as he approached middle age

The big things that jolted his head into action were of course seeing Hannah and Paul again, looking exactly as they did when he first met them twenty years ago. A shock yes, but it relighted a fire in a long disused part of his brain.

Wasn't just the big things like your first love or your dead best friend now being alive, but also the little things. Things that when you're in the time seem insignificant but you really notice them when they've been gone for a while. Like Buildings. Derby had been redeveloped so much in the last twenty years it was almost unrecognisable, now all the old buildings that had been knocked down were back. The old hospital he woke up in, the old shopping centre and the old bus station.

Having had to use the old bus station a lot until he passed his driving test in 2004, Simon remembers hating it with a passion. It was dirty, draughty and a haven for alcoholics and people who kept mistaking it for a public toilet. He remembers being quite happy when it was cornered off for demolition. But seeing it again filled him with delight.

Same feeling seeing his former favourite coffee shop The Big Blue back open, and all the other brands he used to love that had been discontinued in the two decades that had passed. He sat on his younger self's bed watching The Simpsons on BBC Two. Another small fact that delighted him. He forgot The Simpsons used to be on BBC Two.

Simon was in his younger self's flat alone; he checked his Apple watch. It was 6:16pm. He was getting a tad concerned.

'Swear he said he'd be back at six' he thought to himself.

'What if he's dead?'

'it's been getting worse, what if a new one got to him?'

Simon starred at his hands to see if he was starting to fade from existence. Nope. Still solid. Either than means his younger self is fine or Back to the Future got it wrong.

To break his negative thought spiral he decided to stand up. Through force of habit, he tried looking for the pause button on the remote, forgetting that he wasn't able to pause live tv. He tutted when he realised what he had done and he just hit mute, stood up and stared out the window and the courtyard of Peak Court.

It was getting darker noticeably earlier. The deep purple dusk light was filtering over the square patch of skyline above the courtyard. He saw the green and white branding of the Unibus pull off and a smattering of students came through the entrance, some chatting, some carrying books, some on their phones. He was straining to see if his younger self was with them when there was a knock at the door.

Simon froze. Although he had a cover story of being his own dad he still panicked like a shoplifter when he saw the security guard.

'Who is it?' he said slightly high pitched

'It's me mate' said Paul from the other side of the door, who took 'who is it' as sign that it was ok to come in. As he opened the door, he was a little taken aback by seeing the man who he believed was Simons dad. They hadn't interacted much since the hugging incident.

As ever with potentially awkward situations, Paul tried to charm his way out of it.

'Simon Snr' he beamed falsely 'Sorry you sounded just like Si then'

'Yea. We sound alike' replied Simon in very measured tone. Trying hard to keep a lid on his emotions.

'Si's not back yet, I was expecting him at six' he continued trying to sound parental

While he was talking, Paul couldn't help but wonder why someone as confident as Si would need his dad to stay in his halls for the first two weeks of uni? He looked at Simons eyes. He never noticed it before, but it hit him now. The eyes! They were identical to Si's. Not just alike but identical!

Come to think of it, didn't Si's dad seem a bit young to have a nineteen-year-old son? Paul's gut feeling he was getting about his new friends dad was spot on. He was younger than he looked. Paul snapped out of this train of thought when he noticed Si's 'Dad' had stopped talking

'Few of us are going to Zanzibar later, was just gonna see if Si fancied it' before Simon could formulate a reply Paul carried on and said something that took him by surprise.

'Come with us if you like?' Paul was suddenly intrigued by this man stood before him, he had a hunch and he wanted to know more. Before anything else could be said the front door intercom buzzer sounded.

Paul pointed in the direction of the front door and mouthed 'I'd better get that' and backed out of the room. He picked up the receiver

'Y'ello' he answered

'Paul, is that you?' it was the younger Si, sounding a tad gruffer than normal. An unexplained chill went through Paul. Si sounded identical to the man he just spoke to in his room. There was a pause.

'Paul, you there?' Paul stood for a second 'Can you let me in forgot me key' Si broke the silence with his impatience

'Sorry mate' Paul jabbed at the door switch to let Si in, left the front door on the latch. He went to the kitchen to grab a four pack of lager from the fridge and went back to his room.

The elder Simon was sat back on the bed with the TV on, flicking through the folder Rhonda gave them for the thousandth time when his visibly distressed younger self entered the room.

Although there was no visible evidence, he could tell his younger self had another run in.

"What happened?" asked the elder Simon

"A new one, disguised as a tramp at the bus station, flame thrower' replied his younger self slightly out of breath. He sketched in the rest of the details and how he was dispatched by a FATE sniper who was on the roof of The Eagle Centre.

The younger Si slumped down on the bed next to his older self. He didn't even take off his jacket or bag, as collapsing in a heap was the first thing on his to do list.

He slumped width ways on the bed, his feet hitting the floor and his head being propped up by the wall his bed was next to. When he glanced over, he couldn't help but notice the difference in the size of his stomach compared to his older self who was sat upright to his right. It was getting increasingly difficult to hide his disgust when he thought about what he'd become in twenty years.

Ever since his thirty-nine-year-old self had showed up, he'd been having the same recurring nightmare where he was in a boxing ring with him, and with very punch he hit square in the face of his older counterpart, the younger Si screamed vile abuse at him.

'WHAT THE HELL HAPPENED TO YOU'

'YOU LET ME DOWN'

'YOU RUINED MY LIFE'

Were some of the more family friendly phrases he threw at him. His older self just stood there and took it. Never at any point did he fight back. Si shifted his glance to the TV and dismissed the negative thoughts entering his brain. He needed something to take his mind off of everything.

It had been a hard week for the younger Simon. He had all the emotion of finding out what he turns into when he's knocking forty, but then he finds out his girlfriend is a potential assassin, and he then had to string her along with a series of half-truths so he could delay seeing her until his older self had gone back to 2022, and his memory of these few weeks were automatically buried.

First, he said he'd gone home for a couple of days due to a 'family emergency'. An excuse given to him by his older self who called it a 'belter of a reason' due to its vagueness and how people never question it.

This made the younger Si wince when his older self said it. At what point in the future did he become such a prat?

Then he was back in Derby but was bed ridden with the flu. Real flu, not man flu. For some reason, he always felt the need to clarify that whenever he spoke to a woman.

He got Paul to cover for him when Hannah inevitably came up to try and see him and to see if she could help.

Paul agreed without question, but Si could see suspicion mounting at the back of his mind.

He sat in his room alone with the lights off when Hannah came to the front door. His older self was out at the uni library. He heard the creek of the fire door hinge as it opened

'Hannah! Hello lovely, how are you?' beamed Paul

'How is he?' Hannah replied curtly, not returning Paul's cheerful greeting

This seemed to shake off Paul's false charm as he got to the agreed cover story.

'Sleeping, he's not great to be honest'

'Is his... dad still about'?

'Yea' replied Paul 'That man's still here'

Si lifted his head up from the pillow. What did he mean by that? Paul continued

'Do you want a cup of tea?' Paul offered, there was a silence where Hannah shuck her head

'Vodka?'

She suppressed a laugh, she really didn't like Paul and she hated herself a little bit for succumbing to his charms.

'Tell him I'll call him, and' She paused... she got louder as she finished off the sentence. Raising her voice and moving her head in the direction of Simons room

'...it's not what you think. We were made for each other.'

Si sat bolt upright in his bed. "Shit! Did I just hear that right? Does she know I know? What the hell did THAT mean?" he thought slightly frantic.

This was very clever wording as Paul misread it as they'd had a bust up and Si was avoiding her.

A cavalcade of mixed emotions raced through Si's head. His heart was pounding. He wanted to Laugh, Cry and punch the wall in rage all at once. Meanwhile, in the Uni Library at the same time the memory of what he overheard came racing back to his older self, rendering Simon Snr completely catatonic.

As if this wasn't enough, the assassination attempts had increased just as FATE had predicted. The documented ones weren't so bad, as plans were in place to keep the two Simons out of harm's way were working, but it was the brand-new attempts that were scary. And these new guys didn't seem bored. They were new and they meant it.

The flame thrower wielding tramp tonight at the bus station, the man collecting for Amnesty International on Princes Street with a fully loaded AK47, the Rugby ball that was filled with six grenades that blew Leroy's arms off. The list went on. Sheer desperation had driven the organisations and people who wanted either Simon dead to increasingly ridiculous methods.

The older Simon broke the silence.

'Been a shit week, hasn't it?' he said dryly

His younger self managed a singular sarcastic 'Ha' in agreement

'If you fancied a drink Paul's invited us both out tonight'

'Both?' the younger Si lent forward looking at his older counterpart, with one eyebrow raised

'You sure?'

'Yea, seemed keen for me to go' replied Simon putting down the folder on the pillow.

'Nothing in the dossier that says we can't, route from here to the club is well covered, think we need to let off a little steam. Fancy it?'

11:45pm, London Road

Si, Simon, Kirsty and Paul stood in the seemingly static queue to get into Zanzibar which was snaking so far up London Road it almost reached Bradshaw way. The queues was awash with students smelling of a mixture of WKD Blue, cigarettes, sweat and CK One, already half cut and not wearing enough to protect them for the late September midnight chill.

The faint green light of everyone's Nokia screen illuminated their faces as they text their friends to see where they were. The faint base thud of the music on the ground floor level poured out from the front doors and could be felt before it was heard.

The elder Simon was having a wonderful time. The younger Si wasn't.

Simon was enjoying being out with Paul and Kirsty like he did back in the day, but this was better. It was back in the day. He relished every little detail, like managing to get a pint of premium lager in a pub for under £2. The bars he used to love that had closed were back open again, and right now memories were zipping back about Zanzibar Night Club.

He tilted his head towards the door to identify what was playing.

'Almost got it, one sec' he said aloud, a mixture of alcohol and ultimate nostalgia elating him and making him talk louder

'How can you tell what's playing? All I can hear is a thudding' said Kirsty in disbelief.

Simon clicked his fingers when he got it

'Love at first sight by Kylie' he beamed. Zanzibar was a multi-level night club, Ground floor was pop music and cheese, first floor R&B, and on the top floor where they only sold bottled water, dance house and trance music.

'I'm impressed you keep up with the charts Mr R. My dad never did,' said Paul. Misreading why the older Simon was so keen on what was playing.

The younger Si rolled his eyes. It had been like this all night. Paul, Kirsty and his older self had hit it off after a few drinks and were 'bantering' all evening, just as he did with them both just a few weeks ago when they first met. The younger Si's eyes met his forehead when a self-aware thought popped up without warning.

'Are you jealous?' Si was surprised by this. Maybe he was. His older self was always a bit cagey when he asked him if he and Paul were still friends. He'd change the subject and act like he had something to hide. There was something he wasn't telling him.

'Not as good as the music twenty years ago though, is it? Dad.' Spat Si, putting extra emphasis on the 'Dad' bit. Alcohol making him drop his guard and lacing every word with added sarcasm.

The elder Simon was taken aback. It's rare he's in a genuinely good mood so he was frankly offended that someone who would take a pot shot to rob him off it. He was even more offended that this someone was him. This was taking self-hatred to a new level.

Simon was sensitive about his age. Literally living in the past made him forget about this for a while until now.

The elder Simon had found it increasingly difficult to hold his tongue with how his younger self behaved. A lot of his behaviour he'd forgotten and a lot he didn't realise he did.

He always thought of himself as basically good, smart, and respectful. But meeting himself as he was twenty years previously gave him evidence to the contrary. At times he could be stubborn, selfish, vain, snide, and riddled with toxic masculinity. Frankly he was a cocky little prick.

Simon knew thanks to his condition that nobody can hurt you quite like yourself. That inner voice that knew which buttons to press to break you. This planted an idea in his head. If his younger self used his age to get under his skin, he knew exactly how to fire back.

'Not as good as the music from summer last year though, is it eh? Son!' Said the elder Simon, mimicking the speech pattern of his younger self.

Simon left this hanging for effect to see if his younger self would cotton on. Nothing. He decided to up the ante.

'You know when you were seeing that girl. What was her name..' the elder Simon clicked his tongue a few times

'Oh yea, Kim.'

Kirsty had correctly guessed what Si's so-called dad was getting at and was trying to suppress a laugh. The younger Si's face sagged like a bloodhound. Panic started to rise through his body. He wouldn't. Would he? He promised he wouldn't say anything.

'Pretty sure that was your first girlfriend, wasn't it? Son!' The elder Simon beamed, adrenaline from getting back some fight into his system running through his veins, he turned to Paul

'Runs in the family though Paul, I also didn't lose my virginity till I was...'

The younger Si flew forward to cut his older self off and went to grab the lapels on his jacket

'Alright, that's enough!' Si shouted. Paul broke them up

'Fellas, fellas, calm down. We've been in the que 20 minutes you wanna get chucked out before we even get in?... well?'

The two versions of Simon eyed each other dubiously. A line had been crossed.

Paul continued.

'Now. Si, apologise to your dad' Paul gestured with his right hand towards the elder Simon, as usual getting mediation horribly wrong.

Si was just drawing breath to sling a series of obscene phrases at Paul when the queue started moving.

11:59pm

Finally, they reached the front of the queue, a chilly silence between the two Simon's had descended since the argument, which was occasionally punctuated by Paul going into charm overdrive trying to reignite the conversation. Kirsty was trying to distance herself from the awkwardness by looking busy on her phone, when really she was just playing Snake.

'So, bet you can remember when this was a cinema eh'? Said Paul, smiling at the older Simon.

'Nope' was Simon's one word answer.

Paul racked his brains for what to try next. He turned to the younger Si

'You heard from Hannah?' he asked

'Yep' was Si's one word Answer

When he knew both men weren't looking, Paul rolled his eyes.

The queue moved forward, as they got to the front Kirsty made a point of dashing in front of the three men and ducked inside the club at great speed. As she did the doorman put his palm out in front of him to indicate for them to stop. The doorman was over six feet tall with muscles tiered form the neck. Dressed all in black and wearing an earpiece.

Without hearing each other both versions of Simon sighed

simultaneously, then they both spoke the same words in unison

'Sod this, I'm just gonna go back to the fla....'

They both finished before they could complete saying the word flat. They realised they both had the same idea. They both paused for a second, then they gestured for each other to speak first.

'Look, I'll get a hotel' the elder Simon said quietly, conceding defeat. He had the money, as Rhonda has set him up with a funded bank account to use while he was in the past, so he wasn't dipping into Si's student loan. He knew the Pennine Hotel would be safe enough.

He patted his jacket pocket to see if he still had his wallet. The younger Si looked at his older self and suddenly felt wretched for killing the good mood. He was about to open his mouth to attempt to mend the fence when there was a screeching sound.

A high-pitched deafening wail came from the doorman's earpiece. He tapped his ear twice. Just as he was about to draw breath there was the sound of a gunshot. A gushing fountain of blood burst out the left-hand side of the doorman's head followed by a bullet. He dropped to the floor; he was dead before he hit it.

A shriek was let out by the front few people in the queue who witnessed it, alerting the rest. Paul stood open mouthed unable to move with fear, the two Simon's instantly recognizing what was happening. The doorman was used to get their attention, this was another new attempt on their lives. But where did that come from?

They both glanced rapidly around as panic spread was causing chaos on London Road. The queue full of students had quickly dispersed and were causing cars to screech to a halt as they ran into the road without looking. Blood from the dead doorman's head was starting to trickle down the stairs that lead to the front door of the club.

Police sirens could be heard in the distance. Fear and adrenaline had overridden any petty squabble the two Simon's were engaged in. The older Simon turned to his younger self when he figured it out.

'Bullet came out of the left-hand side of his head; door was on the right. It came out of the club' said Simon, having to shout to be heard over the noise.

Without thinking Simon pointed right as it was the quickest way back to Peak Court, he didn't think that this would still leave them in the path of whoever was in the club. As the younger Si gabbed Paul's arm and the elder Simon took one step, a second gun shot came from inside, missing the elder Simon's head by such a narrow measure that he could feel the air ripple by his cheek as the bullet went past.

'FUCKING HELL' Shouted Paul, witnessing the bullet miss Simon. Paul had now regained the power of speech, but he didn't offer much in the way of constructive planning to get out of the line of fire.

The gunman, or rather in this case gun woman exited the club with snipers rifle still trained on the elder Simons head.

'You're new' the younger Si said aloud, the background noise on London Road dying down.

Paul had a mixture of bewilderment and fear on his face as he looked at his friend

'WHAT?' was all he could manage

'Yea, I was dispatched in a bit of a rush' Replied the woman with the gun casually. She turned to the elder Simon 'That's why the sights are a bit off on this thing. I was aiming for your face'

She smiled. A smile that chilled the two Simon's to the bone. In a funny way they had grown so used to the assassins that looked bored. They knew that they caused no harm, or the harm they did cause would be put right so quickly they had become immune to them. But as the day drew closer to when Simon was due to go back to go home, the increase in newbies who didn't look bored was scary.

She wouldn't miss this time.

As the woman went to reload Simon felt a buzzing from his jeans pocket where his keys were. She fired before he could check it. Time seemed to slow down. He couldn't get out of the way in time.

All Simon could so was close his eyes, and brace for the inevitable.

CHAPTER THIRTEEN

Life on Mars?

Tuesday 1st October 2002

12:05am Zanzibar nightclub, front entrance

'Erm, you can open your eyes now' Simon heard his younger self say.

Gingerly he opened his eyes to see the bullet the assassin had fired, suspended in mid-air just 5 millimetres away from his face.

Simon tilted his head to the left without taking his eyes off the bullet. He carefully lifted his hand up and flicked it. The bullet stayed suspended as Simons finger thudded into its side. He looked over in the direction of the gunwoman.

She was static, as were the smattering of students fleeing the drama of the front of the queue as well as the cars that narrowly avoided hitting them. The music had stopped from inside the club. The silence was punctuated by Paul's exasperated plea of.

'Will someone PLEASE tell me what the fuck is going on?'

'Not too sure myself to be honest' said the older Simon, walking up to and examining the gun woman who remained static, aiming at where he was stood.

Simon glanced into the club, the doors to the ground floor were open. He turned to his younger self and nodded inside.

'Think You'd better see this'

His younger self headed to the doors without question. Paul was stuck for something to say apart from 'what the FUCK is going on?'

'It's not just London Road, it's the whole club' Simon said to his younger self as he made it to the top of the stairs. As they walked in they passed Kirsty, stood perfectly still at the cloak room, reaching her arm forward to collect her ticket. Paul tried a few times to get her attention with all the desperation and denial of someone who had found a loved one's dead body.

'Why's he freaking out so much?' Si asked his older self.

'Why do you think?' replied Simon 'remember when he disappeared for 25 minutes when we were in The Bless?'

'Thought he was on the fruit machines' the younger Si said innocently. His elder self snorted

'He wasn't. He was seeing his dealer'

Si had his suspicions about his friends chemical habits, but he unintentionally turned a blind eye as he knew he couldn't cope with the truth. Although mature for his age, the 19-year-old Simon was very sheltered in many aspects of the world. Class A drug use was one of them.

He would wise up Pauls habits in the years that followed, and the part they played in his untimely death. Right now, it was something he tried to put to the back of his mind. There was enough to deal with, and that was before an entire nightclub became frozen in time.

Time, of course! The younger Si checked his watch. Not a smart watch, just a regular watch. It still said 12:05am they'd been inside for almost five minutes; it should say ten past midnight.

The lower level of the club was even more eerie than the cloak room, it was heaving with people five or six deep at the bar and a dancefloor so packed you'd swear the floor would give in with the weight.

And everybody was static. If you see a human statue, or someone pretending to be still there's always a tell. Shallow breathing, the odd flinch. But not here. It was like someone had pressed pause. The music was silent and the club lights and even the smoke from the smoke machine were still.

'I've always wanted to do this' said the younger Si with a grin before he vaulted over the bar. When he landed, he raided the fringe. He popped two beers, one for him and his older self and went to pour something stronger for Paul as he was in shock.

He thought better of it. So, he downed the double whiskey he just poured and got him a bottle of water instead. He shouted to his older self who was walking up to the DJ booth

'Think this was Fate?'

Simon rapidly turned around and told his younger self to shush

'What?' Si said in disbelief

'Paul' His older self-replied in a hushed tone

Si looked at the static bar staff, and then gestured to everyone who was still around him as Paul was moving around the dancefloor looking at everyone with his jaw wide open.

'Mate, I think the cats out the bag' he shouted to his older self as he approached the bar. Simon's face gestured that his younger self had a point and gladly took the beer from him. After he took a swig, he said

'Get us a sidekick will you? I've not had one in twenty years'

As his younger self turned to the bar Simon mentally run through the events that led up to time freezing, just in case there was a clue. Anything that would explain what was going on.

His pocket. He felt a vibration in his pocket where his keys were. He put the beer down on the bar and took out his keys.

The cylinder that Rhonda gave him that he attached to his keys was flashing red from the LED light that was on at the end of the tube. This little thing had caused all of this, really? Can't have! He felt his watch vibrate; he checked the screen. It just said 'Walk towards the speakers'

His younger self was back with him, he told him his theory and they set off towards the DJ booth. Paul, still freaking out was guided over by the younger Si. The red light on the end was pulsating and got to a greater speed the closer they got towards the stack of speakers towards the end of the room. When they were only a few feet away a piercing feedback screech came out of the base bin that almost knocked them over.

A man's voice came through the speaker, sounded like he was in his late twenties. Slightly nasal.

'Right, ok... how do I know that's on. Can you hear me. Simon, are you there?'

'Yes!' both Simons said in unison, sounding identical. Paul looked at Si, then his 'dad' then Si again. Looking like he was in the crowd on finals day at Wimbledon.

'I can't hear them' the unknown voice said through the speakers 'Dave, can't hear them'

In the distance, faintly you could hear Dave, who had a slightly depressed sounding West Midlands accent offering tech advice

'Did you send the message to his watch?' offered Dave

'Yes' said the voice

Both Simons and Paul were looking confused by this point

'Have you flicked the red switch?' Dave replied

'Yes' said the voice impatiently. There was a pause.

'You sure? Dave offered

'That happened once! Gimme a break!' replied the voice impatiently.

In the background Dave could be heard approaching, followed by tutting as he looked at whatever equipment the voice was using, then there was the sound of several switches being pulled and a short burst of static through the speakers, which made the sound a higher definition.

'There' said Dave louder than before, clearly next to the mic. 'Stronger frequency and you need to release the speak button when you've finished'

The voice called after Dave as he left

'Thanks Dave, cheers'

'That's the last time I pull your chestnuts out the fire' replied Dave, his voice fading as he exited and got further from the mic. The unknown voice tried again.

'This is Dr Zac Watson of FATE HQ, Simon Radcliffe do you read me? Over'

The two Simon's again replied 'yes' in unison, with slightly less enthusiasm than before.

'Oh, what's happening now?' moaned an overwhelmed Paul quietly to himself. The younger Si tried to explain to Paul without giving too much away and that there were some people he knew who could fix what was going on.

Dr Zac confirmed that the device that Rhonda gave Simon had activated. The device, which is way more sophisticated than its appearance would have you believe can activate without you having to do anything. In field tests, the engineers at FATE concluded that if faced with mortal danger and you have only seconds to act then the last thing you would want to do would be to fumble about in your pocket and press the on button. So, this device could perform billions of calculations, way up a situation and if an unexpected death was on the cards without any agents around to help, the device would freeze all time with a one-mile radius, allowing whoever was in the line of fire, time to get out the way, and for FATE to properly investigate.

'First job would be to remove you, and anyone else caught in the eye of the device from the scene for processing.'

'Processing?' the older Simon asked, one eyebrow going higher than the other.

'Yup. Stand Still. I need to get a lock on' replied Zac. The sound of furious typing at a keyboard could be heard over the speakers. Three of the clubs rotating spotlights were unfrozen and pivoted round to light up the three men.

'I can't move' said Paul, panic rising again in his voice

'Don't panic Mr Kimmel, we just need to keep you all still for the extraction' said Zac trying to be soothing but sounded distracted as he was concentrating on what he was doing.

And what he was doing, was he was bringing them all to FATE HQ.

All they saw was a blinding white flash that engulfed them, followed by the sensation of floating for a millisecond. Then just as quickly their vision cleaned, and they were standing in the same formation in a different room.

Banks of computers faced the three men in the dimly lit light grey oblong room, FATE's logo was painted onto the back wall that faced them along with the motto 'Don't argue'. The only brightly lit part was the white raised area the three men were stood on, above them were some threatening looking light panels that were radiating heat. The elder Simon lifted his hand for a second, drawn to the heat. Paul who was a closeted Star Trek fan was convinced this was just part of a bad trip and they'd just materialised on the bridge or something.

Zac's bearded face appeared from behind a computer monitor. Paul was secretly disappointed it wasn't Scotty.

'I did it' beamed Zac

'I DID it!' he jumped down from his chair. He shouted in the opposite direction towards an open door

'Dave, I did it!'

'Well done' replied Dave flatly from another room

Zac bounded up to where the Simons and Paul had landed.

He reached up and vigorously shook the younger and older

Simon's hand.

'Simon, good to see you both again'

The elder Simon looked puzzled. He'd swear he'd never seen this man stood before him before in his life. And as he was 4 feet tall at the most, he would have remembered him.

'Erm, sorry.. Zac isn't it?'

Zac nodded

'Don't think we've met'

Zac winced. He wasn't supposed to do that. If you meet time travellers out of sequence, you have to be very careful how you address them. The incident on the green goddess truck was two years ago from Zac's point of view, that was the first time he met the two Simon's. They had not met him yet. He'd just broken a major protocol.

The only thing he was supposed to speak about what the shoe magnets, items in a temporal paradox could be discussed out of sequence. As nobody else was around who heard his mistake who could put him on report (other than Dave, but he wasn't listening) Zac decided to make light of it.

'Quite right, sorry. I've read so much about the case feels like I know you all'

'That sounded convincing' Zac thought to himself 'I'll show that assessor who can't think on his feet'

Zac looked at Paul

'Mr Kimmel, I'm so sorry about all this. Afraid you got caught in the crossfire' he held out his hand 'Dr Watson, pleased to meet you'

The younger Si tried but couldn't hold back on the snigger that came from his mouth

'Something funny Mr Radcliffe?' Said Zac giving the younger Simon the side eye, knowing full well what he was laughing at.

Si slammed his mouth rigid and shook his head

'What was I supposed to do when I got my doctorate in history, change my surname? I've worked here for seven years. Go on, tell me one I've not heard'

There was a silence, Si just looked at the floor. Zac told them to wait there as he'd be back in a second and he left the room

When he was out of earshot the younger Si whispered to Paul

'Must be nice to not be the shortest one in the room anymore, eh?'

The two men sniggered. The elder Simon gave them both a look that brilliantly conveyed the thought of 'Grow up you two' without saying a word.

Zac came back in with a glass of water and what looked like a prescription pill still in its blister pack, he approached Paul and offered it to him.

'Here take this' he said warmly

Asking what it was, Zac explained that it was well documented

what drugs Paul had taken on the evening of the 30th, as the stress of witnessing time freezing and being taken up to HQ was enough to bend anyone's mind, he didn't need to be tripping as well. This pill would locate all the chemicals and neutralise them in an instant.

Paul took it without question.

'Trust me, you'll feel great in the morning' said Zac as Paul handed him back the glass of water.

Zac muttered something about FATE's pharmaceutical department being brilliant, but not quite back to full capacity after a recent 'incident' his face dropped for a second when he realised he said too much again then he outlined the next stage of the plan, it would take roughly two Earth hours before they could be returned back to 2002.

FATE had done this countless times before on the 'first man' case. Every new assailant and the scene of the attempted killing had to be frozen, so that civilians who witnessed it could have their memories wiped and returned to normal, and FATE would take the attacker into custody and process and document where they came from. This generated a lot of paperwork that nobody wanted to do. Thankfully some poor sod on punishment duty locked in The White Room would have to deal with all that. And thanks to the internal post having time travel capabilities Doctor Gavin Dawes would be getting admin work sent to him that was forward dated to two years after he was released.

'You gonna erase my memory?' asked Paul, somewhat concerned.

'yes' Zac held out a hand as if he knew this news would upset Paul 'Don't worry, it's not intrusive, it's an entirely organic process'.

'Organic?' the younger Si questioned. 'How do you organically erase someone's memory?'

Zac kept the explanation short. The human brain cannot cope with witnessing the weird and wonderful things FATE deals with on a daily basis, especially Time Travel, and certainly before the era in which Time Travel is a commercial activity. It would be the equivalent of a cave man finding himself mid Atlantic on a Boeing 747. It would be too much.

FATE had developed a system of mild hypnotic suggestion that utilises the naturally occurring brains chemicals to help when a witness couldn't comprehend what they had seen. An agent sits them down individually and they tell them two truths. One is the full hard to swallow actual truth of what they have seen, the second is a plausible and palatable lie.

Humans will always take an easy to digest lie over an uncomfortable truth. When they have been returned to their own time the brain picks the lie and they forget what they've seen. Usually dismissing it as a dream.

Ever dreamed you have visited another place that's out of the ordinary? Or been back at your old school, in the time period when you were at that school, but with the knowledge and memories you have now? Or maybe you've met with a much-loved relative who's been dead for a few years.

Truth is you did. You didn't dream it. FATE got in the way.

Zac's watch beeped. He looked at it then looked back up at the three men.

'We have a few minutes, fancy a quick tour?'

The main corridor of FATE's northern hemisphere ran outside the room they were all in, which as they left Simon noticed was marked 'Extraction Chamber 2610'. There was no obvious entrance or exit, just a long thin stretch of space that curved around out of view.

The corridor was a curious mix of low and high tech, touch screen computers that seem to appear out of thin air on command, but also printed signage suspended by wire from the ceiling. Agents dashing past them talking in every known and unknown language on the most incredible and impossible looking wearable tech, but they were squeakily walking on a cheap linoleum covered floor that was being mopped by a depressed looking maintenance man.

The elder Simon, who was petrified of Hospitals, was starting to get creeped out by the lino and the smell of the cleaning fluid. This place was like an NHS hospital crossed with the Apple store.

As they walked and made small talk about what goes on at FATE, they came to an intersection where the corridor split into two. One side had a sign marked 'Processing' the other 'Gate's 5-15'

They carried on down towards processing, to the left, banks of windows appeared letting them see outside. In the distance you would swear they were at an airport. Ten or so planes being boarded, all with FATE's logo on the tail. One taxiing to the runway getting ready for take-off.

Simon noticed the terrain. Where was this place? Looked like a desert.

Clearly his younger self was thinking the same thing, he asked Zac where they were.

'Mars' replied Zac casually.

This news caused Paul and the two Simon' to run to the window. Mars? The actual planet Mars?

They stood wide eyed starring out onto the red planet. Zac was talking about something to do with FATE being such a big operation that they needed a base that was the size of a planet. Just the department of historic clothing and artifacts stretched over a continent.

The three men didn't hear this. They were too engrossed in the view

'This is amazing' said the elder Simon, open mouthed.

'Is at first' replied Zac, ' but you get used to it'.

By the time Paul's memory of everything that happened tonight would be erased, they would be all deposited back into their flat. All goes to plan; Paul would appear on his bed in his room and the two Simon's in the kitchen at roughly 12:30am local time. The cover story would be they weren't let into the club, so they all decided to go home.

The tour had ended. Almost all the civilians had been delt with and the gun woman had been put into the infinite loop of failure. Soon she would board rigid at the thought of putting a bullet into the elder Simon's head.

Zac had gone to prepare the room for Paul's two truths. The elder Simon was sat with Paul on a bench outside the room while the younger Simon stood by the window a few feet away, still in awe of the view of the red planet.

Simon looked to his left at Paul. He looked drained. It still felt weird seeing him again, alive, and well. They always said they would travel together one day. Looks like they finally did. 140 million miles away from it all.

Zac appeared at the doorway.

'Won't be long, just need another ten minutes' he was holding two skeletal like metallic devices that made Paul's eyes widen.

'Hope they're not for me' said Paul, pointing at what Zac was holding

'No no, they're for' Zac didn't want to give too much away 'Something else. I just need to have a quick word with' He pointed at the younger Si and headed over to where he stood at the window.

The elder Simon watched them both chatting, he couldn't hear what they were saying but it sounded serious. Zac handed the two metal devices over to Simon's younger self.

Simon was tired. End of a heavy night out level of tired. He didn't have it in him to question what was going on. Right now, he either needed another drink, a strong coffee or bed. He remembered he bought a bottle of single malt whisky that was in his old room. He was visualizing doing some serious damage to it when Paul spoke.

'Not gonna lie, I'm bricking it' As he said this, he rubbed his hands over his face then sighed.

This was it. This was the chance that Simon thought he'd never get. To make amends, to get everything off his chest that he wanted to say to Paul but couldn't. His memory would be wiped any minute. He would never get a chance like this again.

'What's up with you?' Paul asked the elder Simon quietly, registering he was deep in thought

Simon smiled.

'You always could read my mind' he looked at Paul 'Nice to know that hasn't changed'

'Who are you? Paul asked, he'd had his suspicions about this man for a while. He'd guessed correctly he wasn't Simon's dad they were too similar.

'I haven't seen you' Simon took an intake of breath as he tried to phrase this right.

'... in sixteen years'

There was an awkward silence. Simon had to force the words out as he knew he didn't have a lot of time.

'Your friend over there by the window talking to Dr Watson, does something amazing twenty years in your future. He's, for reasons he still doesn't know. Goes back in time twenty years and comes face to face with himself, and all the friends he hasn't seen in way too long'

Paul looked at the younger Si, then down the corridor at all the comings and goings of FATE HQ

'Look at it all, you're on Mars in the headquarters of fate because somethings gone wrong with time' Simon could see the penny drop in Paul's face as he explained this, Paul turned back around and pointed at the elder Simon.

'You mean, you are..' his voice tailed off

Simon smiled.

'It's good to see you again mate'.

The two men hugged excitedly, Zac and the younger Si glanced over to see what the excitement was. They couldn't figure it out and just kept on talking. Paul was full of questions about the future, including the big one.

'You said you aint seen me in sixteen years, how come?'

Simon warned him to not freak out and he could only tell him this as he was about to have his memory wiped. He told him about the planned holiday to Ibiza, the argument over a woman and about Paul's death in 2006. How the guilt had weighed him down so badly over the last sixteen years, and how stupid macho pride had cost him the best friend he'd ever had.

'I'm sorry mate, I'm so sorry' Simon was losing the fight to hold back the tears 'If I'd have been there, I would have stopped you, a. a. and you'd still be here'

Simon was now in floods of tears and found it impossible to talk, emotionally he was rung out but felt like a weight had been lifted.

Just when Paul thought he'd come to terms with seeing time freeze and being in an impossible building on the red planet, he now find out that his best friend is a time traveller, and he is going to die in four years.

Actually, that's three years and nine months as the planned holiday was in May. He was frighted before, but now he was more than ready to get his mind scrubbed. As Zac came back and asked if he was ready, Paul stood up, squeezed the elder Simon's shoulder, and gave him a wink as he walked off with Zac.

The room he was taken to was dimly lit and set up like police interview room. Paul felt a little underwhelmed, it may be an organic process, but he was expecting something a little higher tech than this.

He sat down, Zac jumped up to the chair opposite and he pressed a hydraulic that raised the chair to Paul's eye level. The two men sat in silence for a second. Zac spoke first.

'It's a funny thing, time. From my point of view' he put his hand on his chest as he said the word 'my' 'I've already met Simon'

What was he getting at? Paul sensibly waited for Zac to continue

'I don't need to skirt the issue, I know the older Simon has already told you who he is, I first met him two years ago from my point of view, which from your point of view will be the night of the Freshers Ball, which is still to come'

Zac left this dangling, Paul wondered if this pointless yarn was part of the process of the memory wipe until Zac continues.

'And on that night. Something terrible happens'

CHAPTER FOURTEEN

Hangovers don't get easier

Tuesday 1st October 2002

4:13pm, Peak Court, First floor

Three days till the Freshers Ball

It had been roughly fifteen hours since the two Simons and Paul had got back from FATE HQ. The trip back was as instantaneous as the trip there from Zanzibar. The elder Simon exited the lift alone on the first floor, wearing his man bag and carrying a suitcase. He instinctively walked to Hannah's flat and banged on the door with his left hand. He would have used his right hand but the cuts on his knuckles had only just scabbed over.

Hannah opened the door; she didn't know how to address the older Simon now after everything that happened last night. There might be a chance he didn't know.

'Mr Radcliffe, what brings you her…'

Simon cut her off

'Drop that act, I know you know everything' he barged past her.

'Come in why don't you' thought Hannah, somewhat sarcastically

The door to her room was open. Any other day during his trip to the past, Simon should have felt a melancholic nostalgia wave hit him, this was his first time in this room in nineteen years. But no. No warm fuzzy feeling today.

'Going somewhere?' Said Hannah, referring to his suitcase

'Was gonna ask you the same question' Simon nodded to her case on the bed

'Still, least I get to see you leave this time' he continued. Hannah stood in the doorway and crossed her arms defensively.

Tuesday 1st October 2002

1:20am Peak Court, Fourth Floor

The Simons were assured by Dr Watson that a now comatose Paul would wake up feeling refreshed and with zero memory of the night before when they got back. The truth his brain would latch onto, would be that he was too drunk to stand up straight and the bouncers refused him entry to the club, so both Simon's got him home and left Kirsty in there.

A new assassin, time freezing and a trip to FATE HQ had stopped the two Simon's from bickering and had bought them back together, but both their brains were just about at frazzled with everything they'd gone through. The elder Simon suggested cracking open the single malt scotch he had, to sooth them both before they turned in. They were tired but the adrenaline in their systems was forcing them awake.

One whisky made both men feel a lot more mellow, so they figured if one was good then two must be better. Two turned to three, then four and before they knew it they had done most of the bottle between them. It was now getting on for 4am, although it only felt like they'd been chatting for only half an hour.

The younger Si wondered if that was an after effect of time freezing, but he was reminded by his older self that time does tend to go a lot faster when you're having a heavy session. They had reached the random and silly stage of drink, where to the parties involved in the session think they're being hilarious (but any sober witness would think they're being juvenile and outright dumb.)

They both laughed a bit too much over the notion that

technically they were drinking alone when the elder Simon went to the kitchen, leaving the younger Simon actually alone.

Alone for only a minute or two with his own thoughts, head full of whiskey and the knowledge his future was going to be underwhelming. He started to spiral downwards.

Suddenly he felt quite teared up. His whole life from this point on was going to be controlled and manipulated into mediocrity thanks to FATE and how messed up Hannah's eventual ghosting of him would make him feel.

Anger swelled up inside him He wanted to see her and have it out with her right now. She knew alright, she knew everything. That thing she said to Paul in the corridor outside his room. What was that all about?

Si was pacing the floor, almost felt like the friction caused from the nylon mix carpet was charging up his hurt. With nobody to sit him down and reassure him or talk him out of it, he slammed his drink down on his desk and left for Hannah's flat barefoot and without his keys.

The elder Simon was in the kitchen when he heard the front door slam hoping it was someone else from the flat he raced back to the room to find it empty. He knew instinctively that this was bad, where did his younger self go? New memories started to flicker in his mind.

He was getting a lot more used to his memory's from when he was the younger one being unearthed, he didn't get the sickness or the sweats any more, he just got the visions. He was starting to remember where he went to, and what happened next.

He was confused. This wasn't supposed to happen. Both their lives were mapped out in minute-by-minute detail from the instant he got there. He was supposed to avoid Hannah until the night of the Freshers Ball, and they were due to break up the following Easter as history dictated. Him going down to have it out with her drunkenly at 4am would have a major knock-on effect.

His younger drunken self was about to mess with cause and effect. He grabbed the blue folder that Rhonda had given him and flicked through. Reading was out of the question; thanks to the drink the words might as well have been hieroglyphics. What could he do? How could he stop that hot headed tit of a boy he used to be ruining everything? Then he spotted his younger self's phone.

Hannah didn't wake up in time to let the younger Si in herself, the bloke in the room next hers on the left who didn't say much, Robert (or as they called him, Silent Bob) was raised out of bed by the drunk and angry Si banging on the front door.

She had just tied her silk dressing gown and appeared at the door when she saw Si barge past the stunned looking Bob and charge towards her. She panicked; this wasn't supposed to happen.

How much did he know? What had got him so worked up? She decided to act as if everything was still on the level

'Simon, it's 4am why are you.....'

He cut her off as he barged past her

'Drop the act I know you know everything' he disappeared into her room. She mouthed the word 'sorry' to Bob who was still in the corridor. He checked his phone, put it back into his dressing gown pocket and went into his room.

She shut the door. Si had his head pressed against the window.

'Well, someone's feeling better' she said with mild sarcasm.

'You bitch' said Si with quiet rage, his breath streaming the window

'Why are 21st century boys so emotional?' Hannah thought before saying aloud 'I guess were past the pleasantries then?'

Si turned and bellowed

'I thought it was real, you and me it...' his voice tailed off. He ran his hands over his face

'But no, the woman I love wants me dead like every other tosser with a snipers rifle or poisoned latte in this poxy fucking city'

Sadness was overtaken by rage. He turned back around; in a fit of pique he wheeled around again and punched the window. His fist came off worse thanks to the window being mostly reinforced plastic.

He collapsed on the floor, now in floods of tears. Hannah crouched down and brushed his cheek tenderly.

'It was and is real. I do love you.' She said soothingly.

Overcome with emotion Si couldn't speak, he just shook his head and hid his face

'All I can tell you is, there were hundreds. And I was the best match'

Si drew his hands down his face to reveal his blood shot eyes, hundreds? What did she mean by that?

'I don't want you dead darling. I want you alive and I want to be by your side as you fulfil your potential in the future, not be that waste of space you've been telling everyone is your dad'

A thought flicked through Si's head. 'When has she ever called me darling before now?' His heart and head were at odds with each other. As the intensity built, neither of them registered the man who appeared behind them both with a gun.

'Simon Radcliffe, you have broken FATE mission law 1607 subsection 83, consider this an official warning' said the man with the gun with an authoritative tone

Hannah turned around. It was silent Bob standing pointing the gun at them. With all the weird things Si had witnessed this one was a surprise. Silent Bob worked for FATE? Bob tilted the gun towards Hannah

'Hannah Maberhill, you're cover is officially blown'

Hannah stood up and went to speak, Bob cocked the gun directly into her face.

'Don't even think about it' said Bob quietly. His even quiet tone stopping Hannah in her tracks and making her compliant.

'We're not interested in all-out war with your people, we've got enough on this close to the Freshers Ball. That's why we are giving you 24 hours to pack your things and get back to your own time. If you don't, then we will come for you, and we'll unleash hell....These are our terms nod if you agree'

Hannah nodded. Bob dragged Si up by his collar and frog marched him back to the lifts.

Simon's older self-answered the door, the new memory of Bob's real identity hadn't caught up with him yet, so he was surprised when he saw him and the younger Si stood there, he displayed his warrant card. He wasn't called Bob after all, his was Dr Tree Sturgeon, FATE field agent.

'We appreciate the tip off Mr Radcliffe' said Tree as he pushed the younger Si forward. He turned and left.

'Tip off?' the younger Si slurred quizzically.

Simon told his younger self that he had no choice but to text FATE HQ about what had happened. Even though he couldn't read the dossier, he remembered Rhona said the whole city was crawling with FATE agents.

Si hit back by saying that thanks to his meddling FATE have ordered Hannah out of this city six months early. She would have to be gone within 24 hours. Simon got bits of information from his drunk younger self about what was said and tried to put a positive spin on events by saying with Hannah leaving, he may get over her quicker and that would benefit his mental health in the future.

Si looked his older self-up and down. And said with real spite in his voice.

'What future?'

The older Simon knew what his younger self was getting at, still he decided to push him

'And what do you mean by that eh?' Simon could feel the anger rise in him

The younger Si gestured drunkenly around him

'All of this, why even bother with all of this, why try and be better when I end up like you. I mean. What went wrong?'

The gloves were off now.

'I'll tell you what went wrong' the elder Simon replied through gritted teeth, he leaned forward threateningly, 'You, thinking you could never put a foot wrong, you thinking that the world owed you success, you arrogant entitled little wanker'

The younger Si's jaw was wide open. How dare he say that?

'I'm you' was all he could muster to fire back with

'YES, AND I'M YOU!' the elder Simon shouted back. 'IF YOU WANT TO SEE THE CULPRIT OF WHO FUCKED YOUR LIFE UP THEN I SUGGEST YOU TAKE A GOOD LONG LOOK IN THE MIRROR'

Although his rage had hit def con 6, Simon was feeling pretty pumped-up for firing back at his younger self.

He could see he had upset him. The need to scream at him had past, but he still had things he wanted to say at him.

'I know that look you've been giving me, ever since I've got here. I can see in your face, 'who is this man, and how did he make such a balls up of my future'. Well, I've got news for you pretty boy. I'm just the effect, you my friend are the cause of all this'

The elder Simon gestured towards his stomach to emphasise his point.

The younger Si was trying to find the words to reply, he opened his mouth and nothing, his head drunkenly made a faint circular motion.

'You forget something. I've been you, and memories of everything you say and do during this time are coming back to me all the time now I'm back here, and I know that you are trying to say, 'where did it all go wrong?'

As he finished saying this the elder Simon shrugged. He was stabbing in the dark now, trying to find the answer to why he turned out the way he did. Entitlement? Laziness? Going with the flow?

His younger self mistook the elder Simon's tone and thought this would be a good time to make a joke to lighten the atmosphere.

'Well, looking at you the flow never went past a gym' the younger Si sniggered briefly before he sensed the atmosphere changed.

The elder Simons eyes narrowed; this had been brewing for a while. Triggered by the sensitivity about his weight he span around and punched his younger self in the face with such force that he split the skin on his knuckles and broke his younger self's nose.

Blood spurted out of the hands that covered his younger self's nose, as the younger Si lay on the floor in a foetal position crying in pain. The pain and the shock making him gasp for air.

FATE who were on high alert, and who were monitoring everything they did swooped in efficiently and quietly and took the younger Simon from the scene to a field hospital in the city to do what they could for his nose. They kept him in overnight.

The older Simon woke up alone in his old bed around 3pm. The hangover was bad enough without the throbbing ache from his knuckles, and that horrendous drip, drip, drip effect as his memory of the night before came back in small doses.

He closed his eyes and whimpered when he remembered the fight.

'Oh god, what have I done'

He sat on the bed with his head in his hands. The curtains were open, it was late afternoon the darkness from the grey sky outside reflected his mood. As he lifted his head up from his hands his fingers traced the outline of his nose. He felt the uneven bump.

He sat up straight when he realised. This was how he broke his nose in the first semester. It was him. He did it to himself. He got up to use the toilet when he noticed a letter had been pushed under the door. It was a hand written letter from Rhonda, asking him to call her. No doubt to get his version of events from last night. He put the letter back down on the desk. He couldn't deal with her right now.

After having a shower, getting water and some pain killers he thought it would be for the best to pack his things and stay in a hotel until the night of the Freshers Ball. He'd have to face his younger self at some point, he'd have to be with him on the night he goes back in order for the plan to work.

As he left his room in Peak Court he wished he was able to call on Paul to offload his troubles. That was out of the question. Paul was back to being a ghost of his past.

Simon felt lonely again as he stood in the lift, a feeling he hadn't had since he got here. As the illuminated buttons progressed downwards, he changed his mind from ground floor to first. There's a chance she might be there still.

4:13pm, Hannah's Room

'Still, least I get to see you leave this time' he said looking at her suitcase.

Hannah stood in the doorway and crossed her arms defensively.

'Where will you go?' she asked

'Pennine Hotel. Seeing as the Premier Inn hasn't been built yet' replied Simon as he sat on her bed

He asked where she was going and who she worked for, which Hannah naturally declined to tell him as you never knew who might be listening.

There was a long pause.

'there's so much I wanted to ask you, but there's not much point' Simon's shoulder slumped as he said this. I'm going to forget all of this when I get back'

Hannah tried to empathise. She did still care about Simon, and she hated to see him to defeated by life.

'Bob's not here so I can talk, but only briefly'

She sat next to him on the bed. Simon forgot the perfume she used to wear; the smell swirled around in his head.

'It's not your fault' she whispered looking straight into his eyes

'FATE did this to you, keep you down, All I wanted was to free you from all that. I'm not your enemy, Science picked me to be your best match'

Hannah was cut off before she could finish by the sound of the air breaks from what sounded like a truck came from outside. Hannah on high alert got up and went to the window.

'Why is there an armoured tank outside?'

'Oh, that's my lift' Simon explained about the number of assassins entering the city were reaching a ridiculous level, so his fight with his younger self had required more FATE personnel in order to separate them.

Simon got up to leave, Hannah stood opposite him.

'I know you think it's pointless, but there's always a way around everything' she said

'What do you mean?' Simon asked a little puzzled.

'You've had a trip to the past, use that to change your future'

'How? I'll lose all memory'

'Find a memory that's out of FATE's hands' she leaned in for what Simon was hoping was going to be a kiss on the cheek. Instead, she just whispered two words in his ear, pulled her head back and told him to go.

She watched from the window as he exited Peak Court and headed for the Tank, as he climbed in there was the sound of a gunshot followed by a sniper falling dead from the roof. He splattered on the concrete then faded out of existence.

From Simon's point of view, the Pennie Hotel had recently been demolished. Now here he was standing alone in the doorway of his room. It was tidy and comfortable enough, but it felt soulless in a way. He lay down on the bed, he was under strict instructions from FATE to not leave the room until he is needed for his own protection.

He wasn't sure if it was the hangover talking, but he felt very lonely. Living in halls you're surrounded by people you bond with very quickly. He could still remember where everyone's room was in relation to his.

Now he was alone in a bland hotel room. The novelty of being in the past had gone, he could be anywhere. Remembering his mum's advice, he got up to put the kettle on and he paced the floor for a few minutes, mulling over what Hannah had said to him, especially those last two words.

Die Clock? He wasn't too sure if that's what she said, but it sounded like it. Maybe that's the name of who she really worked for.

The landline telephone started to ring on the dressing table where the mini kettle was boiling, it was Rhonda calling him.

As he went to answer he heard Hannah's voice again inside his mind

'Find a memory that's out of FATE's control'

CHAPTER FIFTEEN

T-Block

Thursday 3rd October 2002

11:11pm, Peak Court

The night before the Freshers Ball

The elder Simon was back on his airbed next to his old desk in his old room at Peak Court. He was chatting with his younger self about the day's events, and various bits about the future with the lights off. Although they were attempting sleep, they were chatting over the events of the day that lead them back here, at the time deadly serious, but now they found quite funny.

'Your face when he hinted about the max prison' his younger self said before laughing

The elder Simon laughed along with him.

'I know, nasty little sod when he get going isn't he?'

The glow of the security lighting in the courtyard outside illuminated the lining of the curtains and gave the objects in the room a dark blue tinge.

His room was fit to burst with flight cases of equipment, props, and clothing both version of Simon would need to successfully get to Kedleston Road without being killed, let alone get the elder Simon back to London Road in time for him to get home.

'You really think we'll need them welding masks?' his younger self pondered, he used his right arm to prop himself upright and arched his body to the right so he could talk to his older self.

'And what's with the boiler suits over the tuxedos? They know something we don't?'

The elder Simon tilted his head to the left in response

'Better to have them and not need them, then you know... get our heads shot off. If someone else's head gets shot off I guess the boiler suits are to stop the tux's getting splattered' Simon chewed his bottom lip as he mentally ran through the list of props and when they might become useful.

'it's the heelies that bother me'

The younger Simon smirked and nodded in agreement. He felt the dressing on his nose was coming a little loose, he got out of bed and headed for the en suite to fix it. Hanging on the inside of the door on the dressing gown hook, was the formal wear both men had to wear tomorrow night. The younger Simon tutted at the black bow ties hanging loose around the collars. He left the door open as he was stood at the mirror

'I thought they'd give us clip on bow ties; I don't know how to tie one of them'

'Don't worry, I do' his older self-responded. Closing his eyes to drown out the light from the en suite.

'Where did you learn to do that?' his younger self asked.

'YouTube' replied the elder Simon.

There was a pause. The younger Simon appeared at the door, as he switched the light out he asked his older self

'What's YouTube?'

11:11am, Kedleston Road Campus, T-Block

Twelve Hours earlier

The elder Simon sat alone in the lecture room. He was in a room in T-Block, most of his lectures used to take place here. The room could easily accommodate 100 students seated on chairs that have a mini fold away desks attached to them, but for some reason all the chairs bar the one he was sat on, and one to his left were all that were in the room.

Simon was relieved to have a change of scenery, as he did not leave his room at the Pennine since he checked in under orders from FATE. Although they said he being there was dangerous, and he had a single guard patrolling the corridor to protect him, it felt like he was in prison. He had every meal bought up to his room and wasn't even allowed to open the window for fear of tipping off another new assassin to his whereabouts.

All he had to occupy him was a nineties TV that received only four channels, and the memory of the deeply personal abuse his younger self had laid at his door. The reason why what he had said had hurt so much was because he was right. It hit a nerve, and his younger self sounded exactly like the inner voice that loves to criticise him and do him a disservice, that voice that had plagued him for most of his life.

He had made a hash of his life. And his younger self was doomed to make the same mistakes he made. The feeling was something similar to parental guilt, he'd made a mess of that young man's life.

Time seemed to slow down being stuck in that hotel room. He spent the majority of the time either using the voice memos app on his phone or lay on the bed with the TV on mute starring at the ceiling, his thoughts swirling and churning.

The last couple of days hadn't been a picnic for his younger self either. The FATE Field hospital, which was housed in an empty warehouse on the outskirts of the city was comfortable enough and they did what they could for his nose, although they said he may have some slight noticeable cosmetic damage. FATE couldn't do anything to rectify this as he caused the break himself. His nose was now officially a paradox.

The younger Si spent the first day mulling over and breaking down what happened in Hannah's room, silent Bob with the gun, and naturally the fight with his older self. His mind replayed the moment his older self's fist made contact with his face.

For some reason, his brain added in a voice with a mocking tone that kept saying 'stop hitting yourself, stop hitting yourself' on a loop. What was this voice? It had never plagued him before. Hopefully it would go soon, probably a symptom of shock.

Si was trying to digest the huge portion of humble pie his older self-had force fed him. He concluded that he had a point, he was getting arrogant, entitled. And there was the proof of what life would be like if he carried on that way. Straight from the mouth of the ghost of Christmas future.

He kept forgetting that he wasn't someone else. It was him. His instinct was to take some comfort from this new knowledge and act upon it. Then memory trumped instinct by reminding him that after this older self went back to his own time, all these memories would be sealed off to him until he was 39 and lay sweating through the sheets in a hospital bed.

Si was feeling the guilt a cocky teenager feels when they insult a parent, and they take it badly.

He wanted to make amends, he didn't know it but so did his older self, who was unlocking a new set of memories of how he thought and felt when he was lay in the field hospital bed.

Time loops, nose paradox's and guilt were starting to make the elder Simons head ache. The novelty of being back in time had worn off and he was keen to get home. That why he was here in T-Block, for an updated brief of the plan for tomorrow night.

Rhonda hadn't shown up yet, even though she told Simon to be there at 11am. Although it had been 17 years since he had last been in a lecture with Rhonda, and she had revealed she wasn't who she said she was, Simon still felt compelled to be punctual when she orders you to be.

He checked his watch. 11 minutes late, he starred at the double doors then drifted to the front of the room while he pondered why she would be so late, that was not like her at all.

He had got the correct room as Rhonda's second in command Dr James Wells, the genial Yorkshireman who enrolled him, who also as it turned out worked for FATE was stood in front of the projection screen checking his phone, the projector was on without showing anything, so the light was illuminating a quarter of his body. He was drinking from a bottle of what looked like sparkling water, but Simon knew for a fact it was a cleverly disguised Gin and Tonic.

Back when he worked at Southampton Uni, following an incident when the social media manager was hiding white wine in an apple juice bottle, the whole department went under some informative yet tedious training about spotting alcoholism and drug use in the workplace. How to spot the signs and triggers, how addicts rationalise their behaviour, and about how they hide their consumption. They scheduled this in on a day long training session after the majority of students had gone home for Christmas, but the staff had yet to break up. Fifteen minutes after the training had stopped at the end of the workday, 90% of the people on the course were in The Slug and Lettuce pub around the corner. Along with the course tutor.

Simon could see it on Dr Wells as he looked him up and down. He wasn't judging, he was far from a saint himself, but he'd always had a hunch that he was a secret alcoholic since the day he enrolled him on his course all them years ago. The clues were there, the complexion, the sheer quantity of fluid he needed on a daily basis. Also, the pungent smell of juniper berries from the bottle he was swigging from that he'd become nose blind too, also tipped him off.

Simon checked his watch again, 11:12am. He drummed his fingers on the fold out desk. The then folded the desk away as he was feeling self-conscious about how it cut into his stomach, and how his stomach spilled over to the desk. He was starting to get impatient.

When Rhonda called him when he'd not long checked into the

Pennie to arrange this meet up, Simon asked her somewhat sheepishly if she knew about the fight he had with his younger self.

“Yea, I know” she said flatly, with a mild undercurrent of disappointment, then she hung up without saying goodbye.

He could see her approaching the door and extending her arm to grab the handle. She paused before opening and glanced back she was talking to someone; he couldn’t hear what as being said. He felt a dull ache in his sinuses, then a new memory started to come back to him.

He glanced at the chair next to him. When he closed his eyes, he could see himself in a corridor behind Rhonda. She paused before opening the door to say, ‘Don’t worry, he won’t hurt you’.

The door opened as the elder Simon was leant forward with his head in his hands. Rhonda turned around and instructed the younger Simon to sit down next to his older self. He stood in the doorway for a moment perfectly still as both men didn’t know what to do next. Gingerly he walked to the one free desk, staying close to the right-hand side wall for as long as he could. Both versions of Simon tried their best to not look at each other.

As the younger Simon reached the desk, he grabbed the arms of the chair to move it. Before he could even lift it up he heard Dr Wells.

‘Leave it’ he said coldly, he then put his phone away and looked at him.

‘Sit’ he barked. He usual geniality absent as he took a long swig from his water bottle.

The elder Simon glanced to his left at his younger self. His confident demeanour completely gone. Zero trace of ego or arrogance, he was obviously uncomfortable. He was fidgeting, shifting his weight in his seat. He’d rather be anywhere but here. Simon was racked with guilt; he was the reason he’d got a slightly wonky nose. He was the reason he snored so badly when he slept.

This was probably the trigger that made his mental health spiral, sure he wouldn't remember why or who broke his nose, but FATE can only erase memory, they couldn't erase trauma. It was too abstract an emotion to do anything about.

FATE had a hand in a lot that went wrong in his life, but the rest he had done to himself. Not only was he the first man to time travel, but he'd taken self-sabotage to a whole new dimension. He looked at the bandages and dressings over the bridge of his younger selves nose. They had done the best they could to straighten it. He could tell he wasn't able to sleep well. The bags the elder Simon had around his eyes had started to show on his younger self.

He heard a clicking noise from the front, it was Rhonda. Locking the door. She strode purposely to the middle of the room. Her usual spot for giving a lecture.

'I will keep this brief and to the point. The fight you too got into has cost us.' She was suing her British accent for effect, as she knew this scared both Simons rigid and made them listen. She folded her arms. Right on que, both Simons started to squirm

'It has cost us time, money, and resources' She said curtly 'Every FATE agent is already in this city, all the time we have is taken up to get you home without a hitch, we don't have any time, money, or resources to spare. Understand?' He tilted her head forward

Eventually the two Simon's nodded.

'The plan to get the older you home requires you both to work together, and to be together from now until you go back to your own time'

She went on to say she wouldn't start the briefing about what to they both needed to do until they had buried the hatchet and put the fight behind them. The younger Simon tensed up hoping they wouldn't leave the room. The elder Simon hoped very much they would leave the room.

Dr Wells walked up to the desks where they both sat and looked down at them both, his angular features seeming to emphases he was in no mood to be messed around. He looked at his watch and started the timer.

'You have ten minutes' he said still looking at his watch

'What, with you stood there?' the elder Simon complained

'Problem with that?' Dr Wells sniped back, he glanced again at his watch.

'9 minutes, 30 seconds' he looked down at the elder Simon

'Don't suppose you saw the maximum-security prison we have on Mars?'

The elder Simon shook he head

'Trust me, you don't want to. Now get talking' he glanced at his watch again

'9 minutes'.

The elder Simon was open mouthed with fear when he remembered FATE's motto was 'Don't argue' he turned to his younger self

'I'm sorry I hit you, what you said hit a raw nerve and I flipped, plus the drink, I know it's not an excuse, but you were right about what you said. I did let you down. You had it all going for you, and I squandered it all'

His younger self turned to him, his eyes on the verge of tears.

'I'm sorry too, I was a cocky little sod' he said, slightly choked

'It was such a shock seeing you, I shouldn't have said what I did'

There was a beeping noise, it was Dr Wells stopping the timer on his watch with a broad smile on his face

'How about that! 7 minutes to go' he put his arms down and beamed that three minutes was a new record for reconciling historical figures, his previous best was reconciling the Wright Brothers after an argument in four minutes.

'You were right about the prison sweetie' Rhonda chimed in from the back of the room, back using her soothing southern American drawl

'What are you talking about?' the younger Simon enquired

'There is no maximum-security prison back the base' Dr Wells cackled with laughter as turned to walk back to the front.

The elder Simon was so stunned he couldn't vocalise the words, instead he just mouthed

'You crafty bastard'

12:45pm

The briefing had ended, the two Simons headed towards the lifts in T-Block, their heads once again scrambled by information overload.

It was all systems go. The operation to get the elder Simon home started now. Every piece of equipment needed would be covertly delivered to the younger Si's room in Peak Court. For safety and logistical reasons, the elder Simon would have to move back to Peak Court for his last night in the past, so an off-duty agent would pick up his things, check him out of the Pennine.

Now the two versions of Simon had made the peace, or at the very least are talking again, it would be easier if they helped to outfit each other and run through the baffling amount of steps to make tomorrow night run smoothly.

As Rhonda had detailed in their first tutorial last week, the amount of people in Derby on the 4th October 2002 that wanted either Simon dead would be at a level only seen during the latter days of a war, 95.8% of the attempts on his life had already been delt with and were stuck in the never-ending loop of failure. But it was the other 4.2% that was the problem, and most of these would strike just getting him to Kedleston Road for the ball.

The timings ran thus,

At 6pm both Simons would get changed, for reasons Simon

never fully understood these student balls were always black-tie events. His tuxedo had been specially woven for the occasion; it was laced with nanobots that would soak up the mental energy of a few thousand students thinking of the future.

After this they would then need to put on the blue boiler suits and the welding masks for protection, as there was a high chance, they would be needed between this and the next step.

They were instructed to not use the lift in Peak court as they could easily fall into a trap with nowhere to run, so they had to use the stairs. They were also told that silent Bob would have opened every window fully in the stairwell, so if needed they can use the window as an escape route, or as an option they could use it to deflect any attackers.

When they reach the courtyard, they would be exposed to a possible attack, they then had to go through several physical role play scenarios of how to dodge a surprise attack or ambush with Dr Wells playing the assassin as he circled them wielding a Nerf gun. Every time one of the Simons complained that this felt ridiculous he just shot them in the face with a foam bullet.

After this they had to try on each outfit, to see if they fit and also so Rhonda could take a 3D scan of them and upload it to the E.H.P. The Emergency Hologram projector. If needed FATE could project a three-dimensional image of one or both Simons to trick any assailant into thinking they have them in their sights.

Projectors were strategically placed at regular intervals along the route they would take from the flat to the front door of Kedleston Road and would be monitored at mission control back at base, during the scans both Simons had to make it look like they were convincingly being attacked. The younger Simon did feel a bit stupid when he was told to pull a 'scared face' pose several times in several outfits, including while wearing the boiler suit and a welding mask. Acting really wasn't his forte.

When he complained that this felt ridiculous Dr Wells just shot him again with the Nerf gun. Rhonda then took it off him and locked it in her desk, much to his disappointment.

They were then told that an armoured vehicle, driven by Dr Zac Watson would be dispatched from FATE HQ and sent to pick them up outside the front. This would be safe as all known attacks would be delt with, and if they were quick getting to the truck, any rogue newbie shouldn't be a problem.

All vehicles from FATE could adapt the outside to match the local time so they could blend in, as long as the outside was programmed in beforehand. When asked what they planned to turn an armoured truck into, Dr Wells said it would be a red fire engine. He wasn't best pleased when the Younger Simon pointed out that there wasn't any about at the moment due to the fire fighters strikes and the army were filling in.

'Alright' he replied, slightly annoyed that he forgot about the strikes, and still annoyed about his Nerf gun being taken off him

'it'll be disguised as a Green Goddess fire truck. Happy?'

Rhonda gave him a telling sideways glace that said 'calm down or get the hell out'

Defeated, Dr Wells reached into his bag for another bottle of 'fizzy water'.

Rhonda continued and said as a precaution, just in case they needed to be pulled aboard the Green Goddess while it was in motion, they would have a gadget in their shoes that could transport them with ease and could match the speed of the truck if they grabbed on, the shoes did this with small set of wheels located in the heel of the shoe that would descend like landing wheels on an aircraft if they detected enough movement and static.

'You're giving me heelies?' The elder Simon said a tad puzzled, looking up from his notes

'Tiny bit more sophisticated than that' replied Rhonda

'How' asked Simon, who was both amused by the notion and

confused

'Well, you don't get heelies on black leather wing tips'

All being well they will be dropped off at Kedleston Road by 7pm, the majority of FATE field agents would be located there so this would be the safest place in town. They calculated for Simon's tux to absorb the right levels of energy, it would take at least four hours where he could just mingle and enjoy the party.

At 11:15pm his lift would arrive to take him back to where the wormhole to the past would be reopened, at exactly the same spot-on London Road where he arrived. By midnight the connection to the ring statue in his own time would be re-established. When he reaches the other end Simon would arrive back on the 22nd September 2022. It would seem like he'd only been away for a few hours.

The lift finally arrived at the 4th floor, both Simon's got in along with Rhonda, who was keeping a close eye on them both, so an argument didn't fire up again.

They entered, both versions of Simon went to press for the ground floor. The older one pulled his hand back and let his younger self press it. The lift doors closed.

As it started to descend, Rhona pulled a puzzled expression

'Simon, remind me what Hannah whispered to you before you left'

The younger Simon shrugged, as he was too drunk to remember. Rhonda clarified she meant his older self.

'Die Clock' replied the elder Simon. Rhonda asked if he was absolutely sure that was what he heard, he said that was what it sounded like, but it didn't make any sense.

Rhonda became eerily quiet which made the rest of the journey down three floor seem very long. As the lift hit the floor the two Simons got out, instead of accompanying them to the secure transport FATE had laid on to get them both back to Peak Court, she simply told them the reg number and make of car and pressed to go back up.

CHAPTER SIXTEEN

The Last Breakfast

Friday 3rd October 2002

8:45am, Kedleston Road

The day of the Freshers Ball

A convoy of trucks and events vans had already moved in to Kedleston Road to set up for the Freshers Ball, much to the annoyance of the majority of the staff as this put a massive limit on car parking spaces. Some did think to question why there were more vans than usual for one of these events, but they didn't take this thought any further as they had yet to have their morning coffee.

If they did explore that train of thought while they were in the queue at Blends coffee shop, and do some light detective work, it wouldn't be too hard to have uncovered the sheer amount of FATE agents who were on campus posing as Students Union or events staff. This event was the perfect cover, nobody is going to question anyone wearing a t-shirt that says 'CREW' across the back while various stages and bars are being erected.

Reading the psychology of locals in any given time period was a strong point of FATE's collective skills, and they knew early 21st century admin workers and lecturing staff had only enough energy to get through the workday on a Friday and didn't have it in them to question who you where and what you were doing here. Simple camouflage did the trick.

Rhonda was in her office and had been since 5am. She was a little concerned about what Simon had told her regarding

Hannah's last words. They had nothing concrete to go on regarding who she worked for, only rumours. FATE was built on a strong academic principal to disregard rumours without hard evidence. She had accessed the servers at HQ and was trying to run a deep background check against what they already possibly know correlated with her last words to the elder Simon. The slower modems of 2002 were taking far too long, plus she had her third-year dissertation group in 15 minutes in the neighbouring block.

She left the background check running and messaged Gavin in the white room to page her bleeper as soon as there was any news. She picked up with white landline corded phone and called Dr Wells' office. No answer. He must be up on the roof already.

She got her keys and picked up a couple of files and got up to head out towards the lifts when she noticed a text message from the younger Simon asking if everything was ok.

8:46am, St Peter's Street

'Heard anything yet?' asked the elder Simon as his plastic cutlery he was holding gleefully tore into the scrambled eggs and sausage patties, and accidentally most of the Styrofoam base the breakfast was served on.

The younger Simon checked his phone, nothing. He shook his head and took a sip of his orange juice.

The two Simons, and by extension for their protection, a small platoon of FATE agents who had to make sure they were safe had gone to the McDonalds on St Peters Street for breakfast, following a conversation the two Simons had before going to sleep about 'The Big Breakfast' from the menu being discontinued by 2016, which the younger Simon was genuinely outraged about. The elder Simon was particularly keen to get a Big Breakfast again. It was his go to order, and he hadn't had one from his point of view for six years. This plus the knowledge that this was his last day in the past had given him a much-needed boost to his mood. Like someone who knows that they are going home from a holiday tomorrow gets a second wind of energy to make the most of the last day.

He forgot what McDonalds used to be like. It was weird seeing the static menus and not the animated ones on flat screen TV's, no Deliveroo Uber Eats or Just eat riders clogging up a couple of tables waiting for the takeaways, no touch screen ordering, just three big queues and a lot of plastic.

Simon used to ponder whenever he passed the St Peters Street McDonalds in his own time how he would feel if he were to go into an old school Maccy's now. They'd given it an urban and trendy makeover, gone were the peach tones and the beige plastic tables. Now he was back in it how it used to be; the novelty wasn't lost on him. Nor were the amount of single use disposable plastic items that were being binned around him.

Simon was by no means an environmental activist, but given the choice between saving the world, or not. He'd go for the first option every time. Plastic use had been phased out so gradually over his time it didn't occur to him that it would be so noticeable now he was back in the past, but it was. Like how strange it feels whenever you see a black and white film from the 40's and everybody is smoking indoors.

As he gleefully tucked into his meal, he smiled to himself as he thought 'if only Greta Thunberg were here'. The smile dropped off his face when he remembered that by October 2002, she probably hadn't even been born yet.

'What does die clock mean?' The younger Simon pondered as he took the lid off his tray revealing his food, which had built up a lot of steam as he sat there. The elder Simon made the gesture that he couldn't answer as he had just taken a mouthful of food, followed by over-the-top chewing to indicate he was doing his best to process the food to give his answer. He swallowed.

'No idea' he said eventually. Both men knew that answer wasn't worth the wait. They theorised for a few moments it could mean she worked for someone who wanted to stop time travel, but that didn't' feel right. And what was all that guff about the pair of them being scientifically matched mean?

The elder Simon mentioned that some dating apps from the future claim to use scientific methods to find someone you'd click with.

'Are dating websites popular in the future?' Asked the younger Simon

His older self-nodded and told him when he is older, and divorced, to avoid Tinder, it would save him a lot of time. Remembering after he said it, that his younger self wouldn't remember a single word he said after he went home tonight. The elder Simon went back to his food and was only distracted when an undercover field agent left a note written on a disposable napkin on his table as he headed out the front door, the message told him to not use any brand names in conversation that don't exist yet, as he is in violation of FATE field guidance directive 0711 subsection 22.

The elder Simon had just about had enough of these idiots. He purposely and visibly screwed up the napkin. Can't use a brand name? For crying out loud! He was amazed he was allowed to breath. They spent so long guiding his life so he'd end up in the past just to stick their jack boots on his throat when he was here and tell him what he can and can't do.

With a mixture of annoyance, and the feeling you get when you know you're leaving a place and you don't care anymore, the elder Simon took a deep breath and said as loudly as he could

'BITCOIN'

36 fate agents dropped their food and turned around open mouthed in shock at what he just said, just to see the elder Simon extending his middle finger on both his hands at them all, then he got back to his food.

'Totally worth it' he said under his breath to his younger self, who smiled. Reassured in knowing that he hadn't lost his rebellious streak in the future.

The two men ate in relative silence for a few minutes, a few fate agents left as they knew they would have to fill in a load of paperwork since Simon shouted Bitcoin.

The younger Si mulled over the notion of using science with relationships. Then he remembered an essay he did at college a couple of years ago. It may be nothing, but it might be worth mentioning.

'Eugenics' he said aloud

'What, what about Eugenics?' his elder self asked

'You're talking about science in matching people, just reminded about an essay I did in me last year at college'

A memory flashed in the back of the elder Simon's mind

'Oh yea, I remember that now'

Historically many countries practiced Eugenics as selective breeding to improve the gene pool, by allowing the best possible people to breed and banning marriage and even forcing sterilisation on people deemed unfit to reproduce. The practice fell out of favour after World War Two, as did a lot of questionable things that became associated with the Nazi's.

Now that the notion was in the head of both versions of Simon, they were massively conflicted. They had a hunch that they were right, but they were still hung up on this woman and couldn't possibly place any dark or negative notion on someone they chose to remember as being so sweet and loving.

A thought popped into the somewhat more cynical elder Simons mind that Eva Braun was considered sweet once upon a time and look how that turned out.

They both decided to abandon that train of thought as it was bringing the mood down, besides by midnight the elder Simon was out of here and all this would be a memory that would not be remembered. Hannah was gone. She couldn't do anything now.

As the two men had finished their meals, they got up. Emptied the contents of their trays into the bins and turned to leave. As he did the elder Simon saw several of the FATE agents that were left in the room quietly co-ordinate their exit from the restaurant via various undetectable comms devices. He smiled to himself. Just for pure devilment as he left he, turned back and shouted.

'TIKTOK'

He was still laughing by the time he got back to Peak Court.

9:17am, Kedleston Road

Dr Wells was on the flat roof overseeing the technical set up, he'd arranged cover for the lectures and tutorials he was supposed to give today as the mission was top priority, he was assisted by a hive of engineers and computer experts from FATE HQ, disguised as maintenance staff stripping down locally sourced tech that could be repurposed for the mission.

By an air vent on the top on East Tower there were engineers dismantling Windows XP Laptops and Nokia mobiles and turning them into A/fe-energy conductors, a hive of agents doing likewise on the top of T-Block and the learning centre.

His phone beeped, message from HQ. It was an article from the Derby Evening Telegraph dated from October 2012 that has just been unearthed, about a Derbyshire man who had made millions from Bitcoin after hearing the name randomly shouted one morning in the McDonalds in St Peters Street some ten years earlier.

The article had additional text from The White Room, asking if it was worth checking out. Dr Wells sighed. He needed a drink. Thankfully he had a hot chocolate in a takeout cup from Blends downstairs, he'd drank a quarter of it in the lift on the way up and topped it up with Rum from a hip flask.

He replied to the message simply saying, 'not relevant'.

He had a hunch that is was, and this was down to the elder Simon as he correctly guessed feeling rebellious. But he didn't follow it up for many reasons. 1) He had to concentrate on the mission in hand, 2) he was probably winding up the testosterone filled pistol jockeys that were in the restaurant as backup, which he could fully understand. He enjoyed doing that as well and 3) with Dr Jarvis's 100% unbroken field record Simon would be back at his own time in fifteen hours, who cared if local got rich thank to some future knowledge? Fair play to him. And 4) most importantly he had to concentrate on the mission in hand.

Hang on, hadn't he already said that? Ah sod it. Where's the hot chocolate?

11:11am Peak Court

With just roughly seven hours to go until they had to get changed, the only thing both Simons could do now is wait. The Younger Simon was sat at his desk attempting to type up an essay while quizzing his older self about the future, who was lay on the bed mucking about on his phone. The thought did occur to the younger Si as why his older self was using something that was effectively useless, but he didn't question it. His older self did a lot of seemingly pointless activities when he was bored.

The current topic of conversation, were shops that has closed down in the twenty years since he was at Uni. Woolworths and Blockbuster the younger Simon already knew about.

'Debenhams went a couple of years ago' his older self-remembered

The younger Simon was surprised. Even though he never shopped there, he still felt a little sad it at the news.

'So, it's the internet that causes most of these to shut?' he asked the older version of himself who mulled it over.

'Mostly' he replied

'That and piss-poor management'

As the younger Simon tried to navigate his email, he found it hard to believe that something this slow would have shut so many shops, disrupted television and music and annoyed so many taxi drivers.

Amazon in the future surprised him the most. Couple of months back he ordered a book from Amazon before he started back at Uni. And it took six days to be delivered, and with the delivery cost it would have been easier to just go to a book shop. But in twenty years' time you can pay for a book and its' delivered the next day or you can read it on your phone straight away, or that thing his future self-spoke about. It was like his phone but the size of a sheet of A4 paper, he forgot what it was called but you can also watch TV shows on from the same people. Amazon the slow delivery bookshop is in the future, is also a TV channel where you can select what you want to watch, when you want to watch it.

'what's that thing called you have, like your phone but bigger' he asked his older self

'iPad' he replied 'it's a Tablet computer'

The younger Simon turned back to his desk.

'Tablet? What a rubbish name for something so cool' he thought. He looked down and realised 'Laptop' as a name is also pretty naff.

5:07pm Kedleston Road

Rhonda didn't have the luxury of taking the day off to cover the mission, with Dr Wells already having done so, going direct to HR without confirming with her first. She was annoyed by this at first, but he could handle everything, and it would have caused too much suspicion having two members of the faculty not being about on the day of the Freshers ball.

She needed to know if any more had been found out about Hannah Maberhill. She didn't want to delegate it, as if her worst suspicions were born out, well, that didn't bare thinking about.

Thanks to her having to remain undercover, today had been 'one of them days'. Good intentions, but time kept getting away from her. Given what her real job title was the irony want lost on her.

Between Lectures, marking, department meetings that overran, she barely had time to grab a sandwich as he dashed between various parts of Kedleston road, pretending to not recognise the various FATE staff who were in the field.

She'd made It back to her office and logged in the FATE server to see if there'd been any update. Still nothing, but it was still running. She wanted to think that no news was good news, but her instincts was telling her something was going to happen. Until it did there was nothing for her to do apart from head to the roof.

5:30pm Peak Court

'Ahhh, the Docs not dead?' said the younger Si sitting forward, now intrigued by the trailer for part three.

To kill a bit of time both Simon's decided to watch a few films. The elder Simon suggested Back to the Future, which his younger self hadn't seen, and didn't have it, but he knew Paul did have the first two on VHS, his video collection of pirated videos was huge thanks to his days at Blockbuster.

As the younger Simon had been off getting his nose sorted after the fight, he hadn't seen Paul since the unexpected trip to FATE HQ. He knocked on his door about midday. Paul opened up, looking bleary eyed, his curtains still drawn, and his room was dark, Simon realised that he must have woken him up.

'Sorry mate, did I get you up?' Si said apologetically

Paul rubbed his eyes and said yes but not to worry, trying to force being charming even though he was still groggy, he then noticed Simon's nose. His eyes widened as he asked what had happened.

Si just said he fell over on his way back from the club, bashed his nose on the pavement and had to go to A&E, he asked if Paul was ok as he normally doesn't sleep in this late

'Yea, I think so. Ever since we went out Monday, all I've wanted to do is sleep man, it's weird'

Si asked about the Video, secretly concerned about Paul and the excessive sleeping that he assumed was a side effect of the memory wipe. Simon's older self had told him everything about the future regarding Paul, right up to his death in 2006.

Paul opened the curtains and searched his shelves. They chatted briefly about the Freshers Ball and if Paul was still going. He said yes and replied with something that made Simon feel like his heart was going to stop

"You going with Hannah?"

Si shook his head, he searched for some plausible words, he simply said

"We, broke up"

Paul put a reassuring hand on Simon's shoulder, and said he was sorry to hear that. This small gesture reassured him for a brief moment, then he remembered that as well as Hannah he'd lose Paul pretty soon too.

'we'll have good time tonight though yea?' said Paul, beaming.

Si put his bravest face on and agreed, and somehow managed to hold back the tears until he got back to his room.

CHAPTER SEVENTEEN

The Green Goddess

Friday 4rd October 2002

5:45pm, Kedleston Road, North Tower Roof

Rhonda had covered Dr Wells' shift on the roof for half an hour while he went to get something to eat, which as she saw thanks to the CCTV feed he just so happened to be in The Arms Bar.

She sent a message to his wrist watch just as he was starting on his third beer that said 'I can see you'

She known about his issues for a while, and naturally she was concerned. She let him believe he was great at hiding it as she knew the issue was delicate and had to be approached with some care. She overlooked it as he was a terrific field agent, but she was somewhat annoyed that he was at it today, of all days. She needed him to be on the ball and focused, not out of his head. She saw him read the message, look up to the camera and run out of the bar leaving his drink.

She figured there would be about ten minutes until he got back to the roof, so she checked in with Gavin back in the White Room that the timetable of messages were scheduled and ready to be sent to the elder Simons watch. It was almost time for them to get ready

5:58pm, Peak Court

The elder Simon felt rather stiff in his tuxedo, it looked ok, but he could feel the components and wires and nano tech that was woven in the fabric of his shirt, jacket, and trousers. It felt like he was wearing and electric blanket. Probably overkill weaving the nano tach into his socks, cummerbund and bow tie and boxer shorts as well, but he learned to not argue with FATE.

He was assisting his younger self with his bow tie; he took a step back to take in the full picture.

"Looking good" as he glanced down he noticed the silver looking metal rim around the base of his younger self's black shoes, "what's them things?" he said as he pointed directly at them.

The younger Simon said they were given to him by that Watson fella. He explained that on pain of death he was told he MUST put them on before he left the flat and wear them the night on the Freshers Ball"

"Did he say why?" the elder Simon asked, naturally puzzled. His younger self just shrugged

"Fair enough" he looked around the room for the next part "right, where's the boiler suits?"

The younger Simon found the two blue boiler suits that were hanging up on the inside of his bathroom door.

"Is it me or is it colder tonight?" asked the elder Simon as he struggled with getting the arms of the boiler suit over his jacket. Suddenly aware of how old he sounded. Nobody under 30 complains about the cold

"Stairwell windows are open remember" said his younger self, slipping his boiler suit over his evening wear with ease. He came over to help his older self as the zipper had got stuck over his stomach

"No no, I need that open for a second" the elder Simon waved his hand dismissively

"You get the helmets; I'll check the window"

He looked out on to the courtyard and the exit that took them to the road outside, Lodge Lane, where the armoured truck disguised as a Green Goddess fire engine, which thanks to FATE closing the road off, would martialize from thin air from FATE

HQ on the planet Mars, driven by a dwarf called Dr Watson would pick them up and taken them to the ball.

Simon had experienced so much that was mind bending and random over the last two weeks that none of that appeared weird to him.

His watched buzzed. It was time. He instructed his younger self to wait by the front door, he'd be right out.

A minute later Si was joined by his older self, who's boiler suit was now zipped up and he had his welders mask on. He signalled towards the door.

Outside in the stairwell, from one floor above, a desperate crazed assassin that FATE hadn't banked on lay in wait for the two men, brandishing a machete. He waited for his moment, breathing deeply and maintaining his adrenaline, he could see shadows moving below. This was it; he could see both men open their front door. Now, it's time, now or never, he HAD to stop them.

As he charged down the flight of stairs emitting a piercing death scream, wielding the machete at the men who looked directly at him through their welders mask and looked unconvincingly scared, the younger of the two men threw this hands up in fake horror as the assassin thrusted his blade forwards at speed, it passed harmlessly through the 3-D hologram projecting the recording of both of the Simons, which was obscuring the open window that the assassin failed to see directly behind them. Thanks to the speed in which he was running he fell straight through it, and down four floors. He broke his neck on the concrete floor and died instantly.

The real elder Simon opened the door a second after the holograms were switched off. He turned to his younger self and asked through the masks

"Did you just hear something?"

"What?" shouted his younger self, unable to hear much under the mask.

They proceeded down the flights of stairs, blissfully unaware of the many attempts on them FATE were now stopping, they made it to the door and out into the courtyard. Only a few yards to the exit. FATE had snipers on the roof, there were hundreds of windows of all the other student bedrooms overlooking the courtyard.

They were told that statistically they were 80% sure they would be covered for the short dash to the road, they were told to stick to the sides. But the elder Simon forgot this and went straight down the middle, followed by his younger self.

A man with a gun appeared from behind a university braded van, then another from behind them, then another from the side. The younger Simon looked up. Whoever these guys were had got to the FATE snipers first, as they were all dead, throats cut and hanging by the neck from the roof to send a gruesome message to both the Simons.

It was an ambush, 24, 25 now 26 of them all armed, they encircled them. Stand back-to-back, that was drilled into them in training. Let them think they have you.

Miraculously both Simon's were remembering this at the same time, a new memory of how this turned out was appearing in the elder Simons head. At the minute the platoon that circled them had their weapons cocked the elder Simon shouted 'NOW'

Both Simon's dropped to the floor when the guns went off, the party that made up the ambush were laid to waste by their own bullets, killing each other in the crossfire one bullet only grazing the younger Simon's welders helmet.

Both men lay on the floor, breathless. The elder Simon noticed one of the assassins were suspended in mid-air as they fell back, a fountain of blood bursting out of their chest frozen, FATE had employed a time freeze to clear up the mess and reset the location.

The elder Simon took his welders helmet off and gestured to the body suspended in mid-air. He couldn't' help but think

"Oh yea, freeze it now! Where the fuck were you three minutes ago?"

Simon's younger self, still on the floor and equally breathless took his mask off and asked his elder self if he got the feeling that all wasn't going to plan. They helped each other up, discarded the helmets thinking that the worst was over and headed for the exit.

Big mistake, a sniper that they couldn't pin point started taking pot shots at their feet sending them scurrying to the left. A wrecking ball attached to a crane that was parked in the scrap metal yard that joined the end of Peak Court sprang into life and swung around at the two men who were running towards it. The younger Simon hammered his right arm into his older self-back, both men hitting the muddy pavement chest first as the ball narrowly missed them but they could feel the slip stream of the air as the ball sailed past.

The younger Simon went to get up, he hit the deck again and told his elder self to stay down because of the back swing. They waited. Nothing, where had the ball gone?

6:20pm Mission Time. FATE HQ Garage 1658

The green light appeared above the entrance to where the armoured truck was primed, disguised and ready to go. The light was Dr Zac Watson's que to scramble to the vehicle.

He got into the drivers cab, which at first glance was also disguised to resemble a Green Goddess fire engine but was armed to the teeth with FATE tech. Mission control used the revolving platform to turn the truck around like a prize on a game show.

As Dr Watson started the ignition and put the truck into gear, two sets of rollers on the revolving platform gave the vehicle motion and speed without it going anywhere, then the time window to October 2002 on earth was established, he could then approach.

Watson signalled control that he was ready, the wall he was facing faded to black. A digital read out on his dashboard read

'dialling destination, Friday 3rd October 2002, Earth, United Kingdom, East Midlands, Derby, Lodge Lane, 6:21pm'

The destination faded up into life in front of him, when the green light above the steering wheel flashed the connection was complete. It was that simple. All he had to do was release the hand break and there he would be.

6:19pm Lodge Lane, Near Peak court

Both Simon's were now stood upright, boiler suits covered on the front with mud. They were staring up at the wrecking ball that had now become suspended in mid-air.

Did it swing up into the time freeze they'd seen in the courtyard? Then they noticed the open window from the first floor. Hannah's old flat. It was agent Tree, A.K.A Silent Bob, hanging most of his torso out of the window brandishing a device that looked like a much larger version on the key fob Rhonda had given the elder Simon.

He was pointing it towards the ball, an almost invisible ripple that was manipulating the air was emanating from the front end like the sudden change in temperature you see close up from striking a match in freezing temperatures. Although he was far down the road they could see he was struggling.

"I can't hold it much longer!" Bob shouted at them.

"Watson will have to find you on route, LEG IT!"

Both men needed no further persuasion as they turned to run towards the route that would take them to Kedleston Road. And run they had to, and snipers and drive by shooters were now amassing on a level FATE didn't comprehend.

6:22pm Lodge Lane

In a dazzling flash of light, a picture window twenty feet in length and ten feet high boomed into exitance out of nowhere, showing a high definition view the blinding white garage at FATE HQ. Dr Watson drove the Green Goddess through it at speed and the window closed behind him. As he glanced to left as he made his way up Lodge Lane he saw several dead bodies in Peak Court's car park, and he swear he saw agent Tree holding a wrecking ball in mid-air using a time cannon. He couldn't see either of the Simons. Something had gone wrong.

He flicked on the GPS tracker that would locate the tech in the elder Simon's suit. He could see both men on the monitor at the top of Lodge Lane and heading left to Garden Street. Getting them to stop would make them sitting ducks, if they kept moving however, they would have a fighting chance.

"I can see it; I can see the truck it's coming for us!" The elder Simon glanced backwards, he was still running and was behind his younger self, he shouted, breathless.

Thanks to FATE closing the roads there were no traffic problems to contend with on this route, but they did have other problems.

He felt his watch Buzz, it was a message from Dr Watson, it just said 'KEEP RUNNING' having missed several bullets that were aimed at him, the elder Simon found some incredible stamina that he never knew he had, even though his face was drenched in sweat, and he thought his lungs were going to burn up any moment. Although this wasn't the time, his brain still entertained the thought about how easy running the London Marathon would be if you were being pursued by a sniper.

The Green Goddess was now level with the two men as they approached five lamps, matching their speed, the younger Simon noticed as the front passed him the drivers cab was empty. As the truck went to pass him he sensed without looking back a brilliant white light was coming towards him as well.

Faintly at first, as he couldn't hear him over the engine he could hear Dr Watson shouting something, he looked again. The back of the truck had been opened up fully, the interior was a dazzling white filled to the brim with state-of-the-art technology and some mind-boggling weapons attached to the walls.

Dr Watson was stood in the middle of the back end of the cab

"JUMP!" He shouted at the younger Simon.

The high levels of adrenaline, matched with a fight or flight feeling he's never had before meant the younger Simon didn't need be told twice. He leaped forward grabbing for the rubber coated steel hand rail that was on the left-hand side of the cabs rear end. Dr Watson helped pull him aboard.

The two men fell into the cab, as they sat up Watson extended his hand to Si's.

"Nice to meet you Mr Radcliffe" he smiled

"Didn't recognize you without your beard" Si joked

"I've never had a beard" Watson said puzzled

A gun shot ricocheted off the pavement millimetres from where the elder Simon was still running. Watson figured his elder self would need a bit more help coming aboard. Remembering the full inventory of the tech Simon was wearing Watson had an idea.

"Grab my ankles" he said to the younger Simon

"What?"

"I'm gonna help your older self on, when I leap forward grab my ankles, in 3.."

"3 what?" As Si's adrenaline was returning to normal so was his levels of comprehension

"2" Watson continued to count down, the penny dropped in Si's head

"Oh god no" he murmured to himself

As Watson shouted "1" he jumped out of the back of the cab on a mission to pull the elder Simon aboard, the younger Simon grabbed his ankles just in time.

As Watson shouted to the elder Simon to Grab his hand, the younger Simon heard a voice from the cab at the front of the truck.

"Electromagnetic shoe clamps detected, activating magnetic floor"

The younger Simon, now face down on the floor of the truck felt a force snap his feet into place. He couldn't move them. He was bolted to the floor. He tried screaming "I can't move" but Watson and his older self couldn't hear him.

The elder Simon grabbed Watsons hand, as he did the smart wheel device in his shoes deployed and he was being wheeled along at 15 miles per hour. Then 20, then 25. Then a voice could be heard from the cab on repeat.

"Autopilot malfunction, Autopilot malfunction, Autopilot malfunction "

The Green Goddess started to lurch violently from side to side as the speed increased, the elder Simon still being dragged along from the back at 50 miles per hour. As the younger Simon was locked in position there was nothing they could do.

The truck continued to accelerate, the only reason it stayed relative to its course was thanks to the buildings and townhouses it smashed into and then pinballed off, most of the debris missing the elder Simon, but not all of it.

He felt like his arms were going to be ripped out of their sockets, Watsons hands were getting slippery with stress sweat. If he let go now, he'd be done for.

Just as the elder Simon was starting to lose hope. Just as he felt like giving in, a sharp and sickening metallic crunch from the front of the cab seemingly jolted the Autopilot back into existence. It corrected its course and lowered its speed

Si looked up out of the back of the truck to see they had hit the Victorian Five Lamp post that gave that junction its name, it was now knocked off its plinth and onto the road, glass shattered.

He pulled on Watsons legs to drag the men in, slowly they managed it. Eventually the elder Simon was able to grab the hand rail and pull himself a board.

As both Simons lay flat out on the floor, exhausted and unable to catch their breath, Watson jumped up, wiped his hands dry on his clothes and pulled the lever to close the back of the truck

"Can someone help me, I can't move"

Watson noticed the magnetic field was on. He ran into the cab to switch it off, freeing the younger Simon.

Si stood up and looked at his older self who was now sat opposite him, his hands were shaking.

"You ok?" he asked his older self

The elder Simon looked up, exhaling, and giving a knowing laugh at the same time. He shook his head.

"Never better" he replied sarcastically. His right hand went to massage his left shoulder

"God my arms are killing me" he winced

His younger self nodded and said his were as well. Watson came back from the cab and pointed at the younger Simon's shoes

"Where did you get them?" he asked, referring to the metal coverings.

"You gave them to me" replied the younger Simon "You said they were in a paradoxical loop, you give them to me in the future in your time line, which to us was last week"

Si took them off the back of his shoes, they were still warm. He handed them to Watson.

"And then you give them to me, to give to you"

Watson looked down at the metal covers in his hands and smiled. He looked up to both versions of Simon sat opposite each other on either side of the cab.

"Right, well. Best get back behind the wheel"

As he disappeared into the cab, he turned back to say one last thing to both men

"Seatbelts on!" he said with zero trace of irony.

the elder Simon just shook his head.

CHAPTER EIGHTEEN

Get the party started

Friday 4th October 2002

6:35pm Kedleston Road, North Tower

From the roof top, Dr Wells had a clear view of the Green Goddess fire truck as it pulled up the campus drive. Both versions of Simon had clearly made it in ok, as Watson was instructed to go straight back to FATE HQ if the mission had been compromised.

He stood up from the metal vent he was sat on, carefully placed his laptop on the ground, walked awkwardly to the edge of north tower as the blood was trying to flow properly back to his legs, then when he reached the edge he flashed his torch six times in quick succession, to the agent supervising the build on the top of the other block. It was time to switch on, full power.

They couldn't use a radio, or walkie talkie as a side effect of the equipment they were building meant that it jammed the signal. They could use the messaging system FATE agents used but torch signals were agreed upon as being covert, quick, and efficient. As he waited for the return signal he wondered if it would sound too ridiculous to send Rhonda a message to bring up an office chair, or at least a cushion. Sitting on that vent was making his backside sore.

Also, he really could do with that scarf from his office, it was getting a bit nippy up here. He looked out to the other block. Nothing. He checked his watch 6:36pm. He was four minutes early, that means Watson was early. He must have been going at some speed he's never early!

"Oh no, they're gonna think I'm pissed" Wells muttered to himself, he rubbed his hand over his face. His thoughts usually spiralled like this when he made even the smallest error. Although he continued with the charade of disguising how much he drank he knew he had a problem. And he knew that all the other personnel at FATE knew.

His record as a field agent and all the work he did back at HQ was great, but the instant he slipped up, even if it was the smallest of small things he would panic, and he would hear the gossip in his head. "The drinks getting to him" "He's lost control" etc. The agent on the other tower was probably messaging Rhonda right now ordering his instant dismissal.

The agent on the other tower wasn't thinking anything like this, he was fixed on the job and just took his signal that he was ready. He hurried his team for the switch on and returned the six-flash signal at 6:39pm.

6:36pm Kedleston Road Staff Car Park

The Green Goddess truck stopped in the car park that tonight was being used for the events companies, as it had easiest access to the atrium. At this point the car park would be deserted, and they'd be covered well by much larger vehicles. The two Simons' had ditched the boiler suits revealing the tuxedos underneath still thankfully in pristine condition, although the elder Simon did catch an unwholesome whiff of body odour from under his shirt collar. They decided as soon as they got out to head to the toilets to freshen up a tad then go to the bar.

"Before you go" Watson appeared in the back on the truck, addressing the elder Simon

"Switch on will be happening soon, your tux is the receiver so don't be alarmed if you feel a mild..." he put both hands out flat in front of him to emphasize the point, and to take the sting out of what he was about to say.

"..very, very mild" Watson was stalling for time, he left a pause as he tried to find a phrase that was better than what he was about to say

"Yes?" said the elder Simon, getting impatient

"...Electric shock" Watson finally finished

"Electric shock?" Simon repeated in disbelief, he lifted his head up with his mouth slightly open. Well that the just put the cherry on it. Tonight, he'd been shot at several times, dodged an ambush, almost had his arms ripped off and was dragged around Derby at 50 miles an hour in a pair of futuristic heelies.

And now to compound this, the people who he thought were his saviours, who had the technology to travel in time and space and to live and work on the Planet frigging Mars, couldn't wire up some wearable tech properly.

"Oh, don't worry" Watson waved his hands to dismiss his concerns "All part of the process, and the shock is no worse than... you know. What kinky people like"

Watson smiled as he finished the sentence to disguise how stupid he felt using kink sex as an analogy. He explained further that as Simon's brain chemistry was key to time travel, the shock was deliberate. It acted as a switch, so the brain started to produce serotonin to counter the shock, and he needed this coursing around his system to fully absorb the so called 'future energy' that was being farmed from the Freshers Ball.

Explaining a bit more science seemed to calm the elder Simon.

"When do they switch on?" he asked Watson, who checked his watch. It was 6:38pm and 40 seconds.

"At 6:40pm, you've got just over a minute, but don't worry you'll be outside"

As Watson lent over to check the coast was clear to open the back doors, the elder Simon's tux emitted an orange glow as it sprang into life, the electricity shocking him in an instant. This caused him to jump up and bang his head loudly on the roof of the truck.

He screamed 'Arrgh' as he banged his head and fell to the floor.

He lay in the foetal position and cradled his head as his younger self knelt down to see if he was ok.

"Oh, you utter.....bastard!" he said painfully through gritted teeth.

Watson stood awkwardly, his hand still on the release lever. He checked his watch.

"Sorry, they're a minute early"

6:42pm, Rhonda's Office

In quick succession Rhona has received three internal FATE emails. One from The White Room, saying there still was no news about the background check. And if it took this long there was a strong possibility there would be no news.

The second came from Dr Wells from the roof top, saying switch on of all components had happened successfully and one minute ahead of schedule. Additional, please bring up my scarf and a cushion. My arse hurts.

The third came from Dr Watson saying both Simons had arrived safe, but early switch on had caused the elder Simon to bang his head on the truck roof, and where is the best place to get paracetamol?

7:00pm North Tower roof top

Dr Wells sat on the floor leaning up against the vent he was sat on top of earlier tapping away on his laptop, weirdly the flat roof proving to be more comfortable that the metal. Added bonus from this position he managed to catch some warm air from the vent and was shielded from the cold night wind.

As he was ahead of schedule, and the team on both towers were doing their jobs of monitoring everything well, he concluded he had a couple of minutes spare before Rhonda appeared. He minimised the screen he was on and logged into a FATE secure server.

Only the highest personal had access to this server, and as it was encrypted, the data could never been seen by anyone, not even another fate agent. Unless you showed them the screen of course.

From the drop-down list of options, he clicked on 'Civilian search' Under filter he selected Earth, United Kingdom, England, Localised Time.

Then when he got to the name box he typed 'Rachel Morley' as he was about to click 'search' he heard a voice from behind the vent. It was Rhonda

"Keeping on top of things?"

Wells slammed the laptop shut with such force he was worried for a second that he'd broken the screen. He jumped up and faced Rhonda who was the other side of the laptop.

"Sorry Maam' I... I didn't see you"

"Well, that's obvious" she looked him up and down and could tell from his body language he was hiding something or looking at something he shouldn't be. As it would be another five years until Porn Hub launched in local time that lead her to one conclusion.

"She's fine by the way" she said earnestly, Wells' mouth open and closed trying to find the words.

"We've been over this, once your contact is up and you go home she'll never know you've been away"

His mouth stopped flapping, and his body language slumped. Utterly defeated.

He wanted to say 'I miss her' but he couldn't.

Rhonda tilted her head sympathetically and handed him his scarf and a cushion.

"Let's just get through tonight ok, then we'll talk"

8pm Main Atrium

After Watson received a reminder than the first aid kit on board the Green Goddess, had the most advanced pain killers FATE's pharmaceutical division could concoct, the elder Simon's pain diminished, and his mood elevated.

"That can't be just paracetamol, I feel... great" he said smiling"

They got to the gents toilets located below BLENDS coffee shop to freshen up, the younger Simon took a look at the bruise and bump that had appeared on the top of the bald head of his older self, who lent forward to see for himself in the mirror.

"Oh, for god sake, it looks like Mount Snowden, I can't hang about all night looking like......" before he could finish both men witnessed the bump and the bruised areas clear up in front of their eyes.

"Bloody hell" his younger self said in astonishment "They are good pain killers!"

Although it was still early by standards of one of the Uni's events the atrium was filling up, DJ's had already taken to the stages and the bars were open and already one or two deep.

One thing that had got worse over the past twenty years was Simon's ability to deal with a crowd. He wasn't too bad when he was in this twenty's, but as the years had gone on he found them anxiety inducing. So generally, he avoided them. Kirsty and Paul had gone into town first and were going to get a taxi in around 9ish, both mystified as why Simon was already there.

They decided to find a quiet area to get a drink and to kill some time. They went to the exam hall that was opposite Blends which tonight had been taken over to become a pop-up bar and the stage was utilised for the up-and-coming bands who weren't big enough for the main stage. Simon recalls that during the May ball in his final year Girls Aloud and the Scissor Sisters were the headliners. Tonight, they'd have the delights of Liberty X and Gareth Gates.

The elder Simon was sat down waiting for his younger self to come back from the bar, the heat produced by his tech woven garments making him sweat like a man cracking under interrogation.

His younger self came back with the drinks, the elder Simon folded the programme he was reading up and took his wallet out to keep the flyer as a memento, and to give his younger self the paper money that would be obsolete by the time he got home.

"That's £400, you sure" his younger self said in disbelief, and also hoping his older self doesn't change his mind.

"Yea, they're out of circulation, thought I'd best rinse that account FATE gave me, pays you back for helping me out when I first got here"

As he shut his wallet, a blue and white card fell out and landed on the floor. His younger self picked it up.

"Name of vaccine Astra Zeneca, date given 10.4.21, second dose 8.6.21" The younger Simon read aloud, his older self-snatched the card back saying he forgot that was still in there.

"What's coronavirus?" said the younger Si in all innocence. The elder Simon took a deep breath and wondered where he would start with that one.

"You might need to go back to the bar, this'll take a while"

8:45pm North Tower roof top

By this point enough students had started to arrive and produced enough energy for the first wave to be harnessed and relayed down to London Road. An additional wave was sent to the elder Simons tux, who according the GPS he was still in the exam hall with his younger self.

Rhonda and Dr Wells sat side by side on laptops feverishly tapping in the complex calculations and programming the precise amounts of energy and where to send it. Both were discussing what needed doing and when, throwing scientific terms that won't be in use for another 300 years back and forward with such speed you'd think they were speaking in tongues.

Rhonda hit enter on the server that would send the wave down the site where Simon walked back to 2002 two weeks ago to reopen the worm hole.

"Now we wait"

If there was a single bug, the slightest miscalculation in the data programmed for the first wave the whole mission would be thrown into chaos.

Rhonda took a deep breath and she looked at Dr Titor still tapping away. Rhonda knew that he was far from happy. The ever-deteriorating drink problem was a major red flag of course, but it was the signs about his old life creeping in that he clearly yearned for.

Rhonda had an amazing sixth sense for what made people tick. It's what made her an outstanding agent and much beloved leader of FATE. On the one hand she didn't want James Wells to leave, she'd never been so in sync with a deputy before but on the other hand it was pointless keeping him around if he wanted to go back to his old life. She should have trusted her gut instinct that taking him back to a point that was relative to his own time would have been a mistake. But the history books clearly stated he was here and stated what he did. And out of all the people that could argue with FATE she was last on the list.

"You know, as you only have six months left on your agreement..." as Rhonda said this his eyes darted from the screen to meet her gaze

"When tonight's over I can look into giving you early honourable release... I don't have to retire straight away, there's always a little admin to do before they let me go"

Dr Wells genuinely smiled for the first time since they landed on this mission.

"Thank you. Maam" he said quietly

A rapid pinging noise from Rhonda's laptop indicated the energy had hit the wormhole.

"It's there" she said flatly

She looked without blinking at the vector graphic display of the wormhole on her laptop. It felt like forever. Then the pinging stopped. It worked. Relief trickled through her body as the gateway back to 2022 had started to dilate. It was only the size of a pin head for now, but by midnight it would be large enough to get him home.

9:05pm Exam Hall pop up bar

The younger Si was grateful for his older self for giving him a heads up to get another drink, plus something on the side a little stronger before he told him chapter and verse about Covid-19.

He felt his phone buzz in his pocket, it was Paul. He'd arrived and was in the main atrium with Kirsty and a few others from their flat.

The younger Si told his elder self they were here and stood up saying they should go and meet them. The elder Simon said he should just go on his own, he'd cramped his style enough these past two weeks.

"You be alright?" his younger self asked

"Yea" replied the elder Simon, checking his watch "I've got a couple of hours till I get picked up. All I've got to do is mooch about soaking up the.... The" he kicked his fingers a few times trying to remember the proper name for it

"Future energy?" his younger self offered. The elder Simon smiled.

"Yea lets stick with that"

He politely declined the offer from his younger self to have some money back to get another drink, and said when the time came, he would come and find his younger self to say a 'proper' goodbye.

He sat alone as he watched his younger self walk off towards the atrium. He looked at his watch, 9:10pm. No news must be good news, so he was guessing that the worm hole must be opened by now, that plus judging by the frequency the tux had a fresh blast of energy all must be going to plan.

He took out his phone and unlocked it. It was still on the voice memo's app. He pressed the side button to lock it again and the screen went blank. He put the phone back in his pocket and looked up. Another twenty minutes and a band starts playing on the stage, the room was filling up. Students in tuxedos and ballgowns, and the odd non-conformist showing what an individual they are by turning up in a t-shirt and jeans, but still sort of conforming by spending £35 on a ticket.

Simon still had to pause now and again to remind himself that he was back in the past and these people in front of him, would be in their late thirties and early forties by his time. And yet here they were, young and fresh faced, full of hope for the future.

FATE was literally feeding on their high hopes and thoughts for the future and converting it into fuel to make time travel happen. As Simon looked around the room, he wondered how many of the students in here would also be repulsed if they could see themselves twenty years from now?

Not every athlete can win gold, but that's what they aim for. He couldn't be the only one who became timid as they got older. Fell into line, did what they thought they should be doing instead of what they really wanted to do.

He overheard four students chatting on the table next to him with the increased volume booze brings to your voice. They were obviously freshers, and new friends as the conversation was still finding stuff out about each other. The loudest one, a tuxedoed man with pale complexion and dark red hair was talking about the film studies module he was taking as part of his media degree, about how much he wanted to be a film director, and some waffle how he enjoyed About a Boy, he'd never cast Hugh Grant in any of his films as he only play the romantic lead, and he confidently predicted you'd never see that kid in anything ever again.

Simon looked at the wannabe director. He mentally aged him up. Nope. Didn't recognise him. Also, he was totally wrong about Hugh Grant and that kid, whatshisface who played the boy. Clearly someone else with high ambition who came to nothing.

If left alone for long enough, Simon could find a depressing point of view in any situation. If he won the lottery he'd be sure to find an angle that would render him bed bound with depression. He decided to down what was left of his drink and go for a walk.

He couldn't leave the confines of Kedleston Road until he reached peak future energy levels. As he walked out of the Exam Hall that was now a pop-up bar, he felt invisible. Here he was, the first man to travel in time and nobody knew who he is. Funny how you can blend in when everyone in the room is wearing evening wear.

He stopped by the gents toilets where he cleaned himself up earlier, as he washed his hands and looked in the mirror, that old familiar feeling came rushing back to him. He was remembering how lonely he was in 2022.

This was compounded by his younger self having gone off to have Paul and Kirsty to spend the night with. He didn't have that in his own time. He was divorced with no kids; both his parents were dead. He was unpopular at work as he was seen as a budget cutting ogre. Kirsty moved back to Oxford and is married to Mr Fucking-Wonderful, and Paul, well. He'd been dead for sixteen years.

He looked away from the mirror, he couldn't bear to look at himself. He had it all once. These past few weeks had reminded him of that vividly, but also gave him a purpose. To survive and to get home. Pretty soon he'd be going home and would forget all this.

He ran his hands under the dryer. Could he go through with it? Would it work?

He couldn't go back to how things were.

CHAPTER NINETEEN

Until the next time

Friday 4th October 2002

11:12pm, Kedleston Road, Atrium

Si stood with Paul in the queue for the bar, he felt a tap on his shoulder. He looked around, it was his older self, gesturing for him to come out for a word. He told Paul where he was going and instructed him to get the drinks in.

The elder Simon had walked around alone, like a ghost haunting a place where he used to live when he was alive. He'd got orders, literally from above, the roof of the building saying he was at peak energy and his lift was on his way and will be there in ten minutes precisely, but first he had to find his younger self.

They found a quiet-ish spot in the open air between the main building and the Students' Union, the thump of the music from the main stage being heard all around as a high-level base throb.

"Guessing you're off, everything ok?" Si asked his older self.

"Yea, all gone to plan, another five minutes and I'll be off" Simon tailed off as he checked his watch

"When my watch beeps, then I'm at peak levels, then there's a car waiting for me. Takes me up to The Spot" Simon injected as much enthusiasm as he could into the end of the sentence. He sensed the mood changed; they knew this was it.

"I also wanted to say....." the elder Simon paused.

"I wanted to say a proper goodbye. I know we've not seen eye to eye a lot of the time these past couple of weeks, and I know finding out about the future's been a ball ache for ya..."

The younger Simon laughed and nodded knowingly

"Yea, not been easy" he said as he tapped the dressing on his nose.

Simon put his hand on his younger self's shoulder. He conceded that it must have been tricky for someone who had everything going for them, to then see the man they'd become was nothing like they hoped for.

"You're way too hard on yourself" said the younger Simon eventually as he looked his older self directly in the eyes. The elder Simon agreed.

"That's because I've spent, more or less the last twenty years living in your shadow. Every failure I felt like I was letting YOU down". As he said this, he took his hand off his younger self's shoulder and wiped his eyes, he sniffed.

"Don't start" The younger Simon raised his hands to his mouth, getting as emotional as his older self.

"You'll set me off"

They agreed there was no point dwelling on everything that was uncovered, as the younger Simon would forget everything he'd been told the instant his elder self went back. His watched beeped; it was time to go.

"Let me just say this." Simon swallowed hard and took a deep breath. "I.. I really loved being you" He exhaled; he felt a relief as he said that.

His younger self started to look flushed with embarrassment.

"Oh, and you are a lot hotter than you think you are as well. Stop thinking you're still a chubby teenager with a gap in your teeth, and get out there and meet some women who aren't trying to kill you"

"What about Zoe?" asked the younger Si

"Oh, she was different. She was just nuts" they both smiled.

A car horn sounded on the kerb side, just outside the staff car park. Simon turned around to see the FATE agent waving at him from the driver's window.

"My Uber's here" he said to his younger self

The younger Simon resisted the urge to ask what an Uber was, he guessed correctly it was a reference to something from the future. His shoulders slumped as he tried to find the right last words to say to his older self.

"Thanks, for what you said, and you know. Everything else. Wish I'd be able to remember it"

The FATE agent's watch beeped. Simon should be in the car by now. What the hell was he doing? He took his shades off to see him giving his younger self a lingering hug. He tutted; he hadn't got time for this. He looked out of his window. The two men were still hugging. He honked his horn three times.

Simon released his arms and looked his younger self straight in the eye.

"You know what to do?" he whispered. His younger self nodded.

"Good lad. Gotta dash" he turned and started to run for the car.

"Until the next time!" his younger self shouted.

11:25pm, North Tower roof top

Rhonda was still supervising the agents and the equipment when she felt her wrist vibrate; it was a notification from the White Room telling her 'URGENT, New intelligence gathered. LOG ON NEEDED!

An ice-cold sensation flashed through her. Not now, PLEASE not now!

Rhonda had a low-level feeling of dread that HQ giving her new info at the eleventh hour could only mean bad news. So, she left James in charge as she had to log onto her computer in her office.

It was the only one that that could securely receive classified information this sensitive. As she was in the lift heading down to the fourth floor she muttered to herself repeatedly 'please be wrong, please be wrong'. She was hopeful that tonight would be the night her 100% record of her gut instinct being correct would be broken, and HQ were getting worked up over nothing.

She unlocked her office and flicked the lights on, sat down and powered up her computer that was on standby. She cursed the snail like speed of the bloody thing and tried to resist the urge to kick the hard drive tower with every second that passed and every pained whirring noise it made.

The uneasy feeling persisted. She couldn't do anything until she read the information and was clear about why it had to be checked now. If she cancelled the mission over nothing, then Simon would probably be stuck in 2002, unable to get back to his own time. Equally if something bad was bearing down on them, she estimated they'd have at best a couple of minutes to act before it was too late.

She logged onto the FATE's secure server, and clicked the envelope icon that was glowing red. It only took Rhonda ten seconds of reading to grasp the ramifications of what she'd just seen.

Her biggest fears had been born out.

Everything.

Everything was now in jeopardy. Not just the mission, Simon, and the secrets of time travel, literally EVERYTHING was now at stake. Dear god, the rumours were true.

Why didn't they put more people onto this? She now knew the main reason why so many people were here to stop these events from happening, and who Hannah Maberhill really was, and more chillingly who had employed her. She checked her watch. 11:55pm. Whatever Rhonda was going to do next; it would have to be quick.

11:40pm, London Road

The car had dropped Simon off at Albert Street as planned. The FATE agent who was driving didn't say much, apart from 'here' when he pulled up, and to quiz Simon on why he was hugging his younger self for so long.

Simon set off towards The Spot, most of the pubs had now closed and the majority of Friday night drinkers had moved on to night clubs. According to the plan, FATE would block off London Road with a lorry, so the queue of people looking to get into Zanzibar wouldn't witness Simons passage back to his own time.

Simon savoured the sights of the past for one last time as he made his way to his mark. The shops that were still open, the bars and clubs he used to love. When he got back to his own time, the building that survived Derby's mass redevelopment would lie empty, either whitewashed windows or turned over to a pop-up shop that was selling cheap tat.

Part of him didn't want to go back, sure he was literally dodging a lot of bullets these last two weeks, but on the flip side of that, he was well aware of how utterly unique this all was. He felt like he'd just won the lottery and was able to holiday freely in Monte Carlo or be a high roller in Las Vegas. Rhonda assured him that the interference from various agencies who were out to kill him was going to stop when he got home, and he could live his life in peace.

But what life? He hated it as he left it. Now he felt as alive as he did when he was nineteen. He was the first man to time travel, and he was at peace with his past. Trouble was he wouldn't remember anything. Everything would go back to the way it was.

None of this felt fair. This was all wrong.

He mulled this over at length during his stay, and his younger self agreed. But what could be done?

Well, there was something.

After his final conversation with Hannah, the elder Simon came up with an idea. A plan to change his future, and for his younger self to have all the info about the future past his memory being wiped. He set to work during his stay at the Pennie hotel when he could be alone.

Obviously, he didn't tell Rhonda any of this, she'd have hit the roof. And he didn't tell his younger self until we went to hug him goodbye.

The FATE agent who witnessed the lingering hug Simon gave his younger self from a distance, didn't see everything. He didn't see Simon putting his iPhone into his younger self's back pocket, and he didn't hear him whisper

"I've left the charger in your room; I've pinned instructions up on the bord next to your desk. Look for the app called Voice Memo's. Everything you need to know about the next twenty years is recorded and stored"

He heard the car horn being blasted three times, so he double checked that his younger self knew what to do and ran off.

It might work. Although FATE could send him messages to his phone and watch, and put stuff in his calendar, they couldn't edit, delete or even see content added by a user to their device. That was against their code of ethics (which having read it Simon concluded it was as dull as it sounded, but it was helpful)

It might just work. Maybe he would go back to his own time and find a very different life. That the world as he knew it would be re-ordered to favour him. Or his iPhone in his younger self's back pocket would evaporate out of existence the instant he went back, and nothing would change. But he had to try. Hannah said to 'find a memory that's out of FATE's control' maybe this is what she meant? Who knows, she might even be waiting for him on the other side, what was it she said, that they a 'scientifically matched couple' or something along those lines. There was a lot about that last speech she made that was a tad odd. But still nothing ventured.

He stood by the parked lorry that completely blocked London Road, this was his starting point for him to run towards the worm hole when it reached midnight, the wormhole was in the exact same spot as the one that bought him here just over two weeks ago, only this time he be going through it in the other direction. He checked his watch, 11:50. Ten minutes till the off. To pass the time he browsed the windows of the closed shops and stopped when he got to Woolworths.

"Back where it all started" he thought to himself.

He forgot all of his problems while he'd been here, seeing Woolworths again made him think of that awful appointment at the hospital that morning he travelled back, then everything that happened since. Being rugby tackled by his younger self, the escape from the DRI, seeing Paul and Hannah again, Time freezing and the trip to FATE HQ. As he was mentally reliving the last two weeks, he felt a vibration on his watch. He checked it, just said 'Comms Error'. The screen seemed to be glitching. He tapped it several times. He didn't know why exactly he was tapping it; it was an Apple Watch. But it seemed like the done thing to do when a watch is acting up. No use, it was still fuzzy. After getting electrocuted by his tuxedo, he was less than impressed with FATE altered tech right now.

Here was a modified apple watch with tech from far in the future, that could cope with the four-dimensional physics of time travel, and just when he needed it to, it couldn't tell the bloody time! He decided to ask a couple of men who were passing what time it was, he guessed that they were on route to the club.

"Excuse me mate, have you got the time?" asked Simon amiably. The larger of the two men, who was still able to walk straight answered

"Yea, it's time you got a watch!" this for some reason set both men off into hysterics of laughter. Simon could still hear them as the disappeared off down London Road behind the lorry

"I said, pffft, time you got a watch!" exclaimed the bigger man at the top of his voice, when he was able to talk after a laughing fit

"I know mate, I know, classic!" said the smaller of the two.

Simon rolled his eyes and thought 'Twats'.

His watch vibrated again. Still showing 'Comms Error' but at least he got the time back, 11:54. Six minutes. He was walking back to his mark when it started.

First thing he felt was the muscles in his abdomen, mild at first then they were twitching. They felt like electric shocks that made his belly ripple like a cartoon character that was hungry. The rippling intensified; Simon started to Panic. What the hell was happening?

Then quick as a flash, all of his belly fat disappeared. There was no hanging skin, it all retracted. Like a pull cord was ripped and he became, well... ripped!

If it weren't for the braces he was wearing his now overly baggy tuxedo trousers would have fallen down. His head started to feel scrambled, but not like when he feels a depressive episode, this was different. Like something was changing, something changing that had already been changed. This didn't make sense.

A wave of energy coursed through Simon's veins; a rush was overtaking him. He ran back to Woolworths window to see his reflection. His beard had gone. How? An amber light began to emanate from him, his head and most of his body parts started to glitch rapidly. Then just as quickly it stopped. Simon wiped his eyes and looked at himself.

"Hair! Oh my god. I've got hair!" he screamed out loud, he got closer to the glass to take it all in. He ran his fingers through his new hair several times. He'd forgot how that felt. He looked so different. He looked, how could he put this? He looked how his nineteen-year-old self imagined he would look at thirty-nine. No longer like a man beaten down by life, but a man who'd made a success of it. That could only mean one thing.

It worked.

The plan with the voice memos, it bloody worked!

That must have been why the watch was glitching. He looked at himself again in the mirror, and again down at his stomach, or rather lack of it. But if it did work, surely he would have new memories of his younger self acting on his instructions.

He checked his watch again to see how long he had. 11:59:30pm, he had an alert message 'invalid timeline, world disordered' and sixteen messages from Rhonda.

11:50pm, Rhonda's Office

This was an emergency. Rhona, was running out of options. She tried to talk to Simon directly via his watch, nothing. Just kept saying 'Comms Error' She instructed all agents on the ground to locate the younger Simon, who she couldn't find via CCTV.

Finding a skinny student in a tuxedo in an auditorium full of other skinny students in tuxedos was impossible. It was like Where's Wally but with much higher stakes.

Dr Wells buzzed in from the roof, now fully aware of the situation, he'd been instructed to instigate an emergency evacuation of all FATE agents in the worst-case scenario, he was calling down to tell Rhonda it was ready if it was needed. It was increasingly looking like it would be needed. The time line they occupied was starting to unravel.

Rhonda had been in a few situations like this before, but none caused by FATE's intel letting them down so badly. They'd gotten too big, too big and too arrogant. Sure, they were on the right side of the law in terms of policing time, but they got cocky. They'd been tripped up.

She messaged Dr Wells to initiate emergency protocol 2412, he messaged back saying that he didn't know what that was as they've never needed to do it before.

In the unlikely event of something going badly wrong, protocol

2412 scatters random messages backwards along the mission's protagonists timeline warning them to not get into the situation they are currently in. Even with time on their side it would still be a crude scattergun approach, but Dr Wells had his orders, so he dashed off a few quick messages and sent them back as quickly as he could. Many missed both versions of Simon. The one's Si and Simon did see included one hurriedly typed message saying 'it's a trap' which landed on the TV screen of the elder Simon's pharmacy the morning he travelled back, he saw it, but he dismissed it.

Another landed on the younger Simon's phone as a text message the evening when he was alone in the kitchen, but it got scrambled and came through as binary code, so he just deleted it as it was clogging up his sim card, and the last one that hit the mission statement print out that Rhonda gave the two men that just said 'She will cause the end of everything' made the elder Simon think for a second there may be a connection, but the words chilled him to the bone so he ignored them. So much for protocol 2412.

A countdown clock started on Rhonda's desktop. A somewhat unhelpful feature of FATE's server designed to focus the mind in difficult situations. She checked the time 11:54pm. The ticking sound effect from the countdown clock on her computer felt like it was now going faster. As she was sending her fifteenth message to Simon, her computer started fade out. Wavy lines corrupted the screen, the countdown clock and the user interface on the FATE server started to disappear. The text was replaced with EMERGENCY CODE 405. INVALID TIMELINE. Then just as smoke started to plume out of the top of the monitor, filling her office with the acrid stench of burning circuits and components, her computer started to completely fade out, as did the smoke, and they both disappear completely. As did the vast array of shelves in her office and the history text books that they housed.

11:59pm, Kedleston Road, Atrium

Downstairs a drunken younger Si passed through the crowds with ease as he went out to get some fresh air. He was able to move about freely as half the FATE agents who were pursuing him had been erased from existence completely, the rest were in a blind panic trying to stop what was happening. He checked the time, one minute till he'd forget everything. Then he remembered the phone and what his older self said to him. He checked his back pocket and unlocked the phone. He smiled and the apps fell into place. He swiped left and right a few times.

Thirty seconds to midnight. The younger Si smiled and thought,

'here's to the future!'

As the phone was still linked to Simon's watch, a dialogue box popped up, along with sixteen increasingly desperate messages from Rhonda. 'Invalid timeline, world disordered'

Si was pondering what this could mean when he noticed he could see the phones only button through his thumb that was resting still on the fingerprint scanner. He wanted to say, 'what the hell?' but nothing came out of his mouth. He mouthed the words, but no sound came out.

You couldn't hear Si scream as he faded out of existence, not that there were any witnesses. The blinding white flash that emanated from the phone began the process of laying everything to waste.

11:59:50pm Rhonda's Office

A FATE agent worth their salt can do a lot in ten seconds, and Rhonda was the best of them. But the cock sure attitude of the agency was now lying-in tatters. As Rhonda witnessed the white flash that was spreading out from Kedleston Road from her office window, she knew the game was up. Only Rhonda and Dr Wells, who was now in the office with her, were the last agents standing.

She looked at Dr Wells and wearily said.

"Emergency evac. Go."

As he hurriedly initiated the procedure Rhonda took one last look out of her office window, seeing swaths of the world crumbling away to a white blank nothingness. She exhaled.

"Oh Simon"

She shook her head

"What have you done?"

With a blinding flash Rhonda and James disappeared. Evacuated to FATE's panic room, the only place in all of existence that's safe from what was happening.

11:58:55pm, St Peters Street

Although the elder Simon was told he didn't have to run to go through the portal, he was running. At speed. He heard a crumbling noise down St Peter's Street that sounded like a building collapsing

He got down as far as the church when he saw it. Or rather he saw literally nothing. A vast white nothing ness had replaced the rest of the city and was consuming the other half. Simon incorrectly guessed this was part of time being rewritten.

The screams of the locals and the noise of the buildings being consumed were enough to wake the dead, petrified by the speed it was now taking going up St Peter's Street Simon ran back towards The Spot.

The portal was now open, on the other side he could see the Ring statue. Home was in front of him, he snaked around the statue towards London Road so he could approach it from the correct side, his reduced weight giving him increased running speed. He glanced at his watch, he had to extend his arm further to get is oversized shirt sleeve out the way.

five seconds to go.

The Error message had gone, and been replaced with 'Valid timeline identified, New World Order' With two feet to go and reality collapsing around him Simon Jumped through the middle of the ring statue and braced himself. His life as he knew it was over.

Wednesday 23rd September 2022

12:01am, Berlin Road

Simon burst through the Ring poral, seemingly from nowhere when observed by the naked eye, he barrel rolled on the ground as he landed outside the Berlin Road entrance to The Eagle Centre. He picked himself up in in just enough time to see the portal unceremoniously collapsing in on itself and taking the Ring statue with it. The poral healed itself up with a flare of blinding light and a sudden exhale of wind it knocked Simon back off his feet again.

he stood up and dusted himself down, his stained and oversized tuxedo now looking ridiculous. He looked around; the old place looked different from when he left. But the sheer amount of shops that were closed indicated this was the year he came from at least. He checked his watch, nothing was happening. It was dead.

He walked towards where the portal was. He put his hands out in front of him to test if it was still there. Nothing. It was sealed off, for good.

He checked his pocket for his door keys and found nothing. He tried all his pockets, slightly panicked he'd have to get his landlord up at whatever hour this was to let him in. Maybe, just maybe he didn't live there anymore. He checked all of his pockets so see if some sort of clue had materialised to indicate where he was, and who he now was.

He was still checking his pockets when the uniformed chauffeur appeared a few yards in front of him. He politely addressed Simon as 'Mr Radcliffe', and when he'd got his attention, informed him he was here to take him home.

"Home, where's that? And you. You are my driver?"

“Yes sir, I’m here on the instruction of your wife,” said the driver

“Wife?” Simon repeated, with growing disbelief. Panic started to set in.

“Dear god, please don’t be Zoe” he thought, he knew he’d messed about with time a bit, but this would be worse than any punishment Rhonda would dish out.

The driver pondered Simon’s state for a second.

“She mentioned you’d be a little....” He paused, he really didn’t want to cause any offense

“...Tired by your journey you’ve had this evening”.

Simon followed the driver to the black stretch Mercedes that was around the corner. Simon was no petrol head, but he could tell this was an expensive make. The driver unlocked the car with his key fob.

“Wow” Simon said out loud, when he didn’t mean to

“Nice car you’ve got here”

“It’s your car sir” said the driver as he opened the door at the back for Simon.

It worked. His younger self didn’t cock it up and it worked. This was incredible. He had a driver and a Merc that he couldn’t even afford to look at in his old life. Simon couldn’t help but wonder what his house must be like? Or his job, looks like he wasn’t working at Derby City Council any more. And while we’re at it, who is his wife?

He decided he’s already looked as weird as he was going to in front of his chauffeur for one evening, so he decided to go with the flow and find out more from his new life when he got home. With all these thoughts clogging up his brain, Simon missed the salute the driver gave him as got into the back of the car.

CHAPTER TWENTY

Time up

Wednesday 22nd September 2022

6:39am Radcliffe Manor, first floor dressing room

To say that Simon had a restless night would have been an understatement. Despite the luxurious nature of the bed he slept in, there was a lot keeping him awake. Like the excitement of having a bed this luxurious in a room that was basically, a walk-in wardrobe. If this is the bed he keeps in his wardrobe, what must his main bed be like? And who else sleeps there with him?

The house the driver pulled up outside of was so grand that Simon mistook it for the main council building on account of its size, on account of its grandeur and the fact he necked half a decanter of whisky from the bar in the back of the stretch Mercedes. But this wasn't a government building, this was his house, a ten-minute drive from the centre of town. The custom-made iron gates bore the name 'Radcliffe Manor'. Simon hoped to God he wasn't the one who named it. Bit corny.

The driver showed him to the dressing room and repeated his wife's instructions that he will be given a full explanation in the morning, and that his valet will be up at 7am with breakfast. The rest of the house was dark and offered little clue to his new life, all he knew for certain was he had a driver and a valet who'll be bringing him breakfast in bed. With no phone to look thing up on and no sign of a computer Simon gave in to the irresistible urge to sleep.

Not that he got much sleep. So much was keeping him awake.

Like him comparing where he was currently sleeping to his wardrobe in his old flat. Wasn't even a wardrobe, it was portable rail he got from Argos he kept in the corner of his damp bedroom. And who was his wife? What did he do to be able to afford all of this? Even when he did nod off to sleep, he kept having dreams about Rhonda trying to speak to him, but no words came out of her mouth, and another more chilling one where a group of people being trapped in a room, and they were suffocating.

So, he lay there from 6am, his mind clear for once on committing to wake up. No nagging inner voice dragging him down. He watched the sun rise from the window. Desperate to get out to see what's happening but also a little bit scared. He got up, found a silk dressing gown behind the door, he put it on and walked towards the window. Even the dressing gown was so luxurious he felt like he was spending a fortune just wearing it.

The sunrise illuminated the lush and well-kept landscape that formed part of Radcliffe Manor, Simon looked out over it all with his mouth ever so slightly open with amazement. He walked over to what he assumed was his dressing table, an ornate gilded antique table that was so brazen with luxurious accessories even Liberace would think was 'a bit much'. Scanning the table, he found a gold Mount Blanc watch next to the sizable collection of jewelled cufflinks and put it on. It was 6:59am.

Simon put his hands back into his dressing gown pockets and walked back to the window, if he was still looking at his watch he would have seen that the knock at the door took place at bang on 7am.

"Good morning sir, Breakfast" said the voice from the other side of the door.

In his life to date, Simon hadn't even been inside a hotel that offered room service, let alone have staff that attended to his every whim at his home. So, he hesitated, with a mixture of not knowing what to do and desperately trying to run through every episode of Downton Abbey he'd ever watched in his mind to give him some idea about how the correct etiquette to summon one's valet.

"Enter" he eventually said, with a little too much grandeur and a tad too high pitched. The door opened and his valet stood there, in full-service livery holding an ornate silver tray which contained his full English breakfast, coffee and orange juice, a toast rack filled with white toast points and the morning papers.

Although he must have now been around forty-six, an age he never got to in Simon's old timeline. There was no mistaking who the valet was. He didn't look forty-six. He still looked like he was in his late twenties.

"Paul?" proclaimed Simon in disbelief

"Good morning sir" Paul replied breezily, with a received pronunciation he never needed for his old job at Blockbuster video, he walked in and placed the breakfast tray down on the bed.

"Everything ok sir? You normally refer to me by my surname"

"You work here, for me?" Simon put his hand to his chest as he finished saying 'me'.

Paul had been briefed in full about how confused Mr Radcliffe would appear this morning and was told to 'politely guide and answer any questions he may have, no matter how obvious or how odd they may sound'. After some consideration Paul responded.

"You paid handsomely for me to be here sir"

If Simon had have picked apart Paul's answer to that question, and found the hidden meaning in it, he would have had a major clue as to the state of the world, as would one of the newspapers on the breakfast tray, if he'd have opened it up, he would have seen the headlines about 'increased partisan activity ahead of S-Day anniversary celebrations' in that mornings first edition of Die Times.

When he was told that Mrs Radcliffe was taking breakfast in the dining room, Simon asked who that was, when Paul queried why he wouldn't know who his wife was, Simon insisted he have breakfast in there with her. When Paul walked over to his wardrobe and asked how he's like to dress for the occasion, Simon quizzed him as to why he couldn't eat in his dressing gown as he'd normally do. Well, used to do.

Paul led the way carrying his breakfast tray, as Simon didn't know where the dining room was. As they approached Paul nodded to one of the footmen to open the dining room doors. Paul walked in first and spoke to the woman at the other end of the dining room table that stretched the length of the room that overlooked the garden.

"Good morning Maam, Mr Radcliffe insisted on dining in here"

Just a couple of weeks ago if you were to have told Simon that he and Hannah would be married and living in a big house when he got back, he would have been delighted. But something about the last conversation he had with her, some instinct didn't make this feel like a happy occasion. Yet there she was.

He didn't trust her. His gut instinct was he'd fallen for a trap. Something had gone horribly wrong. He stood, rooted to the spot as she got up and bounded towards him from the other end of the room to give him a big hug, it didn't feel like all his dreams had come true.

When Hannah broke away from the hug and asked Simon what was wrong, she followed his eyeline that was transfixed on the ten-foot-tall oil painting portrait of him that was hanging in the dining room behind where she was sat. The location of the painting was obvious, with just a few questionable additions. He was standing, doing his best captain of industry pose outside the palace of Westminster in London. Big Ben just off to his left, trailing a flag from the clockface.

Three things about the background of the picture stood out.

Firstly, the main debating chamber. The houses of parliament were a gutted shell, and in the middle of which a small array of trees filled the centre of what used to be the UK Parliament. Simon had seen something like this before on a school trip. St Luke's Church in Liverpool. Bombed out during World War Two. The shell of the church remained, but over time trees had reclaimed the centre.

Secondly, it was the year 2022. So why where there Zeppelins floating around the centre of London? Thirdly the flag that was on display so prominently from Big Ben. It was the Union Jack, but with green instead of blue, and with a Swastika in the middle. Simon was stood next to all this in his Reichskommissoner uniform. The oh so familiar dress of high rank Nazi military with a few modern touches, with a Union Jack flag on the sleeve.

History they say is written by the winners. And FATE, who were essentially the police of all time were victorious in 99.99% of all their missions. They were responsible for writing the history book on time travel, and according to them Simon Radcliffe, was the first man to do it, all be it by accident.

In truth, he wasn't. The First man to Time Travel wasn't Simon Radcliffe. It was in fact his great uncle.

Although he was the first man to be documented to do it, time travel was cracked many years before 2002. It was by no means perfect, but it did give the organisation behind it hope to turn the tide, and the means in which to secure outright victory across a thousand years.

The name of this top-secret project would bleed through eventually and be dismissed as fantasy or a conspiracy theory. The people behind the project were eventually also behind Hannah's unit when they sent her forward to set a trap for Simon to fall into. The project was called 'The Bell' or in its native language 'Die Glocke'.

Many theorised what Die Glocke was. It was shaped like a bell, and the original version was twice the size of the one in the big ben tower. Some thought it was an anti-gravity device. But few guessed it's true purpose. It was a Time Machine.

The project started in the early thirties and was completed in 1942. The first test run took place in a secret location in an underground laboratory in Osnabrück, Northwest Germany, they successfully sent a randomly selected SS Solider for the experiment, Otto Halder forward in time by seventy years to report back on the world of the future, to see if the Third Reich had prevailed and the extent of the new empire. Otto landed in 2002 not in Osnabruck, but in Derby. England. Die Glocke had succeeded in traveling in both time, and space.

Although not a requirement for the mission, as they didn't think he would land there, Otto thankfully spoke perfect English due to him having an English cousin, Ethel Halder who lived In Derby. Die Glocke must somehow have been sentient and had read his mind and used the family connection to determine his destination, as the settings in the machine were only set for seventy years forward.

He looked up what happened to his cousin after the war. Ethel married her fiancé after he came back from the front and moved to the Derbyshire countryside where they had a son. Jack Radcliffe, Simon's father. After gathering intelligence Otto found out about the outcome of the war, and also about the secrets of more refined time travel.

On completion of his mission, he programmed Die Glocke for a return trip, he missed a bug in his calculation where the interior of the vessel completely burned up on re-entry. Killing Otto instantly and burning up most of the components. But the head scientist found Otto's very detailed field report which he filed in a lead lined locker that survived the fire. Due to the top-secret nature of the operation Otto's name was forgotten, and he 'officially' died on the eastern front during the invasion of Russia, but the Nazi's now had all the information about refined time travel. And the name of the man who's brain waves could guarantee victory.

Hannah Maberhill lied a little bit when she first met Simon at the flat party in 2002. Simon was almost on the right lines when he asked if she was related to Lord Maberhill. In the local time context, she wasn't related to the 7th Lord, she was in fact the daughter of the 5th Lord Maberhill who died in 1950.

Hannah was born in 1922 and was the youngest of five, she had three sisters and one brother who inherited the title of the 6th Lord when her father died. As the Maberhill sisters grew up, they became notorious in society for scandal and for their political beliefs. Her oldest sister Edna was a fully paid-up member of the communist party and fled to the U.S with her husband.

Hannah, and her other sisters couldn't be further from Edna, in the fact that they were all fascinated by the fascist movements that were sweeping Europe and were beyond vocal in their support of Hitler in his rise to power in Germany. When war broke out in 1939, her sisters and their husbands, who were all members of the British Union of Fascists were all interned by the British Government, so they were out of the way for the war. Hannah, who had just turned eighteen managed to smuggle her way to occupied Europe and using money from the sale of family heirlooms she stole from the estate and made her way to Berlin.

The Nazi's welcomed her with open arms and sheltered her in an opulent lifestyle in return for using her as a propaganda tool. She was devoted to the cause and would have done anything to help secure victory so she could return home to a brave new England under fascist rule.

So, when the secret lab in Osnabrück were looking for volunteers for a mission that would eventually see the swastika on Buckingham Palace, Hannah jumped at the chance. Hannah and Simon's compatibility was no accident. With all the intelligence the lab had gained on Otto's great nephew, they had plans to install him Imperial Commissioner for Great Britain with Hannah as a eugenically matched breeding mate.

With the benefit of time travel they could put together the most perfect possible plans for invasion, and pick the best day to cross the channel, and at the weakest defended point.

An unknown date and time in the future
FATE HQ, Planet Mars

Paul Kimmel sat in what looked like an interview room in FATE HQ, waiting to have his memory wiped.

Dr Zac Watson, was sat opposite him giving a long and confusing speech. An hour ago they were in Zanzibar nightclub where time seemed to freeze, since landing on Mars, Zac had given him and his friend Si a tour of the facility, along with a man who he thought was Simons dad, but as it turns out wasn't, it was Simon from the future.

'I don't need to skirt the issue, I know the older Simon has already told you who he is, I first met him two years ago from my point of view, which from your point of view will be the night of the Freshers Ball, which is still to come'

Zac left this dangling, Paul wondered if this pointless yarn was part of the process of the memory wipe, as it was making his head ache until Zac continues.

'And on that night. Something terrible happens'

Watson told Paul about the trap Hannah had set for Simon, about their reality falling apart and a new world that took its place where the axis powers had won World War two. This, on top of everything else had now given Paul a full-blown migraine. He cradled his head in his hands

"Fffff, my heads killing me" he whimpered in pain

"It'll wear off, side effect of that pill we gave you" replied Watson, trying to be as soothing as possible

He showed Paul CCTV footage of the night of the Freshers Ball, of the Younger Simon evaporating and silently screaming in pain, all other students and FATE agents running and screaming and what was clearly Paul, looking to the camera, winking, and fading out calmly

"Was that me? Do I die too?" he pointed to the screen, horrified

Watson slid what looked like a tie pin across the desk

"No, you're safely evacuated to the FATE panic room as you are wearing this"

Paul starred at the tie pin, Watson elaborated that the Tie pin would lock on to the emergency evacuation procedure and get him to safety.

"All this can be undone and does get sorted, or we wouldn't be here now. But we need your help"

Zac leaned in and continued

"I'm not going to wipe your memory. I'm here to recruit you"

Wednesday 22nd September 2022

7:01am Radcliffe Manor, Dining room

Simon was still transfixed on the chilling oil painting when his gaze was disturbed by a polite knock at the door, after Hannah shouted 'enter' Paul reappeared.

"Telephone for you Mr Radcliffe, the secure landline in the main hall"

Simon still not used to the formalities, and with the enormity of what he had done sinking in, it took him a minute to respond.

"Who is it?" he asked

"Orders from above sir" replied Paul conspiratorially

"Ooh, your weekly check in with the führer. I'll leave you to it" said Hannah breezily, she pecked him on the cheek and left to go upstairs.

"Führer? Oh, for crying out loud" thought Simon exasperated.

Who would the führer even be in 2022? Hitler's grandson?

Paul led the way to the red Bakelite phone in the main hall with a flashing bulb that indicated a call on hold. Simon sat down on the satin covered telephone stool that was next to it. He took a deep breath and answered.

"Hello"

There was a long pause, some static and a pipping noise, then the line cleared possibly due to the force of anger of the woman on the other end.

"WHAT THE HELL HAPPENED SIMON?"

Simon stood to attention. Oh, thank God it was her.

"Rhonda? Is that you?"

"Yes, and thanks to you I'm trapped in our panic room, there's only me and two other guys left!"

Rhonda explained that the FATE panic room was all that remained of the world Simon left behind. He confessed everything, breaking down into floods of tears. He never wanted any of this to happen. He just wanted his future, or rather past to go ahead a little more successfully than it did. He didn't want this. To be the head of a puppet government in fascist Britain. If he knew the full extent of everything that had been done under his watch he'd be suicidal. Again.

The effects of this new existence were starting to take hold. New memories, and not very pleasant ones were invading his brain.

"I can feel it, I can feel what's left of my mind and the old me slipping away" he said between sobs. Rhonda, who was back to being her ruthlessly efficient best explained that under normal circumstances FATE would just leave him out to dry as punishment. But as all of time and space was at stake, Simon was their only hope of restoring the old world and erasing this one.

"Were working on a way to sort this out, but it's gonna require some field work from you. And a LOT of patience, understand?"

Simon agreed while trying to get his breath back.

"I can't get out of this room; all I can do is send out some crude bends on to the new timelines in the hope it'll set a chain of events in motion that'll…" the line started to crackle

"Hello…Rhonda?" Simon was panicking

"….and you have to help the resistance in the liberation of …." She faded out again

"Liberation of what? Hello?"

"…hang tight until we can restore FATE and get you out. This is the most important thing. We only have the power to send one …(she faded out then back in)… so I've sent you a….." there were a few pips, and the line went dead.

Simon sat listening to the dial tone for a few seconds

"Rhona?" he said pathetically. Shoulders slumped he hung up the phone. As he exhaled a deep sigh staring at the floor.

He was alone. And slipping away.

He didn't hear the footsteps approach. All he saw was the FATE agent ID card enter his field of vision from the left-hand side.

"Surprise!" it was Paul, no trace of his service accent. This was the old Paul.

Simon looked up at Paul, still holding his ID card and grinning from ear to ear

"What? What the hell?" was all Simon could muster

"From FATE with love, come with me" Paul gestured towards an open doorway off of the main hall that lead to the basement, and he set off towards it.

Simons attempts to abuse time travel to make his future better had gone massively wrong, he was alone in a god forsaken fascist nightmare of a world.

And the former manager of the Derby branch of Blockbuster Video was his only hope.

Simon Radcliffe will return in:

'The First Man to Ruin History'

The End.

Printed in Great Britain
by Amazon

17365678R00139